LET IT BURN

Also by Steve Hamilton

Die a Stranger

Misery Bay

The Lock Artist

Night Work

A Stolen Season

Ice Run

Blood Is the Sky

North of Nowhere

The Hunting Wind

Winter of the Wolf Moon

A Cold Day in Paradise

LET IT BURN

STEVE HAMILTON

MINOTAUR BOOKS

A *Thomas Dunne* Book
NEW YORK

This is a work of fiction. All of the characters, organizations, and events portrayed in this novel are either products of the author's imagination or are used fictitiously.

A THOMAS DUNNE BOOK FOR MINOTAUR BOOKS.
An imprint of St. Martin's Publishing Group.

www.thomasdunnebooks.com
www.minotaurbooks.com

Library of Congress Cataloging-in-Publication Data

Hamilton, Steve, 1961–
    Let it burn : an Alex McKnight novel / Steve Hamilton.—First edition.
        pages cm.
    ISBN 978-0-312-64022-4 (hardcover)
    ISBN 978-1-250-03452-6 (e-book)
    1. McKnight, Alex (Fictitious character)—Fiction.   2. Private
investigators—Michigan—Upper Peninsula—Fiction.   3. Murder—
Investigation—Fiction.   I. Title.
    PS3558.A44363L48 2913
    813'.54—dc23

                                                        2013009810

Minotaur books may be purchased for educational, business, or promotional use. For information on bulk purchases, please contact Macmillan Corporate and Premium Sales Department at 1-800-221-7945 extension 5442 or write specialmarkets@macmillan.com.

First Edition: July 2013

10   9   8   7   6   5   4   3   2   1

To Peter

ACKNOWLEDGMENTS

Thanks as always to the "usual suspects": Bill Keller and Frank Hayes; Peter Joseph and everyone at Minotaur Books; Bill Massey and everyone at Orion; Jane Chelius; Euan Thorneycroft; Maggie Griffin; Mary Alice Kier and Anna Cottle; MWA; Bob Randisi and PWA; Bob Kozak and everyone at IBM; Nick Childs; Shane Salerno; David White; Elizabeth Cosin; Jeff Allen; Rob Brenner; Jan Long; Taylor and Liz Brugman; Larry Queipo, former chief of police, Town of Kingston, New York; and Dr. Glenn Hamilton from the Department of Emergency Medicine, Wright State University.

Special thanks to the Breakfast Bunch of retired cops at the Big Chicken in Levering, MI: Detective Sergeant Tom Collins, Detroit Police Department; Officer Tom Gould, Detroit Police Department; Officer John Hemstret, Lansing Police Department; Chief Larry Holland, Wixom Police Department (and Inspector, Detroit Police Department); Officer Jerry Mallory, Detroit Police Department; and Sergeant Bob Miller, Sterling Heights Police Department; as well as the two "local advisers," Joe Bodzick and Dave Schmalzreid.

And, as always, to the memory of Ruth Cavin.

Finally, to Julia, who doesn't even know how beautiful she is, to Nicholas, who grew up way too fast, and to Antonia, who can do anything in the world.

PART ONE

TWO SUMMERS

CHAPTER ONE

Summers die hard in Paradise.

The first time you live through it, and because this place still has the "MI" as part of the address, you might actually expect the summer to fade away slowly like it does below the bridge. Down there, on a crystal blue day in September, the sun shining hot and bright until it starts to go down, you might feel a slight note of coolness in the air, a note that makes you think of football and back-to-school and leaves turning and all those other bittersweet signs that the season is changing. Something so subtle you might even be forgiven for missing it the first time it happened. Especially if you didn't want the summer to end.

Up here, on the shores of Lake Superior, there's a cold wind that gathers from the north and picks up weight as it builds its way across two hundred miles of open water, and then, on a late afternoon in August—hell, sometimes in July—that wind hits you square in the face and makes its intention quite clear, no matter how much you might not like the message. Summer may not be one hundred percent done, not just yet, but it's been mortally gutshot, and it's only a matter of days until it's gone.

It was late August this time around. Actual *late* August, meaning an absurdly long summer. I've got six cabins stretched along an old logging road, built by my father, and in the summer I rent them out to a particular brand of tourist who wants to get away from everything without actually going to Canada or Alaska. They're mostly repeat customers, because there's something about this place. While they're here, they might go around the corner to Tahquamenon Falls, or all the way up to the Shipwreck Museum on Whitefish Point, stand there and look out at the vast expanse of water, maybe think about the *Edmund Fitzgerald* resting just a few miles out there, five hundred feet below the surface. Come back and spend some time at the Glasgow Inn. That's summer in Paradise.

I was at that very same Glasgow Inn that night. I was sitting at the bar, instead of my usual place in front of the fire, having given up my chair and the chair opposite to a couple from Wyandotte. They were staying in one of my cabins, and when they asked me where they should go to eat, I directed them here for Jackie's famous beef stew. After that and a couple of cocktails, they looked to be quite content, just sitting by the fire and looking at each other.

As for me, well . . . There was nobody for me to look at. I had just felt the northern wind and had come in to inform Jackie that summer was on its last legs, something he never enjoyed hearing. Which might be why I always made a point of being the one to tell him. We have that kind of relationship, I guess. I bother him on a nightly basis, and in return he complains to me about everything in the world, including my own presence in his bar.

Oh, and once a week, he drives across the Internationl Bridge to bring me back a case of real Canadian Molson.

"I don't think I can take another winter," he said to me, as he banged down one of those Molsons on the bar top.

"You say that every year."

"This time, I mean it." He'd been here in Paradise, Michigan going on thirty years now, and yet he still had that Scottish accent. He'd tell you that he'd lost it, of course, that he sounded just as American as I did. Just one more thing he was wrong about.

There was a television above the bar. The sound was off, but I was watching the Tigers play the Rangers. It was a home game, in what I still thought of as their brand-new ballpark, even though it had been a few years now. Comerica Park, one of those new-style parks that opened up into the city, showing off all of the downtown buildings I had once known so well. Three hundred miles from where I was sitting, and what felt like a thousand years ago.

"I hear Arizona's nice," Jackie said. "I hear it's *real* nice."

"They have rattlesnakes there," I said, not taking my eyes off the television. "And scorpions."

Jackie scoffed at that, but I could tell the idea had gotten to him. There weren't any rattlesnakes or scorpions crawling around when he was growing up in Glasgow, and as for Paradise . . . Well, they might have a few eastern massasauga rattlesnakes downstate, but you'd probably never find one in your bed up here.

"Summer's supposed to last more than a goddamned month," he said. "That's the part I just don't know if I can live with anymore."

"I think we had double that this year. Besides, you *love* the winters up here."

He just stood there looking at me, bar towel in hand, like he was ready to smack me with it.

"It's cold as hell," I said, "it snows every day, and it lasts forever. What's not to like?"

He shook his head, looking tired, like winter had already begun.

"Seriously," I said. "You love winter because you know this becomes the best place on earth. This bar, right over there by that fireplace."

"With your sorry backside parked in front of it every night, ordering me around. You're right, it doesn't get any better."

He looked over at the couple by the fireplace.

"How old do you think those two are, anyway?"

"Hell if I know." I turned to give them a quick once-over. "Forty, maybe?"

"Forty years old and they're sitting there looking at each other like they're on their honeymoon."

"Second honeymoon," I said. "That's what they told me. They

wanted to go to the most out-of-the-way place they could find without having to fly."

"Which cabin do you have them in?"

"The last one. Now that I finally have it finished." Meaning rebuilt and refurnished, after somebody burned it down for me.

"End of the line," he said, nodding his approval. "Won't be a soul bothering them there."

"You're sounding almost romantic, Jackie. Did you hit your head today?"

"Smartass." He turned away from me and started cleaning some glasses. This was the man who had survived the worst marriage in the history of mankind, to hear him tell it. Yet here he was, getting downright wistful at the sight of a man and a woman who were obviously married and didn't seem to hate each other.

Then it occurred to me. This was a bar in a town that saw its fair share of hunters in the fall, snowmobilers in the winter. Which means lots of men. Bird-watching had become the big thing in the spring lately, meaning mostly women. Then families in the summertime. A mom and a dad, yes, but also a couple of kids along to complain about how their cell phones don't work up here. The one sight you *don't* see too often in Paradise, Michigan is a moony-eyed couple, whether on their first honeymoon or their second.

The man caught my eye and raised his glass to me. I raised my bottle of Molson in return.

I'd been married myself once. A long time ago, to a woman I met when I went to college after baseball. A woman I didn't have much in common with, aside from the "Mc" in our last names. Jeannie McDonald, who became Jeannie McKnight, who went back to being Jeannie McDonald again. Who may have then remarried and changed her name yet again. I'm ashamed to say I don't even know if she did, or if she still lives in Michigan. If we had had children together, the story would be different, I'm sure. Or if I ever paid a cent of alimony. At least that way I would have had an address to send checks to. As it was, she just left. Just walked away. I got the divorce papers in the mail, I signed them, I sent them back to her lawyer, and then we were done.

I wonder if she feels guilty. Wherever she is now, whoever she's with, I wonder if she looks back at the way she bailed out on me a few weeks after I got shot and has any regrets.

Hell, I wonder if I'd even hold it against her now. I think I knew, way back when, that we'd never last, shooting or no shooting. I think we both knew.

I sat there at the bar, looking at my bottle as the Tigers played in silence above my head. There'd been a few women in that lost year after I left the force. Then I'd come up to Paradise thinking I'd sell off my father's cabins and had ended up staying here. Something about the place had spoken to me. Like this is where you really belong, mister. In the midst of these trees bending in the wind. On the shores of this cold lake. This stark lonely place on the edge of the world, which also turns into the most beautiful place on earth for the few days they call summer.

Then there was Sylvia, the wife of a rich man who thought I was his friend. Then Natalie, a cop from Ontario, someone who'd lost her partner, just as I had. Someone who may or may not have turned out to be the right person for me, if I had ever gotten the chance to find out.

No. God damn it. No.

I put the bottle down. This is not where you want to be going tonight, I said to myself. This is not going to make you feel one little bit better about going back to that cabin alone.

"What's with you?" Jackie said.

"I'm fine."

He narrowed his eyes at me like he wasn't buying it. Which made it feel like the right time to leave. A minute later I was outside in the cold night air, looking up at the stars and listening to the soft waves just behind the tree line.

I got in the truck and took the left turn down that old logging road, deep into the woods, passing my one neighbor's cabin. Vinnie Red Sky Leblanc, a blackjack dealer over at the Bay Mills Casino. He'd gotten into some trouble, and I'd been watching out for him. The lights were on at his place, and everything looked normal, so I gave him a honk and kept driving. My cabin was the first, the one I'd helped my old man build back when I was eighteen years old and on my way to play Single-A ball. Back when I was young, stupid, and full of energy, and I didn't have a nine-millimeter slug sitting half a centimeter from my heart.

When I got inside, I saw the light flashing on the answering machine. I don't get a hell of a lot of calls. I hit the play button and listened to a voice from my distant past.

"Hey, Alex McKnight! This is Tony Grimaldi. Remember me? I was a sergeant in the First Precinct, way the hell back when. I hope you're doing okay, and I hope you don't mind me calling you out of the blue. But I'm really just making a courtesy call, and I'd appreciate it if you could give me a call back."

He gave me his number. Then he signed off.

I stood there looking down at the machine, wondering why in God's name a desk sergeant from the old precinct would be calling me. I checked the time. I was in early, thanks to Jackie being an extra pain in the ass that night. So I figured what the hell, give the sergeant a call back.

I dialed the number, making note of the 734 area code. That was one of the new codes split off from the original 313. If you still had a 313, that meant you were either in Detroit or close enough to see it from your front door.

"Alex, is that you?"

"Sergeant Grimaldi," I said. "How have you been, sir?"

"You can call me Tony now. I don't wear a badge anymore."

A half beat of silence then, as we skipped over my comeback. I wasn't wearing a badge anymore, either. I hadn't worn one in many years.

"How long have you been out?" I said.

"It's over ten years now. Hard to imagine. But most days I don't miss it much, to tell you the truth."

"I hear ya."

"Nothing like it, of course. You know what I mean."

Another half beat.

"I know what you mean," I said. "You're absolutely right. But how did you ever think to get hold of me after all this time?"

"Well, like I said in the message, it's just a courtesy call. I play golf with a few of the actives, and one of them happened to mention you. He was going to call you himself, but I told him I'd love to catch up with you."

"Okay. Glad you did." That's what I said, but it still wasn't making any sense.

"I understand you're still drawing the disability, so obviously they had all of your contact information."

Disability. Not exactly my favorite word in the world, but I guess that's what you had to call it officially. When an officer gets shot on the job, he's eligible for two-thirds of his salary for the rest of his life. I don't make a point of telling most people that, because they'll inevitably look at me and try to see how it is I'm supposedly disabled now. I mean, I can't raise my right arm all the way anymore. I can't throw a ball, which would have been more of a big deal back when I was a catcher, I realize, but not so much now. If you really pressed me, I'd just have to tell you that I took three bullets and only two came out, and I'm supposed to go get periodic X-rays to make sure that third bullet isn't migrating closer to my heart, at which point it could kill me.

I'm supposed to go get those X-rays every year, but I don't. I'm supposed to feel guilt or gratitude or a mixture of both every time I get one of those checks in the mail, but I don't feel that, either. Mostly I just try to forget it ever happened.

"So what did you have to tell me, Sergeant? I've never gotten a courtesy call before."

"I told you, call me Tony, please. But here's the deal. You remember a case you worked on, that last year you were on the force, where you ended up putting away a guy named Darryl King?"

I was confused for exactly one second, because I never made detective and so technically I never really worked on a "case." But as soon as I connected the name to the crime, it all came back to me. You don't see a crime scene like that without remembering it for the rest of your life.

"Darryl King," I said. "In the train station."

"You forgot 'With the knife.'"

"Excuse me?"

"Sorry, bad joke. You know, like in that game? Colonel Mustard, in the library, with the lead pipe?"

That's cop humor for you. A way to distance yourself from the most horrible crimes of all. A way to keep your sanity.

"I've been away too long," I said. "But seriously, why are we talking about Darryl King? Don't tell me he's getting out."

"He is. Believe it or not."

"That makes no sense. He drew a lot more time than that, didn't he?"

"Tell me about it. But remember how he was, what, sixteen years old?"

"I don't remember exactly, but that sounds about right."

"Yeah, sixteen. Tried as an adult. It's been a real thing in the court lately, going back over those cases with youthful offenders."

"Like what, we were supposed to just send him home with a warning because he was a minor? Stop killing people or we'll take away your allowance?"

"Hey, I'm just the messenger here, Alex. You're preaching to the choir."

"Sorry, it's just . . ."

"I know, I know. Believe me. I've seen a few other cases like that. Maybe not as bad as this one. Bottom line, the kid's spent his whole adult life in prison. I don't know where he's going to live, what he's gonna do, but I do know he'll be out in a few days. Not that I expect him to come looking for you or anything."

"No, probably not. Good luck finding me, even if he wanted to."

The sergeant laughed at that. "Yeah, what, you're where, in Paradise? I gotta be honest, I had to look up where that is before I called you."

"It's a long way from Detroit," I said. "I don't think I'll have to watch my back."

"No, like I said, I don't expect this kid to do anything. I keep calling him a kid, I realize, and he's not a kid now. But you know what I mean. You just need to let people know."

"I understand. So you called me . . ."

"And Detective Bateman, yes."

"Wow, Arnie Bateman," I said. "Another name I haven't heard in a long time."

"Yeah, he's off the force now, too. Left right around the same time I did. Things were just getting a little too crazy in the department. More and more politics every year."

"Okay, so me and the detective. I assume you're letting the victim's family know, too?"

"The court system does that. Certainly won't be me, and no thank you, anyway. That would be a whole different thing."

"I can't even imagine," I said. "I remember talking to the husband. It's been a long time, and maybe he's moved on with his life. Gotten married again, I don't know. But in a way it probably feels like it just happened, you know?"

"Exactly. Now they're telling you the guy who killed your wife is going to walk free."

"I still can't believe it," I said. "Was it first degree murder in the end?"

I wasn't there for that part. I was in the hospital when the trial took place, or maybe I was already out of the hospital and off the force and living through my lost year.

"Second degree, I think. After they cut that deal or whatever they did. But still. It's not right."

"Well, I appreciate the call, Sergeant. It was good to hear from you."

"Tony, damn it. And you know what? We have to have a drink sometime. You ever get down this way? I live in Plymouth now."

"Plymouth? Really?" Last I saw it, Plymouth was a little town in the middle of a cornfield or something, twenty miles west of Detroit on the way to nowhere.

"Yeah, you wouldn't recognize the place now. Look who's talking, anyway. At least you don't have to look up Plymouth on the map."

"Fair point."

"But I mean it, Alex, I should have called you a long time ago. It's not right to lose touch like that. You gotta get down here so we can catch up for real. We'll have that drink, and your money's no good down here."

"Next time I'm downstate. I promise."

"You'd better, Officer. That's an order. You take care of yourself, all right?"

I promised him I would. Then we both hung up, and I'm not sure either of us really thought we'd ever see each other again.

An hour later, I was still thinking about the call. That name, Darryl King, which had been so important to me, so long ago. To the whole city of Detroit, really, in that one hot month of June. I had done my small part to bring him to justice, and then my own life had gotten turned upside down, just a matter of days later. I had had no reason to ever think about him again. Until now.

I was in my truck, rolling down to the end of the logging road, past four empty cabins. The family in the second cabin had just left that morning. That left only the couple in the last cabin, the same couple I had seen that evening, down at the Glasgow. The lights were on when I pulled up. I could see that they were inside.

I took an armload of firewood from the bed of my truck and stacked it next to the front door. Then the door opened and the man was standing there, looking out at me.

"Don't mean to disturb you," I said. "It's just getting a little cold tonight, so I thought I'd leave some wood."

"It's August," he said, with some kind of fake outrage. "It's not supposed to get cold."

He thought that was pretty funny. When he was done laughing, he thanked me for the wood.

"This has been such a great week," he said. "We really love it up here."

"Well, I'm glad to hear that."

"It's not even that cold in here, but I think I'll start a fire anyway. It really gets Gloria in the mood, if you know what I mean."

I just nodded at that one. Definitely more than I needed to hear, but what the hell. You're lucky enough to be alone with someone who loves you, in a nice cozy cabin at the end of the road in the most remote place you could ever find yourself in. Your real lives, all of your responsibilities and all of the demands, they're all back home, three hundred miles away. Why not pretend you're newly-weds again?

"You have a good night." I got in my truck and drove back down that lonely road to my lonely cabin. I had already made the decision by the time I got back inside.

I called back my old sergeant, surprising the hell out of him, I'm sure. I told him I'd be coming back downstate to take him up on his offer of a drink.

Then I made one more call.

CHAPTER TWO

Another summer, the one that would turn out to be my last wearing a uniform. Half my life ago. Detroit, back when Detroit was still on its feet. It was a wobbling prizefighter, holding on to the ropes with one hand, but nobody was counting it out yet.

Seven thirty in the morning, on the first day of June. I remember that part because the first day of any month was hell for most Detroit police officers, on account of something they called MAD. It was a three-shift system for patrol officers, *M* for midnight, *A* for afternoon, *D* for day. You did one month on one shift, then you switched over to another. If you were lucky, you got a day off on the switch day, but of course you can't give everyone the same day off, so most of the time you had to do a quick turnaround. Day-shifters going home and grabbing a few hours of sleep before reporting back at midnight, midnight-shifters going home in the morning and then coming back for the afternoon shift, which started at 4:00 p.m. Or on that particular day for me and my partner, coming off the afternoon shift at midnight, stumbling home, and trying to get as much real sleep as possible before that alarm went off and you had to be right back for morning roll call. The smarter criminals in Detroit had a rule—never mess with a cop on the first day of the month.

Sergeant Tony Grimaldi was doing the roll call that day. He was about as Italian as the name would suggest, an eastsider from Warren, where a lot of the Italians seemed to come from. He had been a high school baseball star who went on to play for a small college, so he took a natural interest in my minor league career, and it was obvious he thought both of us had come one inch from making it to the majors, even though he never even got a tryout. It was harmless, of course, and he was a sergeant. So I let it slide.

"All right, listen up," he said, standing up there by the chalkboard. "Welcome back to the daylight, Officers. Hope you all have some coffee in you. Before we get to the announcements for the day, I've got a special guest star who wants to say something to you."

Sometimes we'd actually get a genuine celebrity stopping by the precinct to say hello. One of the Red Wings, maybe, because we were the precinct closest to Joe Louis Arena. I think I remember Bob Seger stopping by one morning when I wasn't there to meet him. But no, today we weren't getting anybody like that at all. The door opened and in walked Detective Arnie Bateman.

"I thought you said we had a special guest *star*," my partner Franklin said. It was the kind of thing he could say, being all of six foot four and a few pounds over his two-forty playing weight.

"Just give him a minute of your time," the sergeant said. "He was so gracious to spare some of his, after all."

The detective nodded at this, with a smile on his face like he really was giving up some of his valuable time just to favor us with his wonderfulness.

"Thank you, Sergeant. Good morning, men."

He was dressed just so, as always, still sporting a Detroit version of the *Miami Vice* look, including the stubble on his chin. His eyes were bright, and he was practically humming with energy, unlike the rest of us overcaffeinated short-shifters, because homicide detectives almost always work regular hours. His gold badge was displayed prominently on his alligator belt. I'm pretty sure he polished that badge at least three times a day.

"As you know," the detective said, "we've got the big annual basketball game against the Thirteenth coming up. They've been taking it to us the last few years, but this is the year we turn it around."

The Thirteenth Precinct was our big rival. The First Precinct extended up Woodward Avenue from downtown, and the Thirteenth was just up the street from us. That left the precincts sitting right on the dividing line in this city, separating the east side from the west side, and it also meant that the infamous "Cass Corridor," where much of the drug activity in the city was concentrated, ran from one precinct to the other. We'd take turns being the precinct with the highest homicide rate. Once a year we'd try to forget that with a basketball game.

The Thirteenth had the nice indoor gym, so it was always an away game for whoever played for us. I'd never taken part myself, but I'd seen my fellow officers limping around the next day, some of them with loose teeth.

"So we really need some help this year," he said, his hands on his hips, jacket open, that gold badge blinding everyone in the room. "Some height, some athleticism . . ."

"Some black guys," Franklin said. "*Tall* black guys. Is that what you're saying?"

Everybody laughed. There were thirty of us in the room, maybe twenty white, ten black, my partner among them. But we were all pretty tight. As a Detroit cop you get over that kind of thing pretty fast. In fact, if you can't deal with the realities of race, talk about it in the open, joke about it, laugh about it, then you're on the wrong police force. For that matter, you're in the wrong city.

The detective laughed along with us. He was one of those guys who had probably never been the butt of a joke, going back to his glorious three-sport high school career, and wasn't about to acknowledge such a possibility now.

"You can say it that way if you want to," he said. "But I didn't, okay? Just see me after roll call if you're interested. We really need some guys with game this year."

Thereby insulting everyone who played last year, I thought, but again, guys like Arnie Bateman get away with that kind of stuff all their lives.

"All right, back to the announcements," Sergeant Grimaldi said. "Thank you, Detective Bateman."

He waited for the detective to show himself out, then he continued.

"We're keeping a focus on Roosevelt Park and MCS this month," he said, MCS meaning Michigan Central Station. "We continue to see some daytime drug activity, both in the park and in the lots by the station itself."

It was a familiar story. A dealer sets up shop, word gets around, the police crack down on it, and maybe a few low-level runners get arrested. Then it all starts over somewhere else. In this case, though, you've got train commuters coming and going, maybe taking a little walk in the park on a nice summer afternoon. Maybe some of them are buyers, but the rest are just people trying to get on with their day. A lot of them don't live in the city. They live in one of the suburbs, and they come downtown to go to work or to see a ball game at Tiger Stadium. It's one of the unspoken rules around here that if people like that turn into crime victims, then it's doubly bad for everyone involved.

And for the city itself.

"We'll be putting together a buy-and-bust later this month," the sergeant went on, "maybe even by next week."

There were a few not-so-subtle groans on that one. Buy-and-busts mean more kids in handcuffs, while the real culprits live to sell another day. Sometimes they ask patrol officers to help out, too— which means you get to dress in street clothes, be bored out of your mind, and then risk your life for a few minutes, all in the same day.

"This is all taking place above and beyond the usual Roosevelt Park activity," the sergeant said. "The solicitation, both male and female. Now that the candy store has moved to the same location, well . . . As you can imagine, it's gonna be a hot spot for a while."

"One-stop shopping," somebody said. "Get high and get off."

"You've summarized the point well," the sergeant said, not looking up from his day sheet. "So just keep an eye on the area whenever you drive by, okay?"

There were a few other announcements that didn't have anything to do with me or my partner, so I tuned out. A few minutes later the sergeant gave us our ten-eight, meaning "officers on duty" and kind of an inside joke because Detroit cops never use ten codes. Then we were on our feet and heading to the locker room for a last pit stop before hitting the road.

My partner was yet another ex-jock on a squad full of them. An ex–football player, once a promising walk-on at the University of Michigan before he blew out his left knee. He still wore a brace, and he took a moment to adjust it while I waited for him. I was just about to ask why the detective hadn't come up to us personally when Franklin slammed his locker shut and there, in a perfect movie moment, was the smiling detective himself.

"You gotta be what, six-three?"

"Six-four," Franklin said. "But I don't hoop anymore."

"I understand you might not move like you used to," the detective said, "but I'd like to see one of those guys at the Thirteenth move you out from under the basket."

"I'd love to help you out, Detective, but the ligaments in my left knee have their own agenda. Why don't you ask Alex? He's the only ex–professional athlete around here."

I was already composing my thank-you note to Franklin when the detective stepped over to look me up and down. "I thought you never made it to the majors," he said.

On a morning when I had a little more sleep under my belt, and a little more patience, I might have taken the time to explain it to him. You get paid to play ball in the minors. You can even make a decent living in Triple-A. Which makes you a professional, by any definition.

"No, you're right," I ended up saying. "I played four years for free. Now if you'll excuse us . . ."

"All right, we'll talk later," he said. "You don't look very fast, but I'm sure you could help us."

With those words of encouragement ringing in my ears, I grabbed my partner and we rolled out into the day.

CHAPTER THREE

I got an early start the next morning and saw the sun coming up as I crossed the Mackinac Bridge. I grabbed a quick breakfast in Gaylord, got back on the road, and kept going. I can drive as fast as anyone, partly because my old Ford F-150 truck still rides smooth going eighty or over, partly because I'm an ex-cop who took three bullets on the job and nobody's going to write me a ticket. Not in Michigan, anyway.

I still wasn't exactly sure that this was a good idea, but I knew if I didn't do it I'd be sitting in front of the fire at the Glasgow that night, telling myself I should have gone. So what the hell.

I rolled through Bay City and Saginaw. Then Flint. The traffic started getting heavier. You forget how empty the Upper Peninsula is, how you can drive for twenty minutes and see one car going the other way. Then you come down here and you realize there are too many people in the rest of the world, and too many cars.

I got off on I-96 and headed southeast, toward Detroit. I remember this road being ripped up and under construction all the time, even way back when. It was nice to see that one thing hadn't changed, at least. A few more miles down a single lane marked with orange cones and I was in Oakland County. I was running a little early, so I pulled off at Kent Lake and parked the truck for a while. I closed my eyes to recharge my batteries. When I opened my eyes again I was looking out over the lake. It hadn't been a conscious plan, just something I gravitated to without giving it a thought. If I ever had reason to move down here again, I'd have to live on a lake for sure, or else I'd probably end up going insane.

It was kind of strange to get an actual good cell phone signal down here, so I took the opportunity to give the sergeant a call while I was sitting there, just to let him know I was closing in. He seemed a little surprised I had gotten down here so fast, but he gave me the address of a sports bar on Haggerty Road and told me he'd meet me there.

I made the mistake of taking the secondary roads to get over to Haggerty, ending up in Novi. There's a huge mall there, plus a million other stores all over the place, and as I sat in the traffic I couldn't help remembering what the corner of Novi Road and Twelve Mile once looked like. Two roads crossing, fields on all four corners. A traffic light. Now that one corner had more retail shopping than the entire city of Detroit put together.

More memories hit me when I finally got over to Haggerty Road. It was two lanes through the countryside back in the day, with a mom-and-pop store and a gas station every mile or so. More old-timer's talk, I know, but damn it all, I swear it wasn't that long ago. A place shouldn't be able to change this much, this quickly. There was another strip of retail on every corner now, and every straight-away with enough dry land was lined with new housing developments. I didn't ask myself where all of these people had come from. I already knew the answer. The people who lived in Detroit were moving out to the first line of suburbs, and the people who lived in those old suburbs were moving out here, in a great second wave. Or hell, maybe it was the third wave by now. Another few years and people would be moving to the moon, just to get away from Detroit.

I found the sports bar. It was right on Haggerty, between a couple of restaurants and a movie multiplex. It was one of those places with seventy television screens. In the men's room there were three more screens above the urinals. When I came back out, I saw my old sergeant standing at the door, looking for me.

"Sergeant Grimaldi," I said. "I would have recognized you anywhere."

I was being kind, I guess. He had lost most of his hair, put on a few pounds. He'd spent too much time outside without putting on his sunscreen. But I did truly believe I would have recognized him, even out of context.

"Alex McKnight," he said, looking me over. "What the hell, you don't look any different at all."

"That means I wasn't much to begin with."

"No, I'm serious. Do they have the Fountain of Youth up there in Paradise or something?"

"Okay, enough flattery. Let's sit down, okay?"

We grabbed one of the high tables, with the high stools you have to be careful not to fall off of. There was an afternoon baseball game on over one of his shoulders. Not the Tigers. On another screen there was a soccer game. On another screen there was a news show. Just two guys talking with a running closed caption at the bottom if you really felt like sitting there and reading it. I ordered a beer, and the sergeant did likewise. I was already preparing myself for the fact that it would not be brewed and bottled in Canada.

"I can't believe you really came all the way down here," he said, looking at me and shaking his head. "I mean, I know I offered to buy . . ."

"I appreciated the call," I said, "and it's been a while."

"It's what, a six-hour drive?"

"Closer to five."

"Okay, so there's another reason you're here," he said. "Me, I'd only drive five hours for one of two things. Money, or a woman."

"Well, there is somebody I'm going to see later . . ."

"Aha. Okay, now we're getting somewhere. Who is she?"

The beers came then. I took a long drink. It tasted good after so many hours on the road, Canadian or no Canadian.

"She's an FBI agent," I said. "I met her when she came up to the UP to investigate a string of murders."

"That does sound romantic."

I had to laugh at that one. "She's a good cop," I said. "Even if she's a feeb."

"God, do you remember how much we used to hate those guys?"

"I do."

"Don't even get me started," he said. "The number of times I had to actively go out of my way just to get something done before those clowns came in to mess everything up."

I smiled and shook my head. It was a topic every local cop could speak to, all over the country. It would probably never change.

"But you say she's one of the good ones," he said. "So okay, I guess that means you're not breaking a code or anything. She's good-looking, too?"

"Matter of fact, she is."

"Okay, then. You may proceed."

He took a hit off his beer. Then he reached behind him and pulled out a little notebook from his back pocket. A real cop move, no matter how long he'd been off the force.

"So, speaking of murder," he said. "I gotta say, I feel really bad about the way I handled this."

"What are you talking about?"

"I called you up, out of the blue, and I had everything right there in front of me. Darryl King, getting out on parole, in about a week. I've got his address, too. Or his mother's address, I guess. Over on Ash Street."

"The same house where we made the arrest?"

"I believe so, yes."

"So what's the problem?" I said. "Looks like you've got it all covered."

"No, I sure as hell don't, Alex. When I got off the phone with you, it occurred to me that I didn't say one word about the woman he murdered."

"You didn't have to, Sergeant. I know what he went away for."

"I told you, I'm Tony now. You see a badge on me?"

"No, but—"

"But nothing. If I was still a good sergeant, I would have remembered the most important thing. Even if you know it and I know it and everybody in the world knows it, the most important thing about Darryl King is the woman he murdered in cold blood."

"Elana Paige," I said. "That was her name."

"Yes," he said. "Elana Paige. You remembered."

"Of course. I was the one who . . ."

"That's right. Not something you're ever going to forget."

We both sat there for a while, thinking about it, while the baseball and soccer games went on over our heads.

"Here's to Elana Paige," the sergeant said, raising his glass. We toasted her, and then we both went silent again.

"The kid who did this," I finally said. "I know you've already told me, but I want to hear it one more time. Maybe it'll make sense."

"He's getting out. Doesn't make any more sense, does it?"

"No, it doesn't."

"I used to know a parole officer," he said. "Going way back. I remember he once told me, when murderers get out of prison, they're statistically the least likely to ever get in trouble again."

"Is that right?"

"Sex criminals, child molesters, those guys are almost guaranteed to end up arrested again, but plain old murderers? They usually stay straight."

"Does that make you feel any better now?" I said.

"No, actually not. How 'bout you?"

I shook my head and took another long drink.

"It's funny," he said. "I called you because theoretically somebody you helped put away for a long time might come after you. But while I'm sitting here thinking about him, walking free like that . . ."

"It's more likely we'd go after him," I said. "I hear what you're saying."

"Okay, good, so it's not just me thinking that."

"Something you think about. Not something you actually do."

"No, I guess not. But if I were her husband? Even after all these years?"

"He's probably remarried now. Maybe with a family. You don't destroy that just to kill the man who killed your first wife."

"I know, I know," he said. "It wouldn't bring her back. I'm just saying . . ."

He waved the whole thing away with one hand. Then he looked up at the screens.

"I never did get the whole soccer thing," he said. "Did you?"

"I've got a friend from Scotland," I said. "He'll talk about it like it's life or death sometimes."

"You've been up there ever since you left the force?"

"Took me about a year. Then I finally wandered up there."

"I know that must have been rough. And you do realize . . ."

He hesitated, looking me in the eye.

"I'll just say it, Alex. You do realize that nobody blamed you for what happened to your partner."

I waited a few beats before answering.

"I did. I blamed myself."

He shook his head. There wasn't much else to say, and he was smart enough not to try.

"So when's the last time you got back down here?" he finally said.

"It was a few years ago. I saw the new stadium, but I don't remember if I drove by the old one."

"You would have remembered, believe me. If you saw Tiger Stadium half torn down . . . That was just the worst. Of course, now it's just a field, and the old flagpole."

"I do remember going by the old precinct," I said. "The building didn't look much different, at least."

"You realize that the First and Thirteenth are combined now."

"Are you serious?"

"Yep. The old rival precincts are now the Central District. They've got six districts now, instead of thirteen precincts."

"That's amazing."

"The city's lost half its people, Alex. I mean, literally half the people are gone now. The population is back at around what it was in 1900. A couple of those precincts, they became like outposts in the desert. No houses around them. Hardly any people. They've even got bears living in some of the old buildings now."

"Bears? Are you serious?"

"That's what I've heard. They've got companies that go around tearing down houses as fast as they can. Whole blocks, just disappearing. When you were down here before, did you drive though any of the neighborhoods?"

"A little bit through Corktown, but not much else."

"What about the train station? Did you see that?"

"From a distance. I never got too close."

"Well, you have to go see it, then. The whole city, Alex. Just take some time today and drive around. You have to go see what's happened to our old Motown."

So that's what I did. After I thanked him for the beer and saw him back to his car, I got in my truck and started driving around. FBI Agent Janet Long was still at work, after all, and I had a few hours to kill before meeting her for dinner.

You have to understand, Detroit is a huge city. Not in terms of population—not anymore, at least—but it's 140 square miles in area. You could fit Boston and San Francisco inside the city borders, and still have room left over for Manhattan. I drove straight east, through Redford, where I lived as a young married cop, just across the border. Then a minute later I was in the city itself. This place I was sworn to serve and protect.

It's so easy to stay on the freeway and to zoom right through it all. As I crossed over the River Rouge I made myself get off and start driving down those residential streets. I had to see it for myself.

I crossed through the northern reaches of the city, turning down one street after another. I saw the abandoned houses. I saw the garbage and the graffiti and the high weeds. I saw the charred remains of houses that had burned down. This is something Detroit had always been known for, of course. Devil's Night, the night before Halloween, when people would come from literally all over the world to watch the city burn. Every fireman on the job would be out that night, and just about every cop, too. It always felt like a losing battle, but now . . .

Now it was like the whole city just said, all together . . . Let it burn.

An hour later, I was still driving. I finally had to stop for a while. I sat there in my truck and looked at an entire row of empty houses. They would be torn down eventually. The demolition companies just hadn't gotten to them yet.

Having worked my way through the west side, it was hard to imagine that the east side could be any worse. But I was wrong. By that time I was getting a little numb, but still I'd see something like a beautiful old church turned into a half-collapsed wreck and it would hit me all over again. A park where children once played. A school with every window covered over with plywood.

As I finally worked my way back to the heart of the city, I came down East Grand Boulevard and passed through the old Packard plant. It had already been abandoned when I was a cop here, but at least then it stood out from everything around it. Now it was just one more forty-acre postapocalyptic wasteland in a city filled with them, with yet more decayed buildings, more graffiti, more garbage, more weeds. This plant where they once made the most beautiful automobiles in the world. It was easy to see how much this one wrecked-out old plant could stand for the whole city, the way it was back in the glory days, and the way it was now.

I hit Woodward Avenue, the center of town, the dividing line between east and west. The old Thirteenth Precinct building, with the indoor gym they were so proud of, was closed now. They had put up a fence with razor wire around the whole complex.

I drove south, feeling a tightness in my chest as I got close to that corner. Even though I knew the building was gone now, that apartment building with the broken elevator and those stairs that Franklin had to climb, complaining with every step. Until we finally got to the top and knocked on that door.

It was gone now, replaced with a Burger King. But it didn't make me feel any better to see it gone, because Franklin was just as much gone himself.

I drove downtown, past the First Precinct building, still open, at least for the moment. Past the new ballpark where the Tigers played now, to Grand Circus Park, where the streets fanned out like spokes on a wheel. It was a weekday. A working day. There were people walking around the place, enjoying the nice day. It was good to see that much. It was good to see that the whole city hadn't been abandoned yet.

I went down to Michigan Avenue, headed west past where the old Tiger Stadium once stood like a huge gray battleship. It was just a field now, like the sergeant said, with only the old center-field flagpole still standing.

I wasn't far from Roosevelt Park and the old Michigan Central Station. I looked at my watch. I still had an hour. Plenty of time to go see the station up close, to see what it looked like now. To see that empty parking lot, those tracks, that desecrated building.

And to remember what happened there.

CHAPTER FOUR

We rolled out onto Woodward Avenue. It was a Thursday, the first day of June, which meant a school day. That's the first box you check when you're on the morning shift, because a school day means there's officially no good reason for kids to be out hanging around on the streets at eight thirty in the morning.

Of course, if you do see kids hanging around on the streets of Detroit, at any time of day, there's a good chance they're not playing kick the can, or rolling a hoop down the sidewalk with a stick. It's just a cold hard reality that the frontline soldiers in this city's drug trade are almost all children. A horribly effective way to run a drug business, when you think about it, because if you ring up a thirteen-year-old for selling, what are you gonna do, put him away for ten years? Even if you did, there'd be another thirteen-year-old to take his place the very next day. The men who are making all the real money, you never touch them.

If they didn't invent the practice here in Detroit, they sure as hell perfected it. Young Boys Incorporated, or YBI, was formed by three teenagers on a playground. A few years later, they controlled most of the heroin trade in Detroit. They were bringing in close to two million dollars a week. In the wintertime, you could spot their runners from a block away, because they all wore the same kind of coat. That's how brazen they were, all of them. Like go ahead, pick off a few of the kids. See how far that gets you.

We finally brought down the gang in 1982. I say we, meaning the Detroit cops, the FBI, and the DEA, actually working together for once. One of the three founding members had already been killed, but the other two were put away for good, along with forty-one of their lieutenants. The kids, they all scattered to the wind, but nobody around here was naive enough to believe that new gangs wouldn't form overnight to take the place of YBI.

Then, on top of everything else this city had to deal with, some genius somewhere figured out how to make a cheap form of free-base cocaine using baking soda. Crack, rock, whatever the hell you want to call it. It hit Detroit just as hard as every other city in America. Maybe a little harder. We still didn't have enough cops in this town, and now with a new, highly addictive form of coke that could get you high for five or ten bucks? It was starting to feel like a losing battle most days.

Franklin and I got about a block down Woodward Avenue before we saw a half-dozen kids walking slowly down the sidewalk. We came up behind them, and Franklin blipped the siren. He was driving that day. As soon as we came to a stop, I got out and rousted the kids, asked them why they weren't in school, dismissing with prejudice their claim that summer vacation had already started. Eventually I just sent them on their way, with me holding only their empty promises to wander over to school.

Franklin was finally getting out of the car to come help me. I waved him back inside as the kids walked away.

"Don't tell me," he said as he got back behind the wheel. "They were on their way to choir practice."

"Not quite. But no big deal. Just a bunch of knuckleheads skipping school on a nice summer day."

"How exactly do you know they weren't up to something else? Did you take one ID from those kids?"

"Did you see me take an ID? You were sitting right here."

"It was a leading question, Alex. Just like in the courtroom."

"I asked them what they were up to," I said. "They answered me, I asked again, and then the second time I believe they told me the truth. So let's go find some real problems to solve, all right?"

"Oh, that's right, I've got the all-seeing swami in the car with me. I keep forgetting that."

"It's not even nine o'clock," I said. "How many times are we going to do this today?"

"That's entirely up to you, Swami. Although I'm surprised you haven't already divined the number in advance."

This is how it went with us. All day long. I had this unshakable belief back then, that I could ask a person a question and I could look in their eyes while they answered me and I could tell if they were lying to me. With absolute certainty. No doubt whatsoever. In the years since, I've found out that some people are gifted liars, and that my supposedly one hundred percent accurate lie detector can be fooled completely.

Of course, if you think I've learned not to put such trust in my own instincts anymore, then you have no idea just how stubborn I am. Or maybe how stupid.

"I need more coffee," I said.

He drove us down through the Wayne State campus, past the great stone edifices of the art museum on one side of the street and of the library on the other. There was a little coffee shop next to the hospital. I went in and got one with cream for myself, one black for Franklin, waiting for the inevitable joke about how he likes his coffee like he likes his women. He was happily married, but some jokes are still mandatory, I guess. And yes, we both had a doughnut. Two cops with two doughnuts.

"What else can we do to fulfill the stereotype today?" he said as the powdered sugar dusted his nice clean uniform. "Too bad neither of us has a badass mustache."

"We could both get out and try to chase down some kid. Climb over a fence and throw him into some garbage cans. Then complain about how we're too old for this stuff."

"The day is young, Alex. I'll let you do that one, though, if you don't mind."

"You really can't run anymore, huh?"

I could see him flexing his left knee, just at the thought of it. "If a bear was chasing me, maybe. But then I'm sure I'd end up in the hospital."

"So I take it you're not going to play basketball."

He was taking a drink of coffee then and just about spit it out. "Are you kidding me? With Detective Jackass as the coach?"

"Coach and star player. Don't forget."

"Star player, my ass. I would have destroyed that boy, back in the day. In fact, if I hadn't been a little better at football . . . I'm just saying. You might have seen me on the hardwood instead of the gridiron."

"Yeah, yeah. I got it."

"Now, if I had played baseball . . ."

"Oh, don't even start," I said. One of our other favorite arguments.

"I won't. My only point is that every sport has its necessary set of physical skills."

"Okay. You're right."

"And then there's baseball."

I shook my head and looked out my side window. There was a line of apartments on my side of the street. By lunchtime there'd be people sitting out on their balconies, watching the traffic. Not exactly the best view in the world, but there were far worse places to live. Across the street was another apartment building, much older and taller. A place we knew well, from repeated visits. Thankfully there were no calls to send us there that day. We wouldn't even set foot in that building for another month.

The downtown buildings were looming in front of us, getting bigger with every block. We passed over the highway, then by the Fox Theater into the canyon formed by the first of the tall buildings. We were downtown now, and there were working people walking around like it was any other city in the world. This one just happened to be built on one thing. The automobile. So as that business went, so went the city. On this particular day, it looked to be holding its own.

That took us past the Opera House and right into Grand Circus Park, with all of the statues and fountains and flowers, and God damn if it didn't all look beautiful in the morning sunlight. Another few blocks and the road curved around another little gem of a park called Campus Martius. It's a big jumble as five roads all converge there, a great place for fender benders, and sure enough, we made the turn just in time to see one happen. One car swinging hard to the outside of the circle, another car in its blind spot. The dull hollow sound of a passenger's-side door being pushed in, then a terrifying moment as the two cars seemed to join together and form a single metal monster that could go just about anywhere, take out other cars or even the people on the sidewalk.

Three wheels jumped the curb. Two front wheels from one car, one from the other. Then everything stopped dead. Franklin flipped on the lights as he pulled up behind. I jumped out and checked on the drivers. Your first priority, of course. Make sure nobody's seriously hurt.

There was a woman in the car to the right. She was black and heavyset, and there was a cross hanging from her rearview mirror. The car itself was a junker. An old Plymouth Horizon that was once blue, now half Bondo and primer. It was the kind of car you could buy in Detroit for three hundred dollars back then.

Her eyes were closed, her hands folded in front of her. She jumped as I rapped on her window. "Are you all right, ma'am?"

"I'm fine," she said as she rolled down her window. "That car just came over, Officer. Right on top of me. I didn't have time to stop."

"You just relax a minute," I said. "We'll be right back to talk to you."

I went to the other car. It was a gunmetal gray Saab, and I'm pretty sure the floor mats alone were worth more than the Horizon. The driver was pounding the steering wheel with both fists. When he saw me, he threw open his door. I had to jump back to avoid getting hit in the knees.

"Take it easy," I said. "Are you all right?"

"I never saw her," the man said. He was wearing a suit, and his tie had been loosened. "She came out of nowhere."

"Well, no," I said. "She was right behind you. I wouldn't call that nowhere."

"I looked before I switched lanes. Then boom! I don't know how it happened."

"You obviously didn't see her. A turn signal might have been useful there, by the way."

"I did signal, Officer."

"We were right behind you. You didn't signal."

"I assure you I did."

Okay, I thought, so this is how it's going to go. Like the old Marx Brothers line, Who you gonna believe, me or your own eyes?

"Let me just get your license and registration," I said. "And your insurance information."

Franklin had called us in as "busy with a property damage accident, no injury." Now he was taking care of the woman in the other car. It was my luck to have Mr. Happy here. He said a couple of half-audible things about the city of Detroit and then about women drivers, and I admit that made it a little easier to write him a ticket for improper lane change. He took that about as well as I thought he would, taking down my badge number and promising me I hadn't heard the last of him.

The tow trucks finally came. By the time we had finished up all of the paperwork, most of our morning was done. Just another busy day in downtown Detroit.

When we were back in the car, I sat there shaking my head for a while. Franklin kept looking over at me.

"Nice guy, huh?"

I didn't say anything.

"Every time somebody acts like that, you take it personally. It's gonna eat you up, you know that."

"I'm not taking it personally."

"You're just a badge to guys like that. You stand for something they need to get mad at."

"I know, okay? Can we just move on?"

"Yeah, with you not talking for the next few hours. That'll be fun."

"You sound like my wife now."

Franklin didn't respond to that. Not at first. We just kept rolling down the street.

"I know we've talked about this before," he finally said. "So there's no use going over it again."

Meaning that's exactly what we were about to do. If the car had been going a little slower, I might have been tempted to jump out.

"Seriously," he said, "you know this job is hard enough, even if everything is squared away at home."

"I know. Believe me."

Franklin and his wife had two young daughters. It all got to be a bit too much sometimes, and I'd hear him complain about it. But I knew he went home a happy man every night. Or day or afternoon, or whenever the hell our rotating shifts would end.

"Is Jeannie still going to school?"

"Yes," I said. "She's almost done."

"So she'll have her degree. In art history."

Oh, we're going to get the full platter today, I thought. Art history being to real areas of study as baseball is to real sports.

"I know I've kidded you about that before," he said, surprising me, "but she's just getting that paper, right? I get it. She wants to have a degree, finish what she started. Then go on to the next thing. I totally get it."

"I'll tell her you're on board."

He looked over at me.

"I'm trying to tell you something important," he said. "Will you just cut it out and listen for a minute?"

"I'm sorry. Go ahead."

"I know we work crazy schedules. I know we can bring the job home with us sometimes. No way around that. But you gotta work through that every single day and you gotta *find* each other. You know what I'm saying? Every day, Alex."

"That's hard to do when I don't even see her."

"So that's why you call her. You set a time and you make it happen. Just see how her day is going, tell her you're thinking about her. That's all it takes."

This was back before everybody had a cell phone. This was back when you had to find a phone connected to a wall and you maybe even had to drop some change into a slot before you could talk to somebody.

"You stop talking to your woman," he said, "you're halfway out the door."

"She has an hour between classes today," I said. "She's usually in a lounge where I've called her before. So I'll do that today, all right?"

"Don't do it for me. Do it because it's the right thing to do."

"Okay."

"Do it because I'm a smart man and I know what I'm talking about."

I didn't get a chance to answer that one. The sergeant came over the radio and asked if we had cruised by Roosevelt Park and the train station yet.

Franklin picked up the transmitter. "We're on our way, Sergeant. We had to handle an accident."

"Copy that."

We cut west on Michigan Avenue, passing Tiger Stadium. There'd be an early game that day. A getaway Thursday game before a road trip. Some of the other cops from my precinct were already out there on the street, getting ready for the sudden heavy traffic and the crush of pedestrians. I nodded to a couple of them as we rolled past.

Then we turned down through Roosevelt Park, really just a flat open field with a few trees and walking paths around the perimeter. The park looked quiet, making me wonder what all the fuss was about. There were probably five hundred vials of crack changing hands all over the city at that moment, and here we were making sure no dogs were taking a dump on the grass.

We made the loop in front of Michigan Central Station, eighteen stories tall, maybe the most beautiful Beaux Arts building in the city. When I came here as a kid, the main waiting room was still open, with the arcade and the shops and the mezzanine and everything else. I'd look up at the high ceilings and think this was the fanciest place I'd ever seen. My father told me this used to be the heart of the city, people arriving on those trains from all over the country.

Now it was half closed down, with only a few Amtrak trains coming through every day. There was some talk about reopening the whole thing, making it look like it did in the glory days, but for now, it was just left hanging in limbo.

We were about to head back out when I noticed a car parked along a side street, just west of the station, by the redbrick church, almost hidden by the high weeds and sumac trees. We pulled up behind the car and hit our lights. I got out and kept an eye on the two male occupants in the front seat. Franklin looped behind me and took the passenger's side. I went to the driver's window and rapped on it.

The driver was white. Thirty-five, forty years old. He looked up at me with a mixture of fear, surprise, and feigned innocence. Like why on earth would you be bothering me when I'm sitting here in my car, minding my own business? It's an expression I saw seven or eight times a week.

"Can I get some ID from you, sir?"

"What's the problem, Officer? We're just sitting here."

"Did I say there's a problem? I'd just like to see some ID, if that's all right."

The passenger was black. Franklin was asking him the same question, and it was obvious the passenger had been down this road before. He just sat there, shaking his head, like he was the most unlucky man in the city.

We got the two men out of the car and put them in handcuffs. The white man started shaking about then and asked me why he was being arrested.

"You're not under arrest," I told him. "We're just doing this for your safety and ours."

"But you don't have probable cause, Officer. You're violating my rights."

I looked over at Franklin.

"You're parked half in the weeds in a known drug-trafficking area," Franklin said to him. "And I'm pretty sure this young man here isn't giving you directions back to the suburbs."

I searched the driver and came up empty, but Franklin started pulling little bags with white rocks out of one of the passenger's pockets. He pulled a large wad of money out of the other.

"That's not mine," the man said. "I don't know where that came from."

"What, the crack? Or the money?"

"The money's mine. I don't even know what that other stuff is."

"This is amazing," Franklin said to me over the roof of the car. "Didn't we just hear about the same thing happening the other day? Somebody going around slipping drugs into young men's pockets? It's like an epidemic around here."

I asked the driver if I could take a quick look through his car. He said yes, and it came up clean. Nothing on his person, nothing in his car. It was turning out to be a very fortuitous day for him.

"So tell me the truth," I said to him, getting close and looking him in the eye. "Were you just down here trying to buy some crack? Or was there something else going on?"

"Hey, hey," the passenger said. "Don't even be saying that now."

"I hear this is the place for it," Franklin said, "and you're sitting in the man's car. What else are we supposed to think?"

"I don't go in for that kind of stuff, man. That's blasphemy."

"No, you just sell crack," Franklin said as he started hauling him back to the car. "Right next to a church. That's not blasphemy at all."

"I'm sorry, officer," the driver said to me. "I don't know what I was thinking."

"Well, I'm pretty sure we both know exactly what you were thinking," I said, "but I appreciate the honesty. If I let you drive away, am I ever going to see you back down here?"

"No, you're not. I swear."

"All right, get the hell out of here."

He got back in his car and drove off. I rejoined my partner in our car. The young man in the backseat was smart enough not to say anything else. He just sat there looking out the window while we drove him back to the station. He looked like he was eighteen years old, maybe nineteen. He lived in a world I'd probably never understand. But he didn't *have* to be hanging around the train station selling drugs to white men from the suburbs. He had a choice. Or at least, that's what I had to tell myself to keep doing this job.

It was already past lunchtime when we got through processing our young dealer. I tried giving Jeannie a call, like I had promised

Franklin, but I just missed her. Then I saw Detective Bateman walking down the hall, looking like he had a few more things to say about the basketball game. So I got the hell out of there and rejoined my partner in the car. My stomach was rumbling.

Franklin had this thing about "Coneys," which were Detroit's version of the Coney Island–style hot dog. There were a dozen different places around town that sold them. Now, I knew all about ex–football players and how they'd often put on too much weight once they stopped playing, but I'd long ago given up. Franklin was going to have his three dogs no matter what I said or did. The diet Faygo Redpop on the side just made the whole meal that much more ridiculous.

"Admit it," he said. "A Coney sounds pretty damned good today. Am I right?"

"Doesn't mean I'm going to eat one."

"You don't understand, Alex. On these short-shift days, you naturally crave comfort food. It would do you great emotional harm not to take care of yourself today."

So of course we ended up at one of the stands on Woodward. Franklin had three. I had two. Principles be damned when you're standing there and you haven't eaten since an early breakfast and you're smelling those grilled onions. When we were done we headed back out on the beat. Back by the stadium, where the game had started. We ended up talking to a man who was pretending to be a game-day parking attendant. He was out in the street, waving cars into a closed private lot, taking ten dollars from every car. When I questioned him, he stood his ground and lied to my face and kept lying even after we got the official confirmation from the lot owner. Yet another man telling me the sky was green. Something that would never stop amazing me.

We would have run him off with a warning, but there was real money involved and apparently this wasn't the first time for him, so we ended up driving him back to the station and processing him. That meant more paperwork, another solid hour and a half in the station, hoping Detective Bateman didn't find me.

Then finally back on the street. That was the afternoon. That's *every* afternoon when you're on the day shift. A whole lot of what-

ever happens next, and you never really know. I honestly don't remember one other thing that happened, until it got close to four
o'clock and we could see the end of the shift coming. Home for
dinner, maybe a few words with my wife, making an effort. A night
of sleep and maybe we'd all feel better the next day.

"Swing by Roosevelt Park one more time," I said to Franklin.
"Just for the hell of it."

We were already halfway down Woodward Avenue again. Over
the freeway and into the heart of the city, one more time before we
called it a day. He made that same turn down that same road. The
train station loomed above us. Here's where time slows down for
me. It stretches out like a long rubber band, and every single event
is stretched out with it.

The whole place was quiet and deserted. Even more so than the
first time we had come by. Not unusual, I guess. They see the cops
taking someone away in a patrol car, that tends to put a damper on
their business. For the rest of that afternoon, at least.

"Swing through the lot," I said.

"This place is dead."

"Just humor me."

With a sigh he pulled hard on the wheel and circled the car
back toward the lot. There were maybe thirty or forty cars there.
Far from the salad days, but at least there was *somebody* still taking the trains. There was so much room in the lot, the cars were
scattered all over the place. I didn't see anybody in any of the cars.
Franklin made one loop through the lot, taking us closer to the
tracks.

That's when I saw him.

A young man, black, jeans and a gray T-shirt. Black baseball
cap. He was walking down the tracks, right at us.

I was out of the car before it even came to a complete stop. He
saw me. He turned and ran in the opposite direction.

"Hey, hold up!" I yelled at him. "Stop right there."

I took off after him. He spun his wheels for a moment in the
gravel of the railroad bed, giving me the chance to close the distance. But he found purchase and started moving fast. His stride
was ugly, but he stayed ahead of me.

"Stop!" I yelled. "Stop right there! Police!"

He glanced back at me for one quick instant. Then his right arm came out from his body. He threw something away from him. I couldn't quite see what it was. Something not that big. A slight flash in the sunlight, maybe a clear plastic bag filled with crack. Big surprise, yet another dealer. At least that's what I was thinking as I chased after him.

I knew that Franklin would be calling it in behind me. Another car would go down Bagley Street to intercept our runner. But then I realized that as we got farther from the station, there'd be fences on both sides of the tracks. Tall fences with razor wire curled along the tops. Meaning there'd be nowhere else for him to run except straight ahead.

"Don't be an idiot!" I said. "It's not worth it!"

Possession with intent, not the biggest rap in the world, and yet here he was adding an evading charge on top of it. Meaning I have to keep chasing you, no matter how much it's killing me.

He was running along the railroad tracks now, somehow managing to hit the ties with each stride. One wrong step and he'd plant his face right on the hard iron of the tracks. I stayed behind him, concentrating on my own footing.

"Stop! Police! I will shoot!"

It was a lie, but worth trying. I was not going to shoot him in the back. If we'd had Tasers back then, I would have pulled mine from my belt and sent those two barbed hooks into him. With a range of thirty-five feet, then fifty thousand volts of electricity, it would have put him on the ground without, as they say, further incident.

But we didn't have Tasers that year. We had guns and we had batons and we had our own bodies. So I put my head down and I kept chasing him. But I had a few years on him, and even though my old scouting report said, "Runs well," that praise was quickly qualified with "for a catcher." You squat down, then stand up a couple hundred times a day, each and every day for an entire season. Then you see how well you run.

The tracks took a slight curve to the right, then went under Bagley Street. I didn't see any helpful backup sitting up there on the bridge. A siren and some flashing lights, and the knowledge that he couldn't keep running down those tracks forever—that's probably all it would have taken. Instead, I saw my suspect disappear into the darkness under the bridge.

When I finally got there myself, I was just about ready to collapse, but I kept moving down the rails, trying to be careful with my footing. Up ahead of me I saw the tracks straighten out and head right for the tunnel that went under the Detroit River, for miles and miles, all the way to Canada. For one horrible second I couldn't help imagining this kid trying to make his escape that way, and then the single bright light from an oncoming train, suddenly bearing down on him. Or me if I was stupid enough to chase him down the tunnel.

I came out from the shade of the bridge, into the sudden glare of the sunlight. I didn't see my suspect.

A movement to my left. I reached for my revolver out of pure instinct. But no, he was up against the abutment, where the fence met the bridge. The bottom corner was loose, and he was working himself through the opening.

"Stop!" I said, running to the spot, just in time to see him slip underneath, feet first. The ragged edge of the fence caught against his shirt, scraping his arm, tearing at his right sleeve. He scrambled to his feet, wincing and looking at his arm. There was a thin trickle of blood on his skin. He looked at me. That one second, the two of us seeing each other on opposite sides of a metal fence. He was close enough for me to see the color of his eyes. Close enough to see the Oakland Raiders logo on his black baseball hat. That close, yet a world apart. I pointed my revolver though the fence.

"Get on the ground! Right now! Or I'll shoot!"

He stood there for another beat, a stone-cold look on his face. Then he turned and ran up the slope, onto Bagley Street. I didn't shoot him in the back, much as I wanted to. I'll be damned if anyone's gonna make me run down the railroad tracks like a maniac, sweating and gasping and generally putting myself into near cardiac arrest. All on the short-shift day, no less.

I crouched down and pulled up the corner of the fence. I couldn't imagine how he could get through there. I couldn't imagine myself even trying. So instead I keyed the radio on my shoulder. I was breathing too hard to speak. I had to wait a moment before I finally got it out.

"Unit Forty-one," I said, by way of identification. "I need two-eleven on a suspected dealer heading east on Bagley Street. Young black male, jeans, gray T-shirt, black Oakland Raiders baseball cap."

I heard a few responses. Cars in the general area, heading closer for a look. Maybe they'd pick him up. Maybe not. It was up to them now.

I stood there with my hands on my knees for a while. When I was more or less functional again, I started walking back down the tracks. Under the bridge, then out into the daylight. I tried to remember exactly where he had thrown away whatever had been in his hand. I replayed the whole thing in my mind. Hand comes out, object in the air. There were two sets of tracks running parallel. I pictured the trajectory of the object, figuring it probably cleared the tracks closest to him, landing right around the near rail on the other side. So I crossed over and looked at the ground as I continued back to the station. When I got to what I thought was the approximate spot, I crouched down and duckwalked along the track, looking carefully. But I didn't see anything. No clear Baggie with white rocks inside. Nothing but the gravel and the usual assortment of trash you find anywhere. Gum wrappers, cigarettes, rain-soaked pieces of paper.

Franklin was waiting about fifty yards down the tracks, talking into his radio. He shook his head as I came closer.

"Are you okay?"

"Why did I do that?" I asked him. "Some dumb kid with ten bucks' worth of crack probably, and I gotta chase him a half mile down the railroad tracks? I could have tripped on one of those railroad ties and killed myself."

"I'm kinda surprised you didn't."

"Nice backup we got there, too. One man standing on the bridge, that's all we needed."

Franklin smiled and looked away from me.

"Excuse me," I said. "Did something funny happen here that I missed?"

"What, besides you running after that boy, like there was any chance in hell of you catching him?"

"So it wasn't a complete loss, is what you're saying. Because at least you were entertained."

"Don't you remember what we were saying earlier? About how all we needed to make the day complete was you chasing somebody, climbing a fence, throwing them into some garbage cans? Then complaining about how we're too old for this?"

"Yeah, so? He went under the fence instead of over it. And I sure as hell didn't catch him and throw him into any garbage cans."

"Well," he said, still smiling and shaking his head. "At least you can still say you're too old for this. Go ahead."

I didn't bother. I walked back to the train station, already feeling the pain in my legs. I knew there'd be hell to pay the next morning.

"What was he doing back here?" Franklin said, looking up at the station. Eighteen empty floors, this whole back end of the station not used for anything. Not for years. The one corner of the station still open was on the opposite end. There was no reason to come down this far.

"You tell me," I said. "Maybe he was meeting somebody back here."

"I didn't see anybody else. Did you?"

I shook my head, looking up at the windows high above me.

"I'm sure he wouldn't be the first guy who broke into this place," I said. "There's probably copper wire and other stuff to steal."

We went inside the door that led to the active part of the building and took a quick look around. There were a few customers waiting on wooden benches, but nobody had seen our suspect. So we went outside again.

We were heading to our car, but then on a whim I walked back down the tracks. There were high-arched windows all along this abandoned section of the station. I couldn't see anything inside except darkness.

"What are you doing down there?" Franklin said.

"He could have been doing something over here," I said. "He might have been coming out right around the time we saw him."

"Why in hell would he do that? It's deserted back here."

A good question. The ground between the tracks and the building was nothing but weeds and trash and old train schedules. I walked toward the windows, keeping an eye out for snakes or God knows what.

Then I saw it.

"There's a door over here!" I said.

"Is it open?"

"One way to find out."

There was a rough path through the thick brush, leading to the door. I tried the handle. It didn't turn, but I could see that the door was ajar. Taking one deep breath, I pulled it open and looked inside.

CHAPTER FIVE

All these years later, to see what this place had become. I parked as close I could, got out, and started walking down the sidewalk. Roosevelt Park was devoid of any life, save for a flock of birds roosting in one of the trees. The birds shuffled and murmured but did not fly away as I walked past.

Michigan Central Station loomed in the sky ahead of me. MCS. The MC Depot. Whatever you wanted to call it. It was half empty back in the day, back when it was part of my beat. Now it was gutted. It was violated. It was torn apart from the inside out. Every window was broken. I mean, eighteen stories high, hundreds of windows. Every single one broken.

There was a high Cyclone fence around the building. Through it I could see the graffiti and the litter, and in some places I could even see the sunlight from the other side of the building. It was the first time I had stood this close to the building since that other summer, all those years ago.

"What the hell," I said out loud. I was looking at the shell of what was once a monument. A palace. And I was thinking of everything else I had seen that day. "How can a whole city come to this?"

There was something more, too. Besides what had happened to this place, this city. Something about the day itself. It was a low-level hum just starting in my head.

I walked down past the station, toward the river. The tracks still looked usable. I was sure the trains still came this way, emerging from under the river and roaring right past the old station. There would be no reason to stop here now. Or even to slow down.

I kept going on the other side of the razor-wire fence, past the big post office building with all the trucks lined up in the parking lot. A sign of life, at least. Some real business still being conducted. I ended up on Rosa Parks Boulevard, looking at yet one more long wreck of a building, a full block of shuttered windows and an old loading dock that hadn't seen a truck in months or maybe years. The street side of the building was tagged with more graffiti. Already today I had seen so many combinations of spray-painted letters. There was a bridge with a battered rusty wreck of a fence on either side, and then the road curved east as it came up against the Detroit River. I kept walking.

I saw the five great towers of the Renaissance Center up ahead as I walked along the river. I could remember back when they built those towers, and of course I knew what the word "renaissance" meant to this city. If we could have looked forward to right now, would the whole idea have felt like a lie? Or was there still hope?

I looked at my watch. The sun was high, but it was pushing five o'clock. Time to get back to my truck. Maybe I'd have the chance to think about the big questions later, but right now it was time to have dinner with Agent Janet Long.

I met her at the FBI offices on Michigan Avenue. They owned one floor in McNamara Federal Building, along with the Department of Veterans Affairs and the Secret Service. The DEA was right across the street.

I waited in the lobby for her. The elevator doors opened, and she came out chatting with another agent. It was her partner, Agent Fleury. I'd met them both at the same time, when they'd come up to my part of the state. Agent Fleury and I had gotten off to a rough start with each other, although I supposed we'd made our peace in the end. Still, there was probably little chance of me inviting him to join Janet and me for dinner.

She saw me and waved to me. She was wearing a dark blue skirt and jacket, with a white blouse. The standard uniform of a female FBI agent. As she came over to me, we both had this moment of sudden bewilderment. Like why are we both standing here as if we're supposed to have anything to do with each other? She broke the spell by giving me a quick hug.

"You remember my partner," she said. "Agent Fleury."

"Nice to see you again," he said, shaking my hand. He was younger than us. His suit was tailored. His hair was perfect. He reminded me a little of Detective Bateman, back in his prime.

He didn't stick around for small talk. He wished us both a good evening, and then he left.

"You look good," she said as soon as he was gone. "But you must be tired. It's a long way from Paradise to Detroit."

"In more ways than one."

"I remember how you drive," she said. "Still using that ex-cop with a bullet angle, huh?"

"It would be a shame not to."

"So I thought we'd have dinner in Greektown. Does that sound all right?"

"That sounds perfect. You want me to drive?"

"This is downtown," she said. "We'll take the People Mover."

We walked a block to the station on Cass Avenue. For fifty cents you can get on this raised monorail that makes a three-mile loop around downtown, stopping at Joe Louis Arena, the Renaissance Center, Greektown, a few other destinations. It's slow as hell, but it gets the job done, and you don't have to drive your car. Maybe even more importantly, you don't have to park somewhere you might not feel that good about.

We hopped on the tram and stood there looking down as the streets passed below us. Everybody was getting off work in the financial district, and in the GM headquarters. Men with suits and briefcases were walking down the street, many of them joining us in the People Mover.

"It's good to see all these people downtown," I said. "You'd almost think the old city was doing okay."

"It can feel that way some days," she said. "Especially in the summer. Especially down here by the river."

When we finally made it to the eastern side of the loop, we got out at Greektown and walked to the restaurant. We passed right by the Greektown Casino, one of the three casinos in the city now. Hard to even imagine back when I was on the police force, going the Atlantic City route and inviting everything else that comes with the gambling money. Yet here they were. I'm sure they were all doing decent business, but I couldn't help thinking they were really just huge monuments to the city's desperation. Once the greatest manufacturing center in the world. Now just a place where you can go to play the slot machines.

"This one was owned by your neighbors," Janet said as she looked up at the bright lights on the Greektown Casino.

"It was," I said, shaking my head. After the Bay Mills tribe started the ball rolling with the first Indian-run blackjack casino in the country, the Sault tribe over in Sault Ste. Marie jumped in with both feet, building the huge Kewadin Casino, and then eventually expanding their operations down here when Detroit passed the new gaming law. Not a year later, the Gaming Board took the casino away from them and gave it to a new group of investors. You can still guarantee yourself an interesting conversation by walking into any bar or restaurant in Sault Ste. Marie, finding a Sault member, and asking him what he thinks of the tribal leaders who let that happen.

The restaurant was just down the street from the casino. A Greek place, believe it or not. We got a table upstairs, and Janet ordered us some wine.

"This is on me," I said.

"Think again, mister. You're the one who drove all the way down here."

We put that fight off for later. I sat there and drank my wine and looked at her. There was a calmness to her face that I had found appealing from the first moment I had seen her. She was up in the UP, trying to solve what would turn out to be multiple murders, going back years. Yet there was always this air of self-assurance about her.

I liked her hair, too. The way it framed her face.

"Remind me again," I said. "How old are you?"

She laughed at that one. "Is that your opening line on all your dates?"

"So this is a date, you're saying."

She shook her head, but she was smiling. "God, we really don't know each other very well, do we?"

"We never got the chance. We were both so preoccupied when you were up there. Then you had to go."

"Yeah, I made you promise to come down and take me to dinner," she said. "I have to admit, I was starting to think you never would."

"I'm sorry. I should have come down sooner."

"So why now?"

"One of the last collars I made when I was down here," I said. "Right before . . . I mean right before I left the force . . . It was a homicide over in the old train station."

"You're the one who caught him?"

"Eventually. I ID'd him, anyway. Was there when he was finally arrested. He's getting out this week, so I got the courtesy call. Not that I think in a million years that he'll be coming for me."

"Then why did you need to come down here?"

"I got talking to the old sergeant," I said. "He said I should come down and see the place. So I figured what the hell."

"Ah, so it *wasn't* just to see me." She had a little smile on her face as she said it.

"A few reasons put together," I said. "Just call it that. Keeping my promise was the best reason of all."

She looked over her wineglass at me, like she wasn't quite buying it.

"I spent a few hours driving around today," I said. "I couldn't believe it."

"I know. It's not like I spend a lot of time in the neighborhoods, but . . ."

"Why are they all leaving, Janet? It's turning into a ghost town."

"Well, I've worked on more than a few corruption cases," she said. "Not that Detroit is the only city where it happens, but you'd be amazed. We seem to have elevated it to an art form."

"But that can't be the only reason."

"The city is broke, Alex. I mean, absolutely flat-out busted. They can't even keep all the streetlights on anymore. They can't run the buses. They want everybody to pick up and move closer together, basically cut the size of the city in half."

"And do what with the rest?"

"Hell if I know. Urban farming? Just let it go wild? Some of the city's half wild already."

"Yeah, I heard about the bears living in the abandoned buildings."

"I think that's just an urban legend."

"Oh, really? It seemed like such a good deal for the bears."

"Just the fact that it sounds almost believable," she said. "That we'd really have that many empty buildings and so much open space . . ."

"I can't believe how many burnt-out houses I saw today. That's one thing we always had to deal with. But then they'd come through the next week and knock them all down. Sometimes even rebuild."

"They don't need people to set fires anymore," she said, looking out the window, like she could take it all in from where we were sitting. "The city is burning itself down."

"How do you mean?"

"In the summertime, when it's dry . . . Sometimes the power lines will come down and start fires. There was one day a couple of years ago, you couldn't even walk down the street without choking on it. There were hundreds of houses burning down all at once."

"All right, we have to stop talking like this," I said. "There must be something good going on around here."

"The Tigers have a nice new stadium."

"Oh, don't get me started on that. I don't care how beautiful Comerica Park is . . ."

"It's not Tiger Stadium. I know. I grew up here, too, remember?"

We drank a toast to Tiger Stadium. Then to the old Olympia Stadium, the redbrick building where Gordie Howe and the Red

Wings once played. We toasted the Bob-Lo Boat that took kids down the Detroit River. We toasted Vernors Ginger Ale, back when it was as strong as rocket fuel. We toasted Greenfield Village and the automobile shows that would bring classic cars and hot rods from all over the world coming back home to the Motor City, to cruise up and down the streets all day long and into the night, while thousands of people gathered along the sidewalks and parking lots to barbecue and drink beer and argue about which cars were the best.

We had our dinner. We eventually got around to talking about our past relationships. It turned out we were both married once, something else I didn't know about her. We started getting closer to the present, and to the unspoken question about what might still happen between the two of us. Even that very night.

"You live really far away," she said as we had our dessert. "You're aware of that, right?"

"Yes, I am."

"It would be next to impossible to do much else besides what we're doing right now."

"If we both stay where we are, yes."

"This is nice, though. I'm glad you came down."

"I'm glad, too."

"But tell me the truth," she said, looking me in the eye. "Why are you really here?"

I had the same two or three answers I'd already given her. I didn't have the one single answer that would really satisfy both of us.

In the end, after we battled over the bill and finally ended up splitting it, we got up and walked outside and into the night. We didn't go into the casino. We just walked down the sidewalk, back to the People Mover. Back to her car and to my truck. She hugged me and gave me a quick kiss. Nobody said a word about us spending the night together, and I have to believe that maybe we were both a little relieved that it never came up. I promised her that I'd see her again soon.

She hesitated as she opened her car door. "Are you sure you're not thinking about moving back down here? Somewhere we could see each other more than once or twice a year?"

"Well," I said, "let's just say I now have one more good reason to do that."

She came back to me and gave me another kiss.

"You're damned right you do."

Then she got in her car and she drove home.

I stood there under the streetlight for a while. Then I got in my truck and drove down Michigan Avenue. A police car cut in front of me, lights and siren going, and for one second my old instincts told me to follow the car so I could help out. It was these same streets, after all. For eight years I had done this.

I turned off into a parking lot next to the first bar I saw. It was just a concrete box, as far away from the Glasgow Inn as you could imagine, but it was all I needed that night. I sat at the bar with a double Scotch and looked at my own face in the mirror.

You will always be alone, I told myself. That's just the way it is.

When I finally left that place, I knew it had been too long a day, with a little bit too much to drink, for a five-hour drive back home. I'd thrown a toothbrush and a few things into a bag, not making any kind of plan, just being ready for whatever happened. I drove a few blocks down to the little motel on Michigan Avenue where once upon a time you could open the drapes and look down the street at the gray walls of the stadium. The stadium was gone now, as I kept proving to myself every time I drove by it that day, still surprising myself every time. But the little motel was still there and now I suppose it was officially the most forlorn place in the world, with no special view from your window to set it apart.

I checked in for one night. I lay on the bed for exactly two minutes, listening to another police car's siren in the distance. Then I got back up and went out to the truck. There was no way I'd be able to sleep.

I got in the truck and drove around the city. One more time, just to see it again. What it had become.

I went to the train station. Of course I did. I parked in the same place, got out, and walked down the same sidewalk, stood on the same piece of cracked pavement and looked up at all of the broken windows. How unnatural for there to be no lights on inside at all, not one single light in an eighteen-floor building.

Something horrible happened here, I thought, and I never really got the time to process it. I never understood it or made my peace with it, because just a month later, in that very same summer, something else happened that obliterated my entire life.

So now that I was here again, standing in this very spot where that first thing happened . . . It was like I finally had the chance to make some sense of it, all these years later.

I was feeling that hum again. Louder this time.

Something is not right. That's the thing that came to me. Something is not adding up for me. Not then. Not now. Not ever.

This is why you came all the way down here, Alex. This thing that you knew deep down but could only start to put words to when you got the chance to stand here in the dark, in this exact moment.

This is why you're here.

CHAPTER SIX

The first thing that hit me was the smell of urine mixed with sweat mixed with a dead animal or two mixed with God knows what else. It should have just been the musty stale air of a place locked up tight, but obviously someone had found the way in and a few others had followed.

It was a small vestibule in this empty corner of the train station, with a half-dozen stairs littered with cigarette butts and trash, leading up to an old waiting room. There, the big arched windows looked out over the tracks. The glass was streaked with grime, and as I turned to look around at the rest of the room, I saw all of the chairs pushed together, covered with sheets. There was an elaborate chandelier hanging from the ceiling, ringed with cobwebs. There was enough daylight coming through the windows that I could see halfway into the room, but then it all turned to darkness.

"Anybody in here?"

I took my gun out, because that's what a cop does when he doesn't know who might be waiting and watching.

"It's okay if you are. I'm just looking around. If there's anybody here, you can come out."

I felt a low rumbling then. In the floor, coming up through my bones. Then the sound. A train was coming. I looked out the window and watched it go by. A freight train. It wasn't stopping here at the station for any of the few passengers that were waiting. It was going southeast, toward the long tunnel that ran under the river, to Canada.

I took the flashlight off my belt and turned it on. In the dark side of the room, it showed more furniture covered with sheets. Nothing moved.

My radio squawked, startling the hell out of me. "Alex, what are you doing in there?" My partner.

"Just taking a quick look. I don't see anybody in here right now. Doesn't mean they're not hiding."

I shined my flashlight on the dusty floor. I could see my own fresh footprints. Then just a few feet away, was that another set? I crouched down low to the floor and directed the light at an angle. Athletic shoes, a little smaller than mine. There seemed to be one set of the same prints going into the room, another set going back out. That made sense. Somebody came in here and then left. That somebody was probably the kid I tried to chase down.

The incoming tracks led to another staircase. As I went closer, I had a perfect angle to see the various footprints on the treads. There were many different pairs of shoes going up and down these stairs. Some recently. Some not so recently. For a part of the station that was supposedly closed to the public, this was a surprisingly popular destination.

The perfect place for a drug deal, I thought. The perfect place to shoot up or smoke. Or the perfect place to meet up with one of the young male hustlers who hang out across the street in the park.

I started up the steps. Stone, maybe even marble, back when buildings were made to last a thousand years. I came to the landing, made the turn, went all the way up to the next level. I was standing on a balcony overlooking the waiting room. The windows cast oblong rectangles of light across the tiled floor. I went to the railing and looked down. Then I turned.

It took me a moment to process what I was looking at. In the corner. Right behind me. I saw the blood first, so dark in the shadows it was like a black void. The body was half sitting, half lying against the wall, the neck at an unnatural angle.

It was a woman. Her eyes were open. She was staring right at me from the other side of death.

I remembered how to breathe. I remembered how to speak as I keyed the radio on my shoulder.

"Code three, code three," I said. "This is Unit Forty-one at Michigan Central Station. I have a one-eight-seven here. All nearby units respond."

A moment of crackling radio silence. Then a voice.

"Where are you, Forty-one?"

"Around the back of the building. One female victim. Suspect as previously reported, a young black male, last seen proceeding east on Bagley Street. Repeat, young black male, proceeding east on Bagley Street. Jeans, gray shirt, black Oakland Raiders baseball hat."

"Wait, this is the same suspect as before? Your call from a few minutes ago?"

"Affirmative. Same suspect."

I could just imagine the confusion I was causing, how many partners were turning to look at each other, shaking their heads, but I didn't have time to worry about it. I was already moving away from the body, back down those stairs, staying to the very edge to preserve the footprints. I went back out the same door I had come in, into the sunlight. Franklin was waiting there on the tracks.

"She's on the second-floor balcony," I said. "Stay here and show them where the door is. I'm going to go find my suspect."

"Alex, wait! He's long gone by now!"

"Yeah, probably," I said over my shoulder, "but I'm the only one who saw his face."

It was a purely instinctive reaction, to get back to that car, to get behind the wheel, crank that engine, take off out of that parking lot and onto the streets. He had been right there in front of me. I had just missed catching him, and then, when he was standing on the other side of that fence, I had looked right into his eyes. I had my gun drawn. I had aimed it right at his chest, then at the center of his back as he turned to run away. I could have shot him down right then.

No, don't go there, I told myself. There'll be plenty of time to second-guess yourself later.

I heard the sirens as I pulled out onto the street. I circled the station and hit Bagley Street. How many minutes had passed since he'd come up from the tracks?

Too many. He could have covered a lot of ground by now. But I needed to give this a shot.

I tried to put myself in his shoes. Running down this street, a long straightaway. I'm thinking I switch streets as soon as possible. Next intersection is Vermont. To the right is back to the tracks, so left.

I took the turn. I was heading north now. But now I was heading back close to the station, so another jog to the right, onto Marantette. Dead end at Rosa Parks, jog left, but stay off this main road, so jog right again.

Now I was in Corktown, the old Irish neighborhood. It felt like a mistake now, as I gunned it down Church Street, lights flashing, siren off, residents out on their porches, watching me go by. A young black man wouldn't run down this street if he had others to choose from. I slowed down as I came up to Trumbull.

Then I saw him. Or at least I thought I did. A young man running. The right size, the right jeans and gray shirt. No black hat, but then losing the hat would be the smart play. He was heading north, moving fast. I made the left on Trumbull and tried to keep my eye on him as I came to Michigan Avenue.

Then I stopped dead at the police barricade.

The Tigers game had ended. All of the people filing out of the stadium clogged the streets. I picked up my transmitter.

"Suspect heading north on Trumbull, just past the stadium. Jeans, gray shirt, no black hat now. All units in the area, please respond."

The officers working the intersection spotted me and did their best to hold off the crowds for a moment. The barricade was moved and I made my way through. But now I had lost sight of him.

"Okay," I said out loud, "you see me coming after you. So do me a favor and try something stupid. Make a break for it. And if you're gonna turn off this street, go right."

I knew that would be a dead end for him no matter which street he took. Everything ended when it came up to the Lodge Freeway.

But now that I was north of the stadium, I was starting to hit the traffic. Everybody walking back to their cars, many of them parked in lots up and down this street. I still had my lights flashing, but when the streets are full enough, there's just nowhere for the cars to pull over.

I picked up my transmitter again. "I've lost touch with the suspect, last seen heading north on Trumbull. Any luck out there?"

An agonizing silence, as I hoped against hope that he was already being arrested by another unit. I pictured the handcuffs slapped on his wrists, a hand on his head as he was put into the back of the squad car.

Answer me, damn it. Somebody out there. Say something.

"Negative so far," I finally heard someone say. "No sight of him."

The cars were lining up to get off the street and onto the freeway. I pulled my car over and got out, locking it and leaving the lights flashing. There were thousands of people on the sidewalk, walking away from the stadium. I started running through them, looking down every side street. Until finally, there, up ahead, a young man's face looking back, then turning away.

I keyed my shoulder radio. "I'm on foot now, in pursuit of suspect. Still on Trumbull, passing over I-75. I need a unit on the other side to intercept. Repeat, I need a unit on the north end of the street as it crosses over I-75."

We'll catch you, I thought. As long as the unit gets there in time, you'll have nowhere to turn.

I kept pushing my way through the crowds as the street and the sidewalk took the long span over the freeway, cars zooming by beneath us. I didn't see him, but I knew he had to be there in front of me.

"Come on," I said out loud, panting as I ran. "Somebody get to the other end so we can head him off."

That's all I was thinking about. That's probably all I could think about and still stay functional. I couldn't let my mind go back to that scene in the train station. I kept moving, kept watching for my suspect, and kept hoping we'd catch him so that at least one thing in the world would make sense tonight.

Halfway over the bridge now, which seemed to go on forever. Police lights ahead of me, finally flashing on the other side. Two cars, then three. Blocking off Trumbull now, not just the cars but a great mass of people backed up on the sidewalk going north. I ran between the cars, and as I finally got close to the other side I saw a figure assuming the position against the side of a squad car. Jeans, gray shirt, legs kicked out, hands on the hood. An officer on either side, going through the guy's pockets. Something being taken out and put on the hood. The handcuffs being slapped on and the young man put in the back of the car. Just as I had hoped would happen.

I slowed down to a walk, tried to catch my breath. The scene in the station already coming back to me, fighting its way back into my head now that the chase was over. The process would begin now. The booking, the arraignment, the visit from the public defender. It would take weeks to get to the end of it. Maybe months. But it wouldn't change what had happened. It wouldn't undo the violence or bring back a woman who didn't deserve to be left for dead in the dusty corner of an abandoned balcony.

I'd probably never understand why it happened, but I'd have the rest of my life to think about it. For right now, I just had to finish my day's work. Go up and thank my fellow officers for the assist on the collar. Take a look at the suspect and confirm he was the same person I saw running from the train station. Then go back and get my vehicle. Find Franklin, make sure the crime scene was secure. Wait for the specialists to arrive, and be glad that part of the operation isn't my job. Go home, maybe get drunk. It sounded like the right kind of night for it.

A sergeant approached me. Not Sergeant Grimaldi, but another man from another squad. He was probably on his way in for the afternoon shift when he heard the call, and he was close enough to be the first supervising officer on the scene.

"I'm Sergeant Schuman," he said, shaking my hand. "I believe we've met before. You okay?"

I nodded. I still didn't quite have my voice back yet.

"We've got a Ronald Jefferson in the backseat," he said, looking at the driver's license in his hand. "We found a few rocks and a fair amount of money on him as well."

I looked over and saw the evidence on the hood of the vehicle. A handful of small Baggies, each one containing a marble-sized chunk of white powder. Next to that was a thick roll of currency.

"Wait a minute," I said, going over to the vehicle. "Why would he still have this on him? I saw him throw something on the tracks."

"Maybe he didn't have time to get rid of it."

"He did," I said, thinking back to the sight of him standing on the other side of that fence. The look of utter calm on his face when he realized I couldn't catch him. "He had all the time in the world. For that matter, why even bother throwing away drugs if he just killed somebody? Unless it was something else entirely . . ."

I think I already knew what I was going to find when I opened the back door to that squad car. A two-bit dealer who just so happened to be wearing jeans and a gray shirt that day.

I opened the door. I grabbed the kid and turned his face to me.

"Hey, what are you doing, man?" Attitude all the way, even now that he was in handcuffs. *Especially* now that he was in handcuffs.

He was around the same age, same build, and wearing, as I had already figured out, the same clothes. Although this kid's shirt was a slightly different shade of gray now that I looked at it. And he didn't have a torn sleeve like my suspect.

I let go of him. I slammed the door shut.

"It's not him," I said.

"McKnight," the sergeant said, "are you sure?"

"I'm sure. It's not him."

"Then where the hell is he?"

I took a quick scan through the other people still milling around on the sidewalk. Then I came back to the car and looked north, up the street. It went up to Pine and Spruce and Perry and a dozen other side streets. He must have gotten across before these cops closed off the bridge.

"He could be anywhere by now," I said. "Pretty much goddamned anywhere."

"Come on," the sergeant said. "Get in my car."

I got in the passenger's seat. He flipped on his lights and headed north on Trumbull.

"Give me a guess here," he said. "Use your gut instinct and tell me where he went."

It was useless. There were blocks and blocks of houses on either side of the street. If we turned down one street we'd see another block and then another intersection. Right, left, or straight, it would just be more of the same. The whole west side of Detroit, all those brick houses lined up in rows. He could have been in any one of them.

"Keep looking," the sergeant said. "But tell me what happened."

I gave him the basic facts. Seeing the young man on the tracks, chasing him when he fled, his escape through the fence.

"You called for backup then," the sergeant said.

"Yes, but at that point it was just trespassing, then evading. I had no idea that . . ." I didn't finish the sentence.

The sergeant shook his head, but before he could say anything the radio squawked, looking for Unit Forty-one. The sergeant picked up the transmitter.

"I've got him right here," he said. "I'll bring him back to the scene."

He put the transmitter back and swung the car south at the next intersection.

"You're the only one who saw this guy. Am I right?"

"I'm the only one who got a good look at his face," I said, looking out the window as we raced back to the train station.

"Sounds like you're going to be a very popular man."

There were a dozen cars at the train station. Our car was one of them. Franklin must have been sent to retrieve it. It was going on six o'clock now, two hours past my shift. I knew my night was far from over.

I took a deep breath as I got out of the sergeant's car. I thanked him. He was officially on duty now, so he stuck around to help coordinate.

There was a train stopped at the station, the air brakes hissing.

I saw Detective Arnie Bateman waving me over. After all the time I'd spent avoiding him that day, this was real business, and I knew he'd be right in the middle of it.

"This is the five forty-five Amtrak," he said as soon as I was in earshot. "We held it up to ask the passengers if they saw anything while they were waiting."

"Yeah, we did a quick pass through the waiting room," I said. "I don't think our suspect ever went in there."

"You might want to take a quick look through the train yourself, before we let it go. I mean, you never know, right? Maybe he's on board right now. We've caught dumber criminals."

"Last I saw him, he was running away. I can't see why he'd double back."

"Just humor me, all right? Maybe you saw somcone else. An accomplice or something. Maybe seeing him will jog your memory."

I knew it was beyond a long shot, but I got on board anyway. I walked down the aisle of every car, giving everyone the once-over. Some of the passengers were clearly annoyed to be kept waiting. One of them actually stood up and asked me when the train would finally be moving. He was wearing a suit, and he reminded me of the man who had wrecked his Saab earlier that day, his time and convenience clearly being more important than anything else. God, how long ago it seemed now, just a routine accident on a day that started out so normal. Now I had this man in my face and I felt like taking him off the train, into the station, up to that abandoned balcony. Here's your reason, you pompous jackass. Now go back to your seat and sit the hell down.

When I got off the train, having looked at every face, it slowly pulled away from the station. It was heading west. First stop maybe Ann Arbor, then on to Chicago.

"Okay, so now that we've got that out of the way," the detective said, "tell me exactly what you saw."

We were standing outside between the station and the tracks. He looked just as fresh and energetic as he had that morning at roll call, but the man who had come looking for basketball players, the man my partner and I had both made fun of, was long gone.

The sun was low in the sky, and I swear that gold shield on his belt was practically glowing.

"Because the last I heard," he said, not even bothering to let me start explaining, "you were asking for two-eleven on a suspected drug dealer running away from here. Then a few minutes later . . . we've got this poor woman on the floor upstairs?"

"Have you identified her?"

"Yes," he said, taking a step back. "Sorry, I'm getting ahead of myself. The victim's name is Elana Paige. She was . . . Well, you saw the crime scene."

"Multiple stab wounds?"

He shook his head. "From what I'm hearing, way beyond multiple. Somebody just stabbed her and stabbed her. God knows how many times."

"What else do we know about her?"

"Twenty-eight years old, married, no kids. Lives in Farmington Hills. Not employed at the moment, but she's taking classes at Wayne State."

Out of everything he was saying, that's the one thing that stopped me short.

"My wife is taking classes at Wayne State," I said. "They might even know each other."

"I suppose that's possible. Although it is a big school."

"I know. I'm just saying."

"It does bring it home, yes. This woman could have been from anyone's family. Yours, mine . . ."

"Any idea why she was here?"

"Not yet. We're contacting the husband right now."

I walked away from him. It was getting harder and harder to keep the scene out of my head. Now I was imagining being the husband, too. Hearing that knock on my door, opening it up and seeing two police officers.

"So tell me," Bateman said. "How did you end up checking out that balcony?"

"I was coming back and I saw the open door. I thought it was worth investigating."

He walked down the tracks to the far end of the station. The door was propped open now. I could see the sudden bursts of flashbulbs from inside. The crime scene unit was up there, doing their work.

"That door right there," he said. "You're saying you didn't actually see him coming out of the building?"

"No. Like I said, he was on the tracks."

He stood there looking at the door, then down the tracks, then back at me.

"I didn't know it went down that way," he said. "I'm sorry if it sounded like I was trying to find fault. Under the circumstances, if you really didn't have any knowledge of the suspect being in the building . . ."

"It's all right, Detective. It's a tough day for everyone."

"This whole back end of the building is abandoned, anyway. How could you have even known? I mean, how did you even think of trying that door?"

"It was just a hunch."

"Okay," he said, nodding like he was deep in thought, his mind already racing ahead to something else. "That's good. But go back to that first pursuit. He goes east down these tracks, right? You were calling for backup at Bagley Street?"

"That's right. I saw him throw something. I assumed it was a bag of crack."

He rubbed his chin. "But that would take him back to being just a dealer," he said. "Why throw away a few dollars of crack if you just killed somebody?"

"In hindsight, it doesn't make much sense."

"Hell, maybe this kid isn't our killer after all. Maybe he just happened to be here at the wrong time, huh?"

"It's possible."

"Are you sure he wasn't throwing away a knife?"

I played the scene back in my head. "I don't know exactly what he threw away," I said, "but a knife I would have recognized. This was something smaller. I didn't even really see it once it left his hand."

"Show me where that happened," he said. "Whatever it was, we should try to find it."

I walked with him, retracing my steps along the railroad tracks. I tried to remember when he had thrown the object, but there weren't any good landmarks to measure how far down we had gotten. It was, after all, just unbroken lines of metal with identical ties at regular intervals.

"It's gotta be around here," I said, slowing down. "I can't be sure exactly. I could be off by a few yards either way."

Detective Bateman was already scanning the ground.

"Which way did he throw it?"

"He was running in this direction." I was thinking back again, trying hard to re-create every detail in my mind. "He threw with his right hand, toward the other tracks."

The detective stepped over the tracks, to the second set running parallel.

"Did he make it this far? To the other tracks?"

"I'm going to say yes. I'm pretty sure he did."

We were inside the fenced-off part of the track now, about twenty feet wide. There was the rough gravel at the base, then the railroad ties, then the tracks on top. The detective was walking right down the center of the rightmost tracks, looking closely at every inch of the ground.

"I don't imagine anybody else got back here to pick up whatever it was," he said. "Not with this fence and all. But if another train came by . . ."

"It did," I said. "I just remembered."

He looked up at me.

"When I was in the building. A train came by. It didn't stop."

"A freight train?"

"Yes."

"Heading in which direction?"

"Into the tunnel. To Canada."

"So on these tracks," he said, looking back down at the ground. "If it was something light, it could have been blown God knows where. Right through the fence even."

He kept looking for another few minutes. Then he pulled the radio off his belt.

"I need some officers down the tracks," he said. "While we're at it, can we get the train traffic held up until further notice? I don't need anybody getting run over here."

An hour later, we were still out on the tracks. There were eight officers, including Franklin, Detective Bateman, and myself. It's exhausting work, bending down low enough to see the ground, tossing aside the random trash and hoping for something significant. Every few minutes I'd stand up and stretch my back. I'd look down the tracks and see the crime unit specialists going in and out of the building. They still hadn't brought out the body.

It was Michigan and it was June, so that meant light until at least nine o'clock. But the sun was getting lower and everything was losing its bright focus. I decided to walk back to the station and to re-create the whole chase scene one more time, second by second, hoping to pinpoint exactly where we were when he threw away the object.

The detective watched me. I went to the exact spot where I had first seen my suspect. Hey, hold up. Stop right there. The kid turns and runs. Stop. Stop right there. Police.

I'm running after him now. My gun, my flashlight, everything on my belt bouncing up and down as I make my way down the tracks. He's opening up a lead. Don't be an idiot. It's not worth it.

No, wait. I hadn't said that yet. He had already thrown the object. Like right around . . . Here.

I stopped a good twenty yards short of my fellow officers and peered at the ground.

"Do we need to shift back?" Bateman said.

"Yes," I said without looking back. "I think we were looking too far down the tracks."

The officers moved closer to me. I glanced up and saw Franklin limping, one hand holding his back as he bent over again. I felt bad for him, but I wasn't about to stop him. The best way to make it easier for everyone would be to just find the goddamned thing the kid threw away.

The detective picked up his radio and listened to it. He said a few words, then returned the radio to his belt.

"The family is on their way down," he said to me. "I need to be there to let them know what's going on. If the crime scene is done, they'll be bringing the body over for identification, too."

He stopped, closed his eyes, and rubbed his forehead.

"These are the worst days," he said. "Makes me wonder why I ever became a cop."

"Tell them we'll find him," I said. "No matter what it takes."

He looked at me. "You know I can't promise that. Half the time, we don't."

"This time we will," I said. "I'll personally go through every face in the city until we find him."

He let out a breath. "I like your attitude, McKnight. But we still can't even put him inside the station, let alone identify him."

I didn't have an answer for that. Not for the first time in my life, I only had a gut feeling and nothing else.

"I have to get back to the precinct," he said. "If you find something, bring it right over, okay?"

That's how he left me. I was down on my hands and knees now, moving along the far set of railroad tracks. I figured I only had a few more minutes before the light went. I didn't want to have to come back and do this again the next day.

"Alex," Franklin said, a few feet away, "we don't even know what we're looking for."

"We'll know when we see it," I said. "I know we will."

He stood up and rubbed his bad knee. I kept looking through the rough gravel bed between the railroad ties.

"She was going to Wayne State," I finally said to him. "Just like Jeannie."

Franklin didn't say anything to that. He didn't have to. He bent back over and kept looking at the ground.

A few minutes later, I grabbed on to the hard metal of the railroad tracks. I dropped my head in frustration.

"I think we're about done for tonight," Franklin said. "We can get right back out here tomorrow morning."

He was right. The sun was too low now. I picked my head up, and as I did, I saw the tiniest flash of light. Probably just a piece of glass or something, but I looked closer. I sifted through the gravel, brushing aside one small gray rock after another.

Then I saw it.

Among the other rocks, pebbles, dirt, sand, cinder, slivers of glass, and all the other small things that by the million make up a railroad bed, that one little stone that stood out from all of the others.

A diamond.

It was just inside the farthest rail, midway between two ties. It had settled into the bed, so I had to get down close to the ground, like an archaeologist brushing away the debris from an ancient artifact. I brushed and I blew my breath on the stones and eventually I found another diamond. Then another. Then finally, against the track itself, I found a long golden strand with several more diamonds still intact. The clasp was broken.

This is what he threw away, I thought. This is what I saw flashing in the sunlight. This is what puts him in that station.

I didn't touch it. I called out to Franklin to go grab an evidence bag. As I waited, I keyed on my shoulder radio.

"Unit Forty-one at the train station," I said. "Please pass along a message to Detective Bateman. Tell him I found what we were looking for."

CHAPTER SEVEN

It was a warm morning. I was sitting on a folding lawn chair on the walkway outside my motel room, watching the traffic going by on Michigan Avenue. Across the street there was a softball game going on in the field where Tiger Stadium once stood.

I took out my cell phone, which was out of date and only occasionally functional. Like myself, I guess. I dialed the number for Sergeant Grimaldi. I'd seen him the day before, of course, but since then I'd seen the train station, gone to dinner with Janet, then seen the station one more time. So by this morning I was in a different state of mind.

The call went to his voice mail.

"Good morning, Sergeant," I said. "I mean Tony. I just wanted to thank you again for the drink yesterday. Also, I had something on my mind I wanted to ask you about. I'd appreciate it if you could give me a call back."

I ended the call. Just in time for a big truck to rumble by on Michigan Avenue, so loud I wouldn't have been able to hear his voice anyway, even if he had answered.

"Okay, now what?" I asked myself when the truck was a block past me. "I can sit here and wait for him to call me back . . ."

Or what else? I could go back to the train station, stand there and feel that same buzzing I had felt the night before. That feeling that there was something important that I was missing. That I had *been* missing for years.

Or I could just go home. Leave right away and be back for a late lunch at Jackie's place. Some of his world-famous beef stew, maybe. With a real Canadian Molson. There were worse ways to spend an afternoon.

Or I could even call Janet. Thank her for having dinner with me, maybe answer her question about whether I'd ever consider moving down here again. Not that I knew what that answer would be.

In the end, I chose none of the above. I checked out of the motel, threw my bag in the truck, and started driving around the city again. I was seeing it in the morning hours now, when every able-bodied person past school age should be at work. But I knew the unemployment rate for black males was hovering around fifty percent here. A staggering number of men without jobs. A good position in an auto plant was just a dim memory, and even a job sweeping a floor for minimum wage was all but impossible to find.

There were young men hanging out on the streets, some of them eyeing me like it was a personal affront for me to be there. I stared back at them, an old cop habit that I'd never get over, and I kept driving around. I was still on the west side of Detroit. I was staying on the secondary streets, avoiding the highways. You get on I-94 and you just zip right through everything, from one end of Detroit to the other, without really seeing any of the city itself.

Eventually, I found myself going down Martin Luther King Jr. Boulevard. This had been such an important street for us, back in that month when we were searching for our suspect. On paper, this had seemed like the northern limit to how far a young man would reasonably run that night. It was dense on either side of the street with apartment buildings. How many man-hours we had spent, knocking on every single door.

I turned south on Wabash, not really thinking about where I was going, just circling through this part of town like a goldfish in a bowl. To the east, the Motor City Casino towered over everything else in this part of town. A strange sight I'd never get used to. I turned my attention back to the road ahead.

Then I saw Ash Street. I stopped dead at the intersection.

Ash Street. I'd been driving around for an hour, not even thinking consciously about where I'd end up. But here I was.

I made the turn. There had been a grocery store on the corner of Fourteenth Street. The building was boarded up, the brick walls tagged with graffiti. A sign in front announced that the building was FOR RENT. As if anyone would see any reason to open a business here now, even if the rent was a dollar a month.

The next block was empty. Not a single building. I thought back and remembered that a few houses had been here once. Now it was just weeds and sumac. Even the sidewalk was almost completely hidden.

There'd been a fire here, on this block. That was a sure bet. A fire right here on Ash Street. It was supposedly just another tree-named street, like Elm and Spruce and Butternut, but no, Ash Street in this particular city meant something else entirely.

I drove one more block, to where an elementary school had been. The playground was still there, and so was the building itself, but the windows were all boarded over. The side of the building was tagged with graffiti, as huge and as elaborate as any I'd seen all morning. An elementary school, the heart of a neighborhood, come to this.

One more block, more vacant lots, an old boat somehow left there on the corner and filled with tires. A neighborhood watch sign, like a cruel joke.

Then finally, the block just past Seventeenth Street. There was one house on the north side of the street now. One single house. Two stories, once white, now a shade of light gray. Some of the siding was falling out of line, and the front porch was visibly sagging away from the house.

It was a small porch, just like I remembered it. Just big enough for one chair. A woman sat in the chair, looking serenely out at the street. A large black woman in a sundress, maybe midsixties, her hair the same color as the siding on the house. I slowed down in front of the house. I had to. If she hadn't been there, I would have kept driving. It would have been a curious little side trip, something I'd shake my head at all the way home. But the woman was sitting right there on the porch, watching me. The same woman I had met all those years ago, on another warm day not unlike this one, on this very same porch.

It was her. No doubt about it. It was Mrs. Jamilah King. Darryl King's mother.

I parked the truck on the empty street. I got out and approached her. If having a strange white man paying her a visit made her uneasy, she didn't show it.

"Can I help you?" she asked me. "Are you lost?"

"No, ma'am," I said. "I was just driving around and I saw you sitting here. I hope you don't mind me stopping."

"If you're trying to sell me some of that frozen food, I'm going to have to say no, thank you."

"I'm not selling anything, ma'am. I promise."

"Then I'm sorry, but I can't imagine what would bring you to this end of the street. Ain't nothing here to see."

"Well, it has changed," I said, taking a quick look around. There was an empty shell of an old house down the street, on the other side. The sumac was so tall and so close, you couldn't even see half of it.

"There used to be houses all up and down this street," she said. "Kids all went to that elementary school on the next block."

"Yes," I said. "I think I remember."

"You were around here then?"

"Yes, ma'am. I'm sorry, I should introduce myself. My name is Alex McKnight. I was a police officer back in the day. The last time I was here at your house, I was, um . . . involved in the arrest of your son."

She processed that for a few moments, looking at me again like she was seeing me for the first time.

"I think I might remember you," she finally said.

"I definitely remember you. I know it had to be a hard day for you."

She nodded and looked down at her hands. "My son will be coming home soon. It's been a long time."

"I know, ma'am."

"Mind you, it's not like I've been sitting here on this porch ever since he went away. I actually went to live with my sister for a while. But I kept the house. Now I'm back. Because Darryl's coming home."

"I understand."

"They've been sending people around to get me to abandon this place," she said. "So they can knock it down. With everybody leaving, the mayor says we need to 'right-size' the city, whatever that means. I guess just move everybody to one side so they can shut down the rest, huh? I understand the part about saving money. I really do. But this is my home, you understand? This is Darryl's home. The only home he's ever had."

"Yes," I said, looking up at the upstairs windows. There was no doubt a bed up there, waiting for its old owner after all these years.

"So you say you're not a cop anymore."

"No, ma'am."

"Then why are you here?"

She put up her hand before I could answer.

"Never mind," she said. "I know why you're here."

That stopped me dead. Because honestly, I wasn't sure I knew myself.

"I think you should come inside for a bit," she said. "Get out of this heat. Do you like chocolate cake?"

I was feeling more lost by the second, but there was only one answer.

"Yes," I said. "That would be nice."

She pushed herself up from her chair and held the door open for me. I followed her inside. There was a small front room with a fan set in the side window, moving the air around. The floor was once a beautiful hardwood. Now half of the slats looked damaged by water.

"You sit right there," she said, indicating one of the two chairs facing the television set. It was one of those old tube-style console monsters that must have weighed half a ton. The sunlight came through the front window, filtered through the white lace curtains. I sat there in my chair, looking around the place, still feeling like I was in a waking dream.

A minute or two later, she came back with a slice of chocolate cake and a glass of milk.

"Gotta have milk with cake," she said. "I'm sure you'd agree."

I nodded and smiled. I wasn't about to argue with her.

She went back into the kitchen and brought back her own slice and her own glass of cold milk. It was now officially the most unlikely thing that had ever happened in my life. Me sitting down with the mother of a murderer, a murderer I'd helped put away myself, and eating a slice of her chocolate cake.

I took a bite. It was pretty damned good. I hadn't had any breakfast, so I had no trouble finishing it.

"That was excellent," I told her. "I really do appreciate it."

"I made this cake as soon as I found out Darryl would be coming home. Right after I moved back into this house. But it was kinda silly of me, because he's not really coming home until the end of the week. So I'll have to make another cake then."

"Yes, ma'am."

"So you're doing me a favor," she said. "Seeing as how I have to get rid of this one. Believe me, I'd have no trouble eating it all myself."

I looked over at her. She was taking her last bite of cake, and clearly enjoying it.

"I know it's going to be a hard adjustment for him," she said, putting her plate down. "A man with a record, that's one big strike against you, no matter what the circumstances might be."

She was right, of course. It was already nearly impossible for a black man to find a job in this city. Add a felony conviction and your chances get much worse.

"There's a man in my church who says he'll give Darryl a chance," she said. "That's a real blessing."

"That is. I hope it works out for him."

She studied me for a moment.

"What was your name again?"

"Alex. Alex McKnight."

"The years have been kind to you. You don't look much older at all."

If only you knew, I thought. It sure as hell doesn't feel that way.

"But like I said, Alex . . . I know why you came here."

"Actually," I said, not sure where to go with this, "I came down here to catch up on things, see a couple of people. I ended up just driving around today . . ."

"To an empty block with one house left standing," she said. "On the way to nowhere. You expect me to believe it was just an accident you ended up sitting here in my living room?"

"I admit," I said. "When I saw this street . . . I mean, it all kinda came back to me. After all that hard work, we were just about ready to give up. But then . . ."

"But then you found my son."

Yes, I thought. We found your son, after finally catching a break, one of the most unlikely breaks ever, a break that led us right to your front door. Then you lied to us about him being here. A forgivable lie, but a lie just the same. Then the way you wailed as we put your son in handcuffs and dragged him away.

I wasn't about to say any of that, of course.

"Now you've come back," she said. "Just like I knew you would. Someday. It must have been hearing the news about Darryl getting out that made you finally come here. Am I right?"

I just looked at her.

"You didn't have to wait so long. You could have come years ago. You might have even helped get him out, you know."

"Ma'am, I'm sorry. You've totally lost me."

"You came here to apologize," she said, her voice fortified with resolve now. "And it's about damned time. Pardon my French."

"Ma'am, apologize?"

"For taking my son away. Even though you *know* he didn't kill that woman."

I looked at her for a while, then down at the plate I was still holding in my lap.

"I'm so sorry," I finally said. "I've accepted your hospitality, but I don't think I've come bearing the message you wanted to hear."

"Listen to me," she said, moving forward to the edge of her chair. "Look me in the eyes and listen to me."

I leaned forward in my own chair. I looked her in the eyes.

"My son did not kill that woman. As sure as there's a God in heaven. As sure as the sun is going to come up tomorrow morning."

"Mrs. King . . ."

"There's a lot of things my son was capable of doing back then. But killing somebody was not one of those things. Dragging some woman into a train station and cutting her up with a knife was *not one of those things*. Do you hear what I'm telling you?"

"I hear what you're saying."

"Do you believe me?"

I hesitated. "I believe that you believe that. It's only natural that you'd—"

"Oh, stop it," she said. "Just stop that right now. I don't need you to pat me on the head and tell me I'm just blinded by motherly love. I don't need that one little bit."

"Mrs. King, where is your son serving his sentence?"

"He was in Jackson for a while. Then when that got closed down, he ended up in Harrison."

"You went down there to visit him."

"Of course."

"I don't know about Harrison," I said, "but I've been in Jackson. There's a big waiting room there, right? Lots of people waiting to see their loved ones?"

"Yes, with all the guards' shooting trophies on display," she said. "I guess that's in case you're getting any ideas about helping somebody escape."

"I do remember that. But let me just ask you this. I don't mean to be rude, and you can ask me to leave your house right now, but when you were sitting there with all those other family members, how many of them do you think believed their sons or fathers or husbands were guilty of the crimes they were convicted of?"

She thought about it for a second. "Not more than a few, I would think. I'm sure even if they knew their man was involved with something, it was probably all a big misunderstanding. Being in the wrong place at the wrong time or whatnot."

"Exactly. And even those prisoners who were in the visiting room when you finally got in there to see Darryl . . . If you'd asked them, how many do you think would have told you they were innocent?"

"I know what you're getting at, Alex. But to tell you the truth, Darryl never said anything one way or another about it. Not to me, anyway."

"He never said he was innocent?"

"No," she said. "Never once."

"And he did confess to the crime. You realize that."

She shook her head.

"Mrs. King," I said, "I wasn't there to see the confession, but I know for a fact that you were. You *had* to be, because he was a minor. Am I right?"

"I was there, yes."

"So you heard him say that—"

"I don't care what some detective made him say."

I let out a long breath. I knew we could keep taking laps on this same track all afternoon, and we'd still get nowhere.

"He promised he'd look after his little brother and sister," she said, finally looking away from me. The resolve in her voice was gone, replaced with what sounded like a hundred years of misery.

"Mrs. King . . ."

"He promised me, Alex. He never broke a promise. Not ever."

I sat there and watched a tear run down her cheek.

"Now his little sister is dead from drugs. His little brother ran away not long after Darryl went to prison. I haven't heard from him in years, so God knows if he's even alive. I've got nothing left."

"You have Darryl now. He's coming home."

"Most of his life is already gone," she said, shaking her head. "How much bitterness is my boy carrying in his heart now?"

"Can I give you my phone number?" I said. "I mean, for any reason. If you want to call me, I'll be there to listen."

"You could do that, yes."

I took out my wallet and found one of my old business cards.

Prudell-McKnight Investigations, with the two guns pointed at each other, from back when I had a partner who really wanted to be a private investigator. Who *lived* to be a private investigator. I still had my license, technically speaking, but I never really wanted any part in the business. Now Leon Prudell was working at a microbrewery in Sault Ste. Marie, and I was back to renting out my cabins and occasionally getting into strange situations like this one.

I turned the card over and wrote down my cell phone number. I handed her the card. She took it without looking at it.

"Any reason at all," I said. "If you call me, I'll be there to listen. Just keep in mind, though, I don't get very good cell phone service up there."

"Up where, Alex?"

"I live in the Upper Peninsula. In Paradise."

"That's a long way from Detroit."

"You said it, ma'am."

She stood up slowly. She was wearing sandals, and you could see every year of standing and walking and hard work in her feet. She took the plate from me, put it on top of her own, and took them to the kitchen. I waited for her, looking around the room, seeing all the little touches she had added, trying to make this a real home, even if the floor was damaged and there were God knows how many other problems with the place if you bothered to look for them. On top of the television set, there were pictures of her three kids when they were young. No pictures of a father. Another woman trying to do her best, all by herself. Such a sadly common story in this city.

But she was still here, in this same house. She was still trying. That said something about her.

She came back from the kitchen and showed me out the front door. I thanked her again for the cake. When I got in my truck, she stood there on the front porch watching me. I was about to pull away, but she waved at me to stop.

She came down the stairs, slowly. She came to my window. I rolled it down. She put her hand on my arm.

"I bet you had a lot of people try to lie to you when you were a cop," she said. "I bet you got pretty good at telling the difference between a lie and the truth."

"Yes," I said. "As a matter of fact, I did."

"My son did not kill that woman."

I just looked at her. The day was getting hotter. There were insects buzzing away in the tall weeds on either side of her house.

"That's a bone fact," she said, squeezing my arm harder. "That's the bone truth."

CHAPTER EIGHT

To this day, I still don't know how the news stations do it. Maybe they have somebody sitting around, listening in on the police band radio, but somehow they always seem to know when something significant is happening, anywhere in the city.

Now, a murder was not significant. Not in a city that would see over five hundred murders over the course of the year. During that hot summer, we'd see two or three a day, easy. But those were usually results of the gang wars, casualties in the fight for control of the drug trade. One black man killing another, whether you want to come right out and say it or not . . . That didn't make the six o'clock news with Bill Bonds.

But a white woman from the suburbs, found dead in the abandoned section of the old train station downtown . . . That was worth scrambling the trucks for. Which is exactly what Franklin and I saw as we came back down the tracks. Channel 2, Channel 4, Channel 7, they were all there. There were remote newscasters standing in front of cameras and lights, and there was crime scene tape strung all across the parking lot, from the station to the tracks, to keep everyone away from that back door.

Sergeant Schuman was still on the scene. He already looked a little frazzled and ready to tee off on the next reporter who asked him a question.

"McKnight," he said as soon as he saw me. "Get down to the station ASAP."

"That's where I was heading."

Nobody asked Franklin or me any questions as we ducked under the tape and headed out to the parking lot. They probably figured we were just two officers helping to secure the crime scene. Nothing special here, let's go bug the sergeant again.

I followed Franklin to our car. I sat in the passenger's seat while he got behind the wheel. He didn't say anything as he started the car and headed out to Woodward.

"Tell me what kind of world we live in," he finally said, "where a woman gets killed just because she's wearing a diamond bracelet."

I shook my head. Did it even matter now? Was there a better reason that would make more sense?

"They call those eternity bracelets," he said. "Those bracelets with all the diamonds. They're pretty expensive."

I shook my head again. I didn't know anything about expensive jewelry. I'd come to find out that it was, in fact, an eternity bracelet, bought for Elana Paige by her husband on their five-year anniversary. A couple of years later, Chris Evert would stop a tournament to look for her bracelet, and that's how they'd come to be known as "tennis bracelets." But that summer they were still eternity bracelets, and if Elana's husband thought he'd have anything resembling an eternity to spend with his wife, he was horribly mistaken.

The sun was going down when we got to the police station. It was already feeling like the longest day of my life. Sergeant Grimaldi was still there, and when he saw me he put his hand on my shoulder and asked me how I was doing. It was a small gesture, but it meant a lot to me. It would be something I'd remember even after I left the police force.

"You're gonna be pulled in about five different directions at once," he said to me. "But first things first. We've got all the current mug shots ready for you. You need to look through them carefully.

If we're lucky, you'll spot the guy and we'll have him in custody before the night is over."

He led me to one of the interview rooms. The mug books were there waiting for me. Four faces per page, each face shown from the front and then from the side. I'd led my share of arrestees to the same wall against which these shots were taken. Now it was my turn to go through a tall stack of them. The hope was that the man I'd chased today had been arrested in the past. And that I'd be able to recognize him.

Franklin came in after a while and asked me how it was going.

"Nothing yet," I said, pausing to rub my eyes.

"You need some coffee?"

"That would be great, thanks."

I went back to the mug shots. He brought my coffee. Then he sat down across from me with his own cup.

"You don't have to stay here," I told him. "Your family must be wondering where you are."

"I called them. They know I'm working on something important."

He wasn't really working on anything, of course. He was just keeping me company. But I didn't call him on it.

"You should talk to your wife, too," he said. "Let her know what's going on."

"I will. Next time I take a break. I think she might have class tonight anyway."

A few minutes later, Sergeant Grimaldi stuck his head in. "Any luck?"

"Not yet," I said.

"Detective Bateman would like to steal you for a few minutes," he said. "The family's still here, and he'd like you to talk to them."

I looked over at Franklin. The night was about to get even tougher.

If you work in a police station in the heart of one of the most murder-prone cities in the country, you're going to see your share of devastated families. They get led into the room with that same look on their faces, helpless and drained of blood. They sit down. They hardly ever accept anything. No coffee or even water. They just sit there and wait for the nightmare to end. But it doesn't. They get shown a photograph, taken at the crime scene. A close-up of the face, from above. The eyes usually open.

You need to prepare yourself for what you're about to see. That's the standard line, as if it's even possible. They take the photograph. Something goes out of them, like a sail losing its wind. There's no longer any doubt, but they still have to say it. They have to give you the verbal identification. Yes, that's him. That's my boy. Nine times out of ten, it's a male.

I'm sorry for your loss. The next standard line. They hardly ever break down when they're in the station. They must save that for home. While they're here they summon up the strength to keep it under control. It never fails to amaze me.

The sergeant led me to another interview room, just down the hall from where I had been going through the mug shots. He opened the door, and I stepped into that drywall box of absolute misery.

The husband was sitting on one side of the table. He was wearing a golf shirt, and his hair was pressed down where he'd obviously been wearing his golf hat. I pictured two cops having to go out onto the course and find him. Interrupting him right in the middle of his round to give him the news. Or maybe he was already done. Heading for home, heading for dinner with his wife. Now he was here in this room, looking down at a clear plastic bag on the table. I recognized the pieces of the diamond bracelet I had found. He was framing the bag with his hands, like he wanted to pick it up. I was sure the detective had told him not to touch it. Not until it had been processed for fingerprints. He kept staring at the bag, not even blinking when the door opened.

The father and mother stood together behind him. The father was wearing casual clothes that looked expensive. The mother, too. I didn't get a good look at her at first, because she stood with her face against her husband's chest. He stroked her hair, and otherwise had the same faraway look as his son-in-law.

A young man sat in the corner, by himself. More nice clothes, another blank stare. He was working his hands together, like he was getting ready to hit somebody.

That left Detective Bateman. He was sitting at the far end of the table, writing in a notebook. He looked up as the door opened.

"Officer McKnight," he said. "Thank you. I'd like you to meet Tanner Paige, Elana's husband. These are her parents, Mr. and Mrs. Grayson. And her brother, Ryan."

The husband and the father looked at me. The mother kept her face hidden. The brother kept working at his hands and ignoring everything else in the world.

"You saw him," the husband said to me. "The man who did this."

I looked at Detective Bateman. He gave me a slight nod.

"I saw the man who we believe is the suspect," I said. "We're going to do everything we can to find him."

The husband wanted to say more, but he seemed to be struggling to find the right words. I was waiting for him to lash out at me. To ask me why I hadn't caught him.

"Can you tell me . . ." he finally said. "I mean, why would anyone do something like this? For a diamond bracelet?"

"I don't know, sir. I'm sorry."

"I told her not to wear this down here. It was just asking for trouble."

I noticed the brother glancing up for one moment. He stared at the husband, then closed his eyes and went back to working his hands together.

"You need to find him tonight," the father said, still stroking his wife's hair. "He could be a thousand miles away by the morning."

"Yes, sir. Like I said, we're gonna do everything we can."

"It's something we don't usually have," Bateman said. "A police officer who'll be able to give us a positive ID. When we catch him, and we will catch him . . . it'll be an airtight case."

"Like that will do any good," the brother said, finally speaking up. "Some gangbanger goes away for life. Is that going to bring her back?"

His mother looked at him, taking her face away from her

husband's chest. Her face was ruined with tears, and there was a great stain on her husband's shirt.

"Ryan, please," his father said. "Of course it won't bring her back. But at least . . ."

"At least what?"

"He has to pay. Whoever did this. I'll spend the rest of my life making sure he pays for this."

The brother waved this away, getting to his feet and starting to pace up and down his side of the room like a caged animal. I watched him, waiting for him to punch the wall. Or something. I wouldn't have blamed him for anything at that point. I honestly could not even imagine going through what these people had to go through that night.

"This isn't happening," the husband said. He was still staring at the bracelet in the plastic bag. "I'm going to wake up and she'll be right there next to me."

"It's happening," the brother said. "It's happening because you can't even walk down the street in this city anymore. Why the hell would you even let her take a class at Wayne State, for God's sake? Some ghetto school in the middle of the worst city in the world."

The husband was looking at him now. In about two more seconds, the brother would launch himself over the table and we'd have a full-blown melee on our hands.

"This is not helpful," Bateman said. He stood up and put himself in the brother's way. He grabbed both of the young man's shoulders and looked him in the eyes.

"Let go of me."

"You need to calm down. You need to respect everyone else in this room. And you need to let us try to solve this horrible crime."

The brother seemed to run out of steam then. He dropped his head and brought one hand to his face. He started to cry.

Bateman hugged him. It was not something you were supposed to do in a case like this, but as soon as he did I could see it was the right play. The brother cried for a while, and then he stopped. He sat back down in the chair.

"Officer McKnight," Bateman said to me, "I know you have work to do. I'm glad you got the chance to meet the family. The next time you see them, I hope it'll be when we tell them we've made an arrest."

"I'm sorry for your loss," I said to everyone else in the room. One of those standard lines you say, but I couldn't think of anything else.

Then I went back to the mug shots.

Franklin left for home eventually. I thanked him for everything he'd done that day.

"Just doing my job," he said.

I kept looking through the mug shots. Detective Bateman came in a while later. His tie was loose. His eyes were red. It was the first time I'd ever seen him looking like something less than a human dynamo.

"I take it you don't have an ID yet," he said to me. He sat down in the chair Franklin had just vacated.

"I'm afraid not."

"Then we need to get the sketch artist in here. Get this down on paper while it's still fresh in your mind."

"I can't believe this guy hasn't been in the system before," I said, flipping through more pages. "He gave me a pretty stone-cold look on the other side of that fence. Like he was about to laugh in my face."

"Jeans and a gray shirt. Nothing on the shirt? No logos or anything?"

"No. Plain gray. He did have an Oakland Raiders hat on."

Bateman nodded. "That's how you do it if you're street smart. No markings, no weird hair. A hat you can throw away in a second. Just blend right in."

"Are you telling me he's so smart we've never had him in the system before?"

"That would be just our luck," he said, rubbing his eyes.

"Why cut her up so bad?" I said, the scene at the station coming back to me, whether I wanted it to or not. I knew it would be there in my head forever.

"What do you mean? He wanted her dead."

"This is way beyond wanting someone dead. This guy destroyed her."

He thought about that one. "We'll never know why he did that. Not until we catch him. Even then . . ."

"Any idea why Elana Paige was at the train station in the first place? That's a long way from the college."

"Her car was in the parking lot. The crime scene guys found a camera bag about ten feet from the body. Nice camera inside, but it was damaged when it hit the floor."

"Why leave the nice camera if you're already stealing her jewelry?"

"Too hard to carry, I guess. Or too obvious if you're trying to blend into the crowd."

"So she was a photographer, you're saying."

"Well, she was taking a photography course at Wayne State, at least. Maybe she figured she could get some great shots at the old train station."

"I though you handled things well with the family," I said. "The brother was about to go off."

"You realize," he said, "that you belong to me now. Until we catch this guy. I'll clear it with your sergeant."

"Anything I can do. Of course."

He nodded. "I'll let you keep looking. Let me know if you get a hit. I'm not going anywhere."

Neither was I. Another hour passed. Maybe two. It was hard to tell at that point. I had gone through all of the mug shot books. I hadn't found my man. They got the sketch artist in, and we worked out a sketch. Problem was, although I could still picture him exactly in my mind, the sketch came out looking like a young black man with high cheekbones and a short afro. In other words, like half the male population in the city.

We tried refining it, but in the end we had to send out what we had. Five foot ten, 170 pounds, muscular build. Jeans, gray shirt with a torn right sleeve, basketball shoes. Last seen fleeing north on Trumbull Avenue. We sent it to every precinct in the city, and to every neighboring suburb. We sent it to the Michigan State Police. We sent it to the FBI.

Elana Paige had now been dead for six hours.

It was going on eleven o'clock when I finally left the station. I had processed an official statement, describing everything I had seen and done. I had tried to eat some dinner. I had gone back over the mug shot books. Detective Bateman told me to go home, to get some rest, and to be back at the station early the next morning. We'd see if we picked up any hits on the bulletin overnight and then go from there.

"We'll start working the neighborhoods," he said. "Somebody saw this kid. I promise you that."

"I hate the fact that he'll sleep in his own bed tonight."

"Let him sleep. Let him believe he got away. If he does, he won't leave town. Or he won't hide. Either way, we'll get him."

I said good night to the detective, and to all of the four-to-midnight-shifters I saw on the way out. They were almost done with their day. Mine had lasted fifteen hours.

I got in my car. I had an eight-year-old Chevy Celebrity back then. About all I could afford on a Detroit cop's salary, with a wife who had quit her job to go back to school. I started driving down Woodward, to hit that freeway that would loop me back through the city and then west to Redford, but then I blew right by the on-ramp and cut over to Corktown. I drove by the stadium one more time. A dark gray monolith now. I drove up Trumbull, daring my man to be outside walking around in the night air, confident that he'd gotten away with his crime today. I slowed down whenever I saw someone. Usually two or three of them at a time, smoking cigarettes, drinking beer, staring back at me in my civilian car. I didn't see the man I was looking for.

I got home at midnight. I lived in a little brick house on a block of little brick houses, in one of the original Detroit suburbs, now a working-class enclave for folks like me, who didn't want to live in the city itself but didn't have the money to move out to Livonia or Dearborn Heights.

I parked the car in the thin little driveway that ran between my house and the house next to me. I got out and took a breath. The dog was barking next door, just like every other time I came home.

I went inside, took off my clothes, and lay on the bed without turning the lights on. I could hear Jeannie breathing on the other side of the bed.

"I'm sorry," I said. "I forgot to call you."

She didn't say anything for a while. I thought maybe she was asleep.

"I was worried," she finally said. "You promised me you'd call if you were going to be late. You remember? "

"There was a murder. A woman who's taking classes at Wayne State. Her name's Elana Paige. Do you know her?"

"Doesn't sound familiar, no."

"She was taking a photography class."

Another few moments of silence. The dog stopped barking.

"Who killed her?"

"Some kid. Seventeen, eighteen years old."

"Did you catch him?"

"No. Not yet."

That was the last thing I said before I closed my eyes. There was nothing else to say anyway.

In my dreams I was standing over the dead body again, but a strong wind was blowing through the building. Then I was chasing the young man in the jeans and gray shirt again. Chasing him and chasing him and never catching him, down a set of railroad tracks that went on forever.

CHAPTER NINE

I had left my cell phone in the truck, as usual. I picked it up as I drove away from Mrs. King's house. I had a voice message from Sergeant Grimaldi. I pulled over and listened to it, then called him back. He answered on the first ring.

"What can I do for you?" the sergeant said. "You're not back in Paradise already, are you?"

"No, I spent the night down here," I said. "It was a long day, and I didn't feel like driving five hours."

"That sounds smart. So where are you now?"

"I'm just driving around the city a little more. I still can't believe what I've been seeing."

"Yeah, I know what you mean. It's like postwar Berlin or something. Although, at least, they rebuilt Berlin. Detroit, I guess they're just gonna let it rot."

"Well, I hope not, but . . ."

"Alex, what's on your mind?"

"Listen, this is going to sound a little crazy."

"I can do crazy, believe me. Let me have it."

"You said you called me and you called Detective Bateman, right? About Darryl King getting out?"

"I did."

"How is the detective, anyway?"

"He's not the man he was," the sergeant said. "Put it that way. But I'm pretty sure he still sees himself as the star of his own personal prime-time crime drama. Even now that he's retired."

You didn't spend enough time with him, I thought. You never saw the other side of Detective Bateman, when he turned off the charm and got down to real police work.

"Well, he was a character," I said, figuring this wasn't the time to be the detective's publicist. "But do you think there's any chance I could talk to him?"

"I'm sure he'd love to hear from you. You want his number?"

"I'd appreciate it."

A moment of hesitation. "Why do you want to call him, anyway? Just to catch up? Or is there something else on your mind?"

"If you want to know the truth," I said, "something's been bothering me about that old case."

"Yeah, see, I wasn't even going to go there, but now that you mention it . . ."

"Wait," I said, "how do you even know what I'm talking about?"

It was the same feeling of disorientation I'd felt at Mrs. King's house. How come everybody thinks they know what's going through my mind today, when I don't even know myself?

"I know what's bothering you, Alex, and I don't blame you. That was a high-profile case, probably the biggest of the year. Bateman made a lot of hay out of it. You might even say it made his career."

"I'm not following you."

"Come on, you know exactly what I'm talking about. Bateman was all over the television after King was arrested. He even got that award, remember? But what did you get?"

"You know what I got."

"Yeah, you and Franklin. I know. But that was a totally separate thing. You should have gotten a lot more credit for tracking down the man who butchered that woman."

"Well, that's not where I was going at all," I said. "I honestly haven't even thought about it that way, not once in all these years."

"Then I'm sure I have no idea what you're talking about, Alex. What exactly is bothering you?"

"Well, that's the crazy part. I actually sorta stumbled upon Darryl King's mother today, and—"

"Excuse me, what?"

"I was just driving by the house where we picked him up. I wanted to see it. She was sitting right there on the porch."

I wasn't about to tell him I went inside and had chocolate cake with the woman. That would be too unbelievable, even if it was the truth.

"That's a new one," he said. "I'm sure she was glad to see you. The man who helped put her son away."

"She couldn't have been nicer about it. And I don't know, even last night . . . I was just thinking about the case, and I guess I just want Detective Bateman to fill in some gaps for me, help me to understand how that case got closed in the end. Because I wasn't there to see it."

"It got closed because he confessed. You know that."

"I know. But I never got to see the tape. I never even read the transcript. So I guess I just want to know how it went, that's all. Call it curiosity, after all these years."

"It sounds like you've got something else on your mind," he said. "More than just curiosity. But I can tell you, I *did* see the tape of the confession. It was airtight."

"Okay, I appreciate you telling me that. That makes me feel better."

"But you're still going to call the detective, aren't you."

"I thought I might. Unless you think it's a bad idea."

"I suppose it might rattle his cage a little bit, you showing up after all these years, wanting to know how he closed out the case. But you know what? That sounds like a good enough reason right there. Hell, I wish I could be there myself."

"You're sounding just like the sergeant we all knew and loved."

"Let me get you the number," he said. I wrote it down as he read it off to me.

"Okay," I said. "I got it. Thank you."

"Let me know how it goes, all right? Let me know what shade of red his face turns when you ask him if it was a clean confession."

"It's a deal."

"Oh, by the way," he said. "I know I said he's not the man he used to be, but you should know, he's really had some health problems over the past few years. So don't be surprised when you see him, is all I'm saying."

"I appreciate the warning."

"You take care of yourself, Alex. It was good seeing you again."

I thanked him again and hung up. Then I sat there for a while on the side of that empty street. It was a clean confession, I told myself. The sergeant saw it himself, and he would know.

So why do I still have Mrs. King's voice in my head, telling me her son was innocent?

I picked up the phone again and dialed Detective Bateman's number.

A few minutes later, I was on the road, driving north. I took the Lodge Freeway out of the city. When I hit Eight Mile Road, the infamous northern border, I had a strange moment of regret and something almost like heartache. This city wasn't a part of my life anymore. I lived over three hundred miles away. Yet it had meant something to me, once upon a time. I grew up rooting for its sports teams. I went to work here every day for eight years. I saw a thousand terrible things here back in the day, but I also saw what the people of Detroit were really made of. When people tell you this city essentially won the Second World War, it's not crazy. Even back in the eighties, when things were really starting to fall apart, I still felt like the people who lived here could put the city back together. Now it felt like most everyone had given up on the place. I couldn't even imagine what it would look like in another twenty years.

I was heading back to Paradise, but with a little detour in mind.

When I had reached the retired Detective Arnie Bateman, after exchanging the standard pleasantries, he had told me that he lived "up north" now. "On the lake." I was already wondering if he had ended up in Marquette, or maybe Eagle Harbor. That was the real "up north," after all, and the real "on the lake." But no, he lived on Houghton Lake, the inland lake right in the middle of the mitten. It was about halfway home for me. Hell, not more than a few minutes out of my way, so we ended up arranging to grab a bite to eat on his boat.

He would no doubt want to show me the lake, and I'd have to act like I was impressed. I'd have to resist the urge to tell him that *my* lake was a thousand feet deep and bigger than ten states.

It took me less than three hours to get there, through Saginaw and Bay City. I got off at the exit and worked my way around the southern shore to the town of Houghton Lake. There were plenty of lakeside motels, restaurants, bars, places to buy fishing tackle. There was a week left until Labor Day, so the place was still moderately busy.

I passed another Ash Street. The day winking at me, if you believe in that sort of thing. Soon after, I left the main road and found the marina. Another quarter mile up the shoreline, I found the address. I'm not sure what I was expecting. Maybe a big white Cape Cod with a sign up front bearing the house's name, BATEMAN'S BEACH HOUSE or something like that, but I was surprised to see nothing but a mailbox with a number and his last name assembled with those reflective letter decals you buy at the hardware store. I turned down the driveway and pulled up next to a Jeep. The house was a simple log cabin, not much different from my own.

When I got out of the truck, the side door to the cabin opened, and out stepped a man I wouldn't have recognized in any other context. I mean, I knew Sergeant Grimaldi gave me the heads-up, but the man I saw was at least fifty pounds heavier than the detective I remembered, and he was walking slowly, gripping a cane in his right hand. As he got closer, I could start to see that old face from the precinct, but there wasn't one single bit of flash left to the man. He looked, honestly, like he was seventy years old.

If Sergeant Grimaldi had lost a step or two with age, then Detective Bateman had lost a whole staircase.

"Officer McKnight," he said, looking me up and down. "I swear, you don't look any different."

I shook his hand. He still had some strength left, at least.

"I'm afraid I'm not moving around quite as well," he said, looking down at his cane. "But they're gonna give me a new hip soon, so I'll be good as new. I told the doctor he should keep going, just turn everything bionic."

"I could use some of that myself," I said, rubbing my right shoulder.

His smile went away for a moment, as he made the connection. The reason my shoulder should need such attention when the rest of me seemed to be holding up just fine.

"Yeah," he said. "How are you doing with that, anyway? I never really got to talk to you after . . . You know."

"I don't even think about it anymore." Half a lie on my part.

"I heard they left one inside you. Was that just for a souvenir?"

"Something like that."

The smile came back as he patted my other shoulder. "Come on," he said. "Let's have a little something on the lake."

I followed him around the cabin, down to his dock.

"You live in Paradise now? Is that right?"

"I do."

"Well, then, I know this lake is just a pond to you."

Another surprise, from this man who once lived to one-up everyone around him. At least a hundred times a day.

"It's a nice lake," I said, looking out over the water. I could see maybe a dozen boats, not nearly as many as I would have thought. "You've got a nice quiet place here."

"Hell, you should see this lake during the Bud Bash."

"What's that?"

"Every summer, they get thousands of people here, all these boats tied together in a big flotilla down the shoreline a bit. People drinking like crazy, just going insane."

"Funny, we don't get that in Paradise."

"It's enough to drive an ex-cop out of his mind, Alex. All those drunks driving their boats around. Then later on their cars when they're going home. It's a miracle they don't have a dozen people killed every year."

The final surprise came when we got to his dock. I would have guessed a sleek speedboat for good old Detective Bateman. Instead, I saw a big fat lazy pontoon boat, with deck chairs, a full roof, and a motor just big enough to move it along at two miles per hour.

"I know what you're thinking," he said. "This thing is just a floating gazebo. But on this lake, it's perfect. I can anchor anywhere, throw a fishing line out, catch a few walleye, maybe take a little nap."

"Nothing wrong with that."

"Come on, I've got the cooler packed already."

He opened up the little gate and stepped onto the deck. I followed him. The boat barely dipped as I stepped on board.

"Rock solid," he said, sitting in the captain's chair and pushing the electric starter. I untied the front end and we were off, backing out into the lake. When we were clear of the dock, he put it into forward and gunned it. A baby duck could have paddled faster.

We moved north for a while, Bateman pointing out resorts and bars on the western shore. Then he cut over by Houghton Point, and we started on a great loop that would keep us out here all afternoon. The sun was hot now, even with the awning over our heads.

"So why did you look up your old buddy Detective Bateman after all these years?" he finally said. "Let me guess. It has something to do with that call we both got from Sergeant Grimaldi."

"Well, I did come down to have a drink with him. Your name came up once or twice."

"I bet it did. Grimaldi never did like me that much."

"I wouldn't go that far. He just never got to know you like I did."

Bateman looked at me. "We spent a lot of time together that month, didn't we? I'm glad it all paid off in the end. Although now that he's getting out . . ."

"Nothing we can do about that," I said. "But the thing is, I never got the chance to see how that case was closed. With what happened to me . . ."

"The only thing that happened after you left was his plea and then his sentencing."

"I never heard his confession."

He looked at me again. "You didn't see the tape?"

"No, I didn't."

"Too bad. It was my finest hour."

He was smiling when he said it, but I knew he wasn't completely joking. It was the biggest case of his career, for all the obvious reasons, spoken or unspoken. A photogenic white woman from Farmington Hills, stabbed two dozen times by a young black male. That same pretty face on the six o'clock news, and in the paper, every day for most of that month. The frustration building every day we couldn't find our suspect. The pressure from every direction. Until finally we had our man and he was locked in a room with a homicide detective who did things his own way. If this was a television show, you might even say he played by his own rules. Of course, it wasn't a television show, and the blood on the floor of that balcony was very much real.

"I've always wondered how it went down," I said. "That call from the sergeant was sort of a reminder, I guess."

Bateman nodded his head. Then he cut the engine. He got up, fished out the anchor, and threw it overboard.

"I take it we're stopping?"

"Good a place as any," he said. "It's only fifteen feet deep here. Most of the lake's about that. I'm guessing Lake Superior gets a little deeper."

"Just a little."

"Interest you in a cold beer?"

"You could twist my arm."

He opened up the cooler and pulled out two bottles of Sierra Nevada. Not bad if a Canadian isn't available, especially in the summer.

"I've got some sandwiches in here, too."

The only thing I had eaten that day was the slice of Mrs. King's chocolate cake, so I was ready for a real lunch. We sat there and had our ham and cheese sandwiches while the other boats on the lake zoomed right by us.

"Okay," he said, when he was done eating and was wiping his hands on his napkin. "You want to know how I got that confession."

"If you don't mind telling me."

He smiled. "You know how much I hate talking about myself, but I'll see what I can do."

I took another hit on my beer, squinting at the sunlight reflected off the water. I ended up closing my eyes, all the better to listen to him, and to bring back that summer and the case that would bind the two of us together forever.

"So we've got this kid," he said. "Remember how we were thinking he was seventeen, eighteen years old? And he turns out to be sixteen?"

"I remember."

"Sixteen on paper, but he was already a hard case. That day we finally caught him, when he just stood there in the doorway with a dozen cops all aiming their guns at him? The way he didn't even blink?"

I thought back to that day. That strange, almost anticlimactic arrest, after everything we'd gone through to get there.

"It wasn't my first confession," he said. "You know that was sorta my thing."

"So I had heard, yes."

"The secret is approaching each suspect on their own terms. Everybody's different. Everybody's got their own story. Something that might work on one person will get you nowhere with the next one. So you can't go in already married to one strategy. You gotta react to the situation and you gotta be *quick*."

He gave an ironic grimace of pain as he resettled his bad hip on the chair. The man's last quick day must have felt like a distant memory.

"So remember, the clock is ticking here, right? We got the kid in the room. His mother's there with him, because that's the law. Darryl's not saying a word, but Mama's telling everybody to let them go because her little boy ain't done nothing."

Having just spent time with Mrs. King, I knew she was a hell of a lot more articulate than that, but I let him go on.

"I know we're running out of time before we have to charge him or let him walk. I think you'd already gone home at that point, right?"

"Sergeant Grimaldi told me to go home, yes. He didn't think there'd be anything else to see."

"That's right," Bateman said. I could tell he was happy to hear it put this way. Like fourth and long from your own one-yard line, just a few seconds left on the clock. So everybody's already on their way out of the stadium.

"So I finally go in the room," he said. "I sit down in front of him. His mother starts talking, but I tune her out. It's just me and Darryl. I don't try to get real close to him like I might to some guys. Get right in his face or anything. I just sit back and I don't say anything for a while. He's looking right back at me. I had to remind myself he was only sixteen years old."

Another boat roared by. He took a sip of his beer and gave the boat a quick glance. Then he was back to that day in the interview room.

"Finally, I just say to him, 'You think you're a man already, don't you.' He gives me a look, doesn't say anything. I say, 'Some people might look at you and say you're nothing but a little punk gangbanger, not even seventeen years old yet. Think you're so bad and everything.' Notice I'm not saying that I think that. I'm just saying some people. That was the important part. Make it all indirect, you know?"

I nodded, even though I wasn't quite sure what he was getting at.

"I say, 'I'll tell you what a real man does. A real man stands up and admits when he's done something wrong. A real man tells the truth, no matter what. While a little punk gangbanger, on the other hand, you know what he does? He runs away crying like a little girl.' Which started to get his attention, I could tell. And then I say, 'So how come you ran away like a little girl, Darryl?' I don't even give him time to answer. I just say, 'You're not even that fast, you know that? That cop who was chasing you, that old white guy? He used to play baseball. He was a catcher. You know how slow catchers are, right? That's who was chasing you, and he almost caught you.'"

He stopped and put his hand up to me.

"No disrespect, Alex. It was all part of the story I was building."

"I got it. Go on."

"I say to him, I say, 'Look, we've got you on this, Darryl. We've got a cop who'll take the stand and testify that he saw you on the scene. Not just some Joe Schmoe from Hamtramck, Darryl. A cop who'll sit there in his shiny uniform and tell everybody how it went down. If that's not enough, we've got your fingerprints on the bracelet. You understand what that means, don't you? We could take this whole thing to trial right now, and I'm pretty sure we could get anything we want.' Which was a bit of a stretch, I realize. But you know how it works. Then I say, 'Here's your chance, Darryl. To stand up like a man and to make this a whole lot easier for everybody. If you do that, I'll make sure it gets taken into account.' This kid's just sitting there. His mother's telling him not to say anything, but I can tell he's thinking it over. Me, I keep ignoring her, so maybe *he'll* ignore her, you see what I mean? And I just ask him flat out, I say, 'Come on, Darryl. Are you a man or not?'"

He paused for effect. Then he took another sip of his beer.

"That was the first time he spoke," he said. "He sits up in his chair and he says, 'I'm a man. Don't forget it.' So at this point, some guys would think they've got him on the hook, right? Yeah, you're a man, that means you're gonna tell me the truth now. Let's have it. And then they get a big lie. So instead of that, I just had this gut instinct that I should keep pushing it. You wanna know why? It was something you said to me."

"Me?"

"Yeah, when you were telling me how you were chasing him down those tracks, and he finally got under that fence, and he's standing there on the other side. You said that as soon as he knew he had you beat, he just stood there and looked at you. Ice cold, you said. Like he was daring you to shoot him. Knowing that you wouldn't. You remember that?"

"I do."

"That's all I needed to know about this kid. He ran, but he didn't *want* to run. The second he didn't have to run anymore, it was like he was pretending he never ran at all. So I say to him, 'I don't believe you, Darryl. I don't believe you're a real man. Because you ran down those tracks like a little girl, and you even threw that diamond bracelet away. You probably left a trail of piss all the way down the tracks, too. I don't know, because we didn't actually test for that. We didn't run the forensics test for a little girl running away and pissing herself.' I could tell I was getting to him. It honestly felt like he wanted to get out of his chair and start something. Which I would have been ready for, believe me. But instead he just says, 'I'm a man, and if there's something I need to do, I do it.' Those were his exact words."

He let that hang in the air for a moment. It didn't sound exactly like the beginning of a confession to me, not any I'd ever heard. But I knew there was more.

"Now his mother's having a fit, and he just tells her to be quiet. At that point I *knew* I had him. Don't get me wrong, I knew I was cutting the mother right out of the equation, but this guy was a child in name only. Only by the letter of the law. So I told him, I said, 'Okay then, just between you and me, the two *men* in this room right now, you gotta tell me what happened. Start at the beginning and lay it all out for me.' So he did. He said he was there at the back of the station when this woman came by."

"What was he doing back there?" I said.

"What?" The interruption seemed to throw him off track for a second. "He was looking to rob somebody. It was a popular spot for young hustlers to bring their johns, he said. A perfect setup to rob somebody because they're not going to go to the police."

"Okay, I got it. Continue."

"He said he saw her taking photographs of the building, and he told her there were some even better shots inside."

"Wait, seriously? She went along with that?"

He looked at me like I was an idiot. "No, of course not," he said. "It was just his first play. When she refused to go inside with him, he pulled his knife."

"And what, dragged her inside? She didn't scream?"

Bateman looked at me again. I wasn't playing the rapt audience he was accustomed to when he told this story. And I knew he had told it, many times.

"The place was deserted back there," he said. "Darryl was a strong kid."

"Okay," I said, still not quite seeing it. "Go on."

"He takes her inside and up the stairs to the balcony."

"Why go upstairs? That's a lot of extra work, isn't it?"

"He knew there were people coming in that door," Bateman said. "He wanted to be out of the way, all right?"

"All right."

"Then he stabs her with his knife. She was screaming at that point, so he just kept stabbing her. Then he took the bracelet off her wrist. He would have taken her money, but she'd left her purse in her car."

"But he didn't take the camera bag."

"No, he didn't. He said no way he's gonna carry around an expensive-looking camera case. Might as well put a neon sign over his head."

"Okay, that makes sense."

"When he went outside," Bateman said, "that's when you showed up. The rest is history."

"Did you ask him why he threw the bracelet away?"

"Pure reaction at that point. It connected him to the murder. So he threw it away."

"But he didn't throw away the knife."

"Not when you were chasing him, no. He threw that away later."

I sat there on his boat and worked it over it in my mind. There was a question I wanted to ask, a question that would get to the heart of things and make it all fall apart if it wasn't really true. But I couldn't come up with the question.

"The knife was in his pocket," Bateman said. "He wasn't about to try to take it out while he was running. It would have been a foolish move, even if he could throw it."

"But he did throw the bracelet. That wasn't in his pocket? And that wasn't a foolish move?"

Bateman looked out at the water. I could tell he was getting frustrated. "Alex," he said, "he threw it away on the spur of the moment, this thing that didn't belong to him. He kept the thing that *did* belong to him. Then he threw that away later, when he had time to think about it. It's really not that complicated."

"Okay," I said. "Okay. So that was his confession."

"Yes. That was his confession."

"He didn't try to take it back later? Say you tricked him or you forced it out of him? I know that happens all the time."

"No, he stuck by it all the way to the end. The prosecutor worked out a plea to simple second degree homicide, on account of his age, and I don't know, maybe because he didn't want to have to bring you back to testify."

That stopped me dead. "Why wouldn't I want to testify?"

"I seem to recall, you had more important things to worry about. Like not dying from your gunshot wounds."

I wiped my forehead with the back of my sleeve. There was no breeze, and it was getting too hot out there in the middle of the lake.

"All right," I said. "Thank you for telling me all that."

He sat there looking at me for a moment. "Alex," he said. "It was a clean confession. I saw a few before that, saw a hell of a lot after that. This one was Grade A kosher."

"Okay. I got it."

He turned his chair and started up the engine. "Let's get you back to shore," he said. "It's hotter than hell out here."

We made our way back to his dock, taking a direct line now so it only took half of forever. When we had the boat tied off and I had carried the cooler up to the cabin, he shook my hand.

"Before you go," he said, "I have to say one more thing to you."

"What's that?"

"I should have let you make the arrest. It's bothered me ever since."

"Detective, you can stop thinking about it right now. Because I did a long time ago. It was a pleasure working with you back then. And it was a pleasure seeing you again today."

"Thanks," he said. "That means a lot to me."

As I turned to my truck, he called after me.

"We got our man, eh? That's the important part."

I didn't answer him one way or another. I just gave him a wave and then I left. As I drove back to the freeway, I knew the whole thing should have been resolved in my mind. Every question was answered, I said to myself. You can let it go now.

So how come I still couldn't?

CHAPTER TEN

I got up early the next morning. I didn't wake Jeannie. I let her sleep as I left the house in the pale light of dawn. I drove to the station on Woodward Avenue, not sure if I was ready for everything that would happen that day.

Detective Bateman was already there. He was shaved, showered, caffeinated, smartly dressed, and ready to roll. He said good morning to me, and then two minutes later we were in his unmarked Plymouth Gran Fury, driving to Corktown.

"We've got two sets of prints back on the clasp of the bracelet," he said as he drove. He didn't have lights or a siren, but he still drove like he owned the road. "One was Mrs. Paige herself. The other was presumably our suspect, although we didn't get a hit on it. So he's not in the system."

"That would explain my big swing and miss on the mug shots."

"I still can't believe he's been under the radar his whole life," Bateman said, shaking his head. "I don't care how young he is. If he's capable of doing something like this . . ."

"I'm out here every day," I said. "Sometimes it feels like we only catch the dumbest ten percent, and everybody else is just doing whatever they want."

"I'd hate to think that's true."

He took us right to the train station. There was still crime scene tape along the back side of the station. A pair of night-shifters in their last hour of duty were standing guard.

"They'll keep working the crime scene," Bateman said, "now that the sun is up. But really, I think it's all going to come down to hustle. As usual."

"So why are we here at the train station?"

He stopped the car in the lot. Then he got out and looked up at those mostly empty eighteen floors. I did the same.

"When in doubt," he said, "start at the beginning. Now show me again exactly where he ran."

We got back in the car. I directed him over to Bagley Street, to the bridge over the tracks where our man had scrambled up from the fence. From there, we went up Rosa Parks Boulevard, where I had thought I had spotted him when I went after him in my car. We cut over to Trumbull, up to the stadium. Then across the freeway where I was sure I had him trapped. We stopped at that same intersection where I had stood looking off into the distance. West, north, or east, all of the streets he could have taken at that point. It was hardly more than twelve hours ago, and yet it felt like he could be anywhere in the world by now.

"There aren't many houses until you get up past Temple Street," he said. "And you'd have to cut all the way over past the high school if you lived east of here."

He moved his finger in the air like he was drawing a map.

"The freeways sort of isolate this one part of the city," he said. "Like a big horseshoe. West, east, and south. So pretend you're him for a minute. You're running away and trying to get back home. Would you risk coming up Trumbull and getting yourself trapped in this horseshoe if you didn't live here?"

"Probably not. Not if I was thinking straight."

"You said you usually only catch the dumb ones. Hell, he led you right through the stadium traffic, didn't he? A great way to lose you. So let's assume he knew exactly what he was doing."

"Okay, so he's in this horseshoe," I said. "That's still a lot of real estate."

"Get back in the car. We've got some ground to cover."

We spent the next hour driving, first up Trumbull to Martin Luther King Jr. Boulevard, then cutting west through the apartment complexes. We agreed, this felt like about as far north as he'd reasonably live, assuming he had to start his day here, then walk down to the train station looking for trouble.

"This is good," he said. "See, I wanted to get the lay of the land before we started sending out the troops. Now that we've got it narrowed down, we can get officers out here knocking on doors. Get some handbills up on every telephone pole, too, asking for anybody with information to contact us."

"That would work a little better if people in this city thought we were on their side."

He looked over at me. "We're not asking them to snitch on a drug dealer. This is a psychotic murderer. I'm sure they don't want him living next door."

I raised both hands in surrender, but I wasn't convinced. I knew many people in this city saw us as the enemy. It's something I dealt with every day. On the other hand, it would only take one neighbor to drop a dime on this guy. Just one mindful neighbor. That's all it would take.

He checked his watch. "Come on, it's time for roll call."

A few minutes later, we were back at the precinct. The day-shifters were all sitting there in the room, listening to Sergeant Grimaldi run down the assignments. There was no joking today. The whole building felt different.

Detective Bateman took over for a few minutes, giving everyone the details about our case. Or at least the few details we knew at that point. He wasn't trying to act like a big shot today. He wasn't the basketball coach or the clotheshorse or the man with the big smile. He was a homicide detective, and he knew he wouldn't break this case without help.

"Somebody saw this young man," he said to the assembled officers. "It would be impossible for that not to have happened. We need to get out there on the streets and we need to find that witness.

Officer McKnight and I have identified a likely target area. Now it's time to start knocking on doors."

Everyone had the description of our suspect. Everyone had the sketch, as inadequate as it might be. Everyone knew the stakes. This was not your regular murder case.

"The target area overlaps with the Third Precinct," Bateman said, "so expect to see them. Obviously, we need to respond to every other call, as usual. But the sergeant will be sending extra units to the area throughout the day. So please just be extra observant today. I'd like to tell the family of this woman that we have this man in custody, ideally by the end of the day."

He thanked them. The sergeant dismissed them.

Franklin came up to me then and put one of those big hands on my shoulder and squeezed. He asked me how I was doing. I told him I was thinking about finding this guy and not much else. He went off to do his thing with his new temporary partner.

"I know I don't have to tell you this," Franklin said to me, "but keep your eyes open today, huh? I know you want this guy more than anyone."

I found the detective at his desk a few minutes later. All of the homicide detectives sat together in a random assortment of desks on the second floor. He was reading something. It took a moment for him to even notice me standing there. He asked me to sit down.

"This is the initial coroner's report," he said. "I'm not sure how much of this I should share with the family."

"What does it say?"

"She was stabbed twenty-three times. There were many defensive wounds on her hands. Meaning she fought back. Also meaning it probably took a while for her to lose consciousness."

I took my hat off and held it in my hands.

"She was not sexually violated prior to the stabbing," he said. "But several of the stab wounds were, um . . . let's just say, in that area."

He didn't say any more. He didn't have to. He sat there looking down at that sheet of paper. At that string of words that could never really capture what she went through.

"We're going to find him today," he said, finally looking up at me, "if I have to personally take you to every house in the city."

Of course it wasn't that easy. It never is. By the end of that workday, we had a few dozen leads that went nowhere. The case was once again the lead story on Channels 2, 4, and 7, only now they had a sketch to show and a plea to call the Detroit police with any information. That led to a number of phone calls, none of which panned out. I had been out in the car with Detective Bateman all day. I was still at the station when the calls came in. It was another double-shift day for me.

By the time I went home, it was dark. Elana Paige had been dead for thirty hours.

We went through the same process the next day, although this time there was a backlog of leads for us to follow up on. Information developed by officers on patrol, or tips called in to the station. Toward the end of that day, the detective asked me to accompany him on one more trip. It was starting to get dark now. We were no closer to finding our suspect. The detective was starting to wear his frustration as visibly as one of his tailored sports jackets. God help you if you happened to be standing in his way while he was walking down the hall, or making any noise while he was on the phone.

"Where are we going?" I said. We were heading south, away from our so-called target horseshoe.

"To the train station."

I thought maybe we were going to start at the beginning again, like we had done the previous morning. But no, he had something different in mind.

He slowed down on Michigan Avenue as we got close to Roosevelt Park. He was looking carefully at the people walking on the sidewalk. There were plenty of men out enjoying the warm summer night. A few women. The female prostitutes couldn't have been more obvious, but that's not what the detective was looking for.

When we passed Sixteenth Street, he did a quick U-turn and came up slowly on the opposite side of the street. We were in his unmarked car, so he wasn't turning any heads yet. The detective let the car roll to a stop. There was a young man leaning against an iron fence. He took a quick look up and down the street. Then he came closer. He stopped when he saw my uniform, but by then the detective had already put the car in park and thrown open his door.

"Stop right there!" he said. It was a voice that carried across the entire park, I'm sure. The kid started to run, but the detective caught up to him easily and pushed him from behind. It's the perfect move when someone is running away from you. One good shove and your man is eating dirt.

I was just getting out of the car myself at that point. I was thinking how nice it would have been for the detective to share his plan with me before executing it.

"Open the back door," Bateman said to me. I opened the door, and Bateman threw the kid into the backseat. I wasn't positive that this car had the one-way locks standard on squad cars, but from the look on this kid's face, it didn't matter. He was not about to try anything stupid.

"All right," Bateman said as he got back behind the wheel, "it looks like we've got our murder suspect."

"What?" the kid said, his eyes wide. "Are you crazy?"

I looked over the front seat at him. He was about the right age, but the similarity ended right there. This kid was at least twenty pounds thinner. His eyes were more wide set, the nose was bigger, the hair was shorter. This was certainly not our suspect.

"What do you think, Officer?" he asked me. "Is this our man?"

"I think he might be," I said, wondering how I was supposed to play along. "I guess close enough, right?"

"Damn straight," Bateman said, putting the car in gear. "We just need *somebody* to go down for it."

"I wasn't even around here that night," the kid said. "You totally got the wrong guy."

"Ah, so you do know something," Bateman said, slamming the car back into park.

"No! I don't know nothing!"

"You just referred to the night of the murder. Because you didn't ask *which* murder, I'm assuming you know exactly what we're talking about."

"That woman. In the train station."

"For someone who claims to know nothing," Bateman said, "you sure have a basic working knowledge of the pertinent facts."

"The what? No, man, I just know that some woman got killed in the station two nights ago. That's all I know!"

"You work this park," Bateman said. "You must have some idea who did it."

"I don't work anything," the kid said. "I don't know what you're talking about."

Bateman put the car in gear again. "Look, I don't care what you do here. Drugs, hustling . . . Right now, I don't give one little goddamn about any of that. I'm not going to take you down for anything, as long as you start telling me the truth. But if you don't, we'll go right down to the station."

The kid just sat there, not saying a word. Bateman put his foot on the gas and we started to move.

"All right!" the kid said. "I'll be straight with you, okay? I'll tell you everything I know. Which is pretty much nothing."

The car stopped. "*Pretty much* nothing? What does that mean?"

"It means I don't know anything. I swear. I didn't kill her, and nobody I know killed her. Everybody's freaked out about it. It's been so strange around here the last couple of days."

"Strange how?"

"Just strange. Nobody's doing any business. It's like everybody knows the place is being watched now."

The detective looked over at me. He shook his head and took a long breath.

"Okay, here's the deal," he said to the kid. "You get out of the car and you go find everybody who hangs out here. You hear me? Every single one. You tell them that if they have any information about this crime, they need to contact me immediately. My name is Detective Bateman. You got that?"

"Yes."

"What's my name?"

"Detective Bateman."

"No other questions asked. Just like I told you, whatever else they're doing, I don't care. I just want to find the killer, and I will personally make sure this place is closed down for you guys until I find him. Is that clear?"

"Yes, sir."

"Okay, then. Get out and spread the word."

The kid got out of the car. Turns out the doors weren't one-way locked. He stood there watching us as we pulled away.

Bateman's hands were tight on the wheel as he drove back up Woodward Avenue.

"How many years do you have in?" he finally said.

"Eight."

"You're gonna take the test?"

"The detective's test? Yeah, I was thinking about it."

"I've been watching you the last couple of days," he said. "You've got a good way with people. You keep your eyes open."

"I try."

"Okay, so let me ask you this. Do you have any problem with what I just did to that hustler? You think you could have done that yourself?"

"I honestly don't know if I could, Detective. Maybe that's something they teach you when they give you the gold shield."

He thought about that for a moment, maybe trying to decide if he should take offense.

"I'm going to call the family tonight," he finally said. "They'll want to know if we're any closer to finding the man who killed Elana."

"Yes?"

"That'll be you someday. When you make that call, you're going to ask yourself something first. You're going to ask yourself, 'Am I doing everything I can to solve this case? I mean, no matter what, am I doing *whatever it takes*?'"

I didn't answer. He didn't seem to want an answer yet. Not that night. He drove us the rest of the way back to the precinct without saying another word.

When I finally went home that night, Elana Paige had been dead for fifty-four hours.

CHAPTER ELEVEN

If they had such a thing as an "Indian summer" in the Upper Peninsula, it would probably have to happen in late August, when it's supposed to be turning cold already. Of course, the whole idea of Indian summer borders on offensive, if you think of it as being just a false summer, in the same way that an Indian giver gives you something and then takes it away. There are plenty of real Indians in the Upper Peninsula, including my neighbor Vinnie Red Sky LeBlanc, and I've never heard him use the term. He just says *niibin* when it's summer, and then *dagwaagin* when it's fall. He won't actually put a coat on until it's *biboon* and there's a foot of snow on the ground.

He was there at the Glasgow Inn when I got back home that night. Three hours on the road to get to Houghton Lake, then another two and a half hours after leaving the detective's house. Plenty of time to think about everything he had said to me. I still wasn't sure exactly what was bothering me, but now that I was home it didn't seem to matter quite as much. I was back above the bridge, in another world.

Vinnie waited for me to get my cold Canadian and sit down by the fireplace. "How did it go?" he asked me. "Jackie told me you were going down there to get lucky."

I just about spit out my beer.

"I did no such thing," Jackie said, throwing his bar towel. "I said he was going down to have dinner with that nice-looking FBI agent. That's all I said."

"Five hours down," Vinnie said. "Five hours back. Ten hours round-trip. If it was just for dinner, I hope it was the best meal of your life."

"All right," I said to both of them. "Enough of that. If you must know, it was a nice dinner and that's all it was. We both realized it's a bad idea to start something when we live so far apart."

"I'm pretty sure you could have started and finished in one evening," Jackie said. "I mean, I know you're out of practice."

"I come back home and it's like I'm in high school again," I said. "Why did I bother?"

"Give us a break," Jackie said. "How often do we get to make fun of you?"

"Apparently never," I said, "because I'm leaving."

I got up and left my beer sitting there on the little table next to the overstuffed chairs. It was obvious they both thought I was bluffing. But then I opened the door.

"Where are you going?" Jackie said.

"Believe it or not," I said, thinking this would be the worst thing I've ever said to the man, "I'm going to another bar."

I'd been planning on going there anyway. Seeing the look on Jackie's face as I walked out that door was just a bonus. I got in my truck and drove over to Sault Ste. Marie. I'd had more than enough time on the road the past couple of days, but I had to make this one last trip before I'd be able to sleep.

I took the main road through the empty hayfields. I rolled down the windows to let in the warm air. It was a dark night with no moon.

Sault Ste. Marie, Michigan, or "the Soo" as they usually call it around here, is the last stop on the road to Canada. The bridge was glowing in the night sky as I made my way along the St. Marys River to the Soo Locks. The lighted fountain in the park was on, and there were people walking up and down Portage Avenue. They were out enjoying the night, feeling it a little more than you would in most places for the simple reason that warm nights are a rare thing up here. So when they come, you make damned sure you make the most of them.

I parked the car in the lot next to the Ojibway Hotel. Leon Prudell's new place of employment was right across the street. The Soo Brewing Company. He was standing behind the counter when I walked in. A bear of a man with comb-resistant orange hair.

Leon has always wanted to be a private investigator, going back to when he was a kid. The first time I met him, he tried to take me apart in the Glasgow Inn parking lot, when he thought I had taken his job away. Later, we were partners. That's how I ended up with the Prudell-McKnight Investigations business card that I had given to Mrs. King. But that partnership didn't last long, mostly because Leon's wife didn't like the idea of Leon mixing it up with dangerous characters. Much as she loved me, she still blamed me for almost getting him killed. Believe me, Eleanor Prudell is not a person you want to get on the wrong side of.

Leon tried to go solo as a PI. He even had an office over on Ashmun. That didn't last, either. There's just not enough business for an investigator up here. Besides, most people up here remember Leon Prudell as the goofy fat kid who sat in the back row, from kindergarten through high school. They don't know that he's actually the smartest man in town, and as loyal a friend as you could ever have.

He sold snowmobiles and outboard motors for a while. Then he worked in a movie theater taking tickets and selling popcorn to teenagers. I hated to see him there. Now he had this new gig at the microbrewery. He was learning to make beer, on top of all the other talents you'd never suspect he had. I hadn't even known he was an accomplished guitar player, for instance, until the night he invited me to hear him record at the studio in Brimley. Typical Yooper, good at a dozen things but won't brag about any of them.

"Alex!" he said as soon as he saw me. "Get the hell in here!"

He came out from behind the counter and gave me a big hug. That's almost as dangerous as a hug from his wife.

"What do you think of the place?" he said, gesturing at the shiny brewing tanks. In the front of the store, they had grabbed every old couch and chair and beat-up table they could find and tried to create the ultimate hangout spot. There were a dozen people sitting around, some reading, some looking at their laptops, some eating pizza. All of them had big glass mugs of beer.

"We've got the pizza place down the street to deliver to us," he said. "It works out great for everybody."

"This is impressive," I said. "It sure as hell beats the theater."

"Oh God, tell me about it."

When he introduced me to the master brewer, the two of them exchanged a meaningful look, like yes, this is the man I was telling you about. The brewer drew a little pony glass from the tap and slid it over the counter.

"Okay," Leon said, "this is one of our staples. It's a session ale, as they call it, but it really stands up. Are you ready to try it?"

"Of course," I said. "I'd be honored."

I tried the beer. It was pretty damned good. I gave them the thumbs-up.

"I know your beer heart belongs to Canada," Leon said, "but I'm glad you like it."

"Hey," I said, now that everyone was happy, "can I borrow you for a couple of questions?"

"Of course," he said. "I can use some air."

We went outside. If there had been a freighter coming through the locks, we could have gone up to the observation deck and watched it, but I wasn't here to look at big boats. I was here to get his unique take on this thing that had been bothering me.

"Actually," I said as we walked down Portage Avenue, "before I tell you the details, let me just ask you something on an abstract level."

"This sounds interesting. Go ahead."

"Let's say you were arrested for murder. During the questioning, you ended up confessing to the crime. But for some reason, I have this gut feeling that you didn't do it."

"Okay . . ."

"The biggest question I would have to answer is, why did you confess if you were innocent?"

We walked a block while he thought about it. That was one of the good things about Leon. He wouldn't give you his opinion until he worked out every angle.

"There are a few possible reasons why I might confess to a crime I didn't commit," he finally said. "One, because somebody else has some leverage over me and they're making me confess."

"What kind of leverage could they have? You're talking about going away for murder. What else could they do to you?"

"Prison is better than them killing me. Or, say, killing someone in my family. I'd confess to anything if it meant saving one of my kids from harm."

"Okay," I said. "That makes sense."

"Or maybe it was my wife who committed the murder," he said. "In that case, nobody's actually threatening anybody, but I know what will happen to her if they find out she's guilty. So if I'm a good husband, I might confess to the crime to save her."

I thought back to the stone-cold look on Darryl King's face. The first scenario was possible, *maybe,* if somebody was threatening his family. He had a mother who loved him, a little sister, a little brother. As for the second scenario, taking the fall for someone else . . . I could rule out the mother and the sister. The little brother, from what I could recall, looked like he'd have trouble killing a mosquito.

Would he take the fall for a close friend? Someone he grew up with? That was always possible. But I kept coming back to that face. The way he looked at me from the other side of that fence. Was that the face of a man who would give up his freedom to save someone else?

"Or maybe I confess because I'm being tortured," Leon said. "That's actually quite common, I'm sure."

"You're just being questioned by a homicide detective," I said. "You're not being tortured."

"There's more than one type of torture, Alex. You lock me up in a room for twelve hours, you make it boiling hot in the room, you don't give me anything to drink, then you start yelling at me . . . I'm sure you could turn that into a real hell. I might break and confess just to make that all stop."

"I know what you're saying," I said, thinking back to Bateman's account of the interrogation. "I think we can rule that out in this case."

"Well, then, there's just one more reason," he said. "I might confess because I honestly don't think it matters one way or another."

I stopped on the sidewalk. We had walked all the way down to the power canal that cut through the heart of the city, and now we were standing just before the two-lane bridge that ran across it.

"Say that again," I said.

"I confess because I know it doesn't matter what I say. So I might as well get it over with."

"Because you're a black kid in Detroit, and the victim was a white woman from the suburbs. You know they're going to pin it on somebody, because that's how you think the whole system works. Besides, you're one *bad* man and you can handle it. You can handle prison standing on your head."

"Now we're getting specific," he said. "Someone you know?"

"Someone I helped put away."

"Now you're thinking you should try to get him out?"

"I don't have to. He's getting released in a few days."

Leon shook his head and smiled. "Tell me the whole story."

We turned around and started walking back to the brewery. I laid it all out for him, from the day I chased Darryl King down the railroad tracks to the day we got our break and finally caught him. Then I told him about the confession, as related to me that very day by the retired detective. He stopped me in the same places where I had stopped Bateman. Why had he thrown away the bracelet? Why did he wait until later to throw away the knife?

"This guy sounds like a badass and a half," Leon said when I was done. "Even if he was only sixteen."

"That's why I'm thinking your last scenario makes the most sense. He knew he was going away, no matter what. If he did it or if he didn't do it."

"He was an angry young man going in," Leon said. "Now all

these years later, what ends up coming out? Is he older and wiser? Or is he a ticking time bomb?"

"I guess we're about to find out."

I thanked Leon and let him get back to work. Then I drove home to Paradise. I was exhausted by the time I went to bed, after all of the miles. I still had this feeling that there was something I was missing. One little piece of the puzzle that, if I found it, would make everything else fit together.

I fell asleep listening to a barn owl sounding its otherworldly complaints. I think I dreamed about diamonds at some point. Floating in the sky, falling in slow motion.

Then I woke up. It was after three in the morning. I opened my eyes, sat up in my bed, and suddenly I knew something. I *knew* something for a fact that I had only suspected before. Simple as that, just like Mrs. King had told me. This was the bone truth.

Darryl King went to prison for a crime he didn't commit.

CHAPTER TWELVE

On the third day after the murder, I got to the station early again, expecting to do more legwork with the detective. More time on the street, more knocking on doors, more running down anonymous tips, hoping for that one lead that isn't a dead end.

But no, Detective Bateman had another plan. Or rather someone else had plans for both of us.

He asked me to ride along in his car. He wasn't saying anything else yet. I could see the tension in his arms and in his face as we left the station and drove west for a few blocks. Then we got on the freeway and headed northwest, out of the city.

"At some point," I said, "you're going to tell us where we're going."

"Elana Paige's parents want to have a word with us. Both of us."

"Detective, you have this habit of not telling me what's going to happen until we're already in the middle of it. A heads-up now and then is all I ask."

"I apologize," he said. "This trip has me a little worked up."

"How so?"

"Well, for one, it's taking us away from what we really need to be doing. And two . . ."

I waited for him to continue. He was doing eighty miles an hour in the far left lane, his eyes dead ahead.

"And two," he said, "I don't like not having any news for them. We're honestly no closer to catching this guy today than we were that first night."

"So what are you going to say to them?"

"I was hoping you'd figure something out by the time we got there."

We crossed under Eight Mile Road, and just like that we were out of the city. All of a sudden you had a mall, and a golf course, and nicely manicured lawns. Grocery stores and restaurants instead of a cheap fast-food wasteland.

The Graysons lived just off of Twelve Mile Road. Exactly four miles from the city line, it might as well have been a different country. There were houses packed in tight on every street, this being one of the original suburbs, where space was at a premium, but the Graysons had one of the larger lots on the northern edge of Southfield, with a long tree-lined driveway.

Detective Bateman parked the car and sat there for a moment, working his hands together. "Okay," he said. "Let's go talk to these poor people."

We walked up to a big brick house with tall white columns on either side of the door. The detective rang the bell. We waited for a while. Then a Hispanic woman opened the door. She wasn't wearing a maid's uniform, but we saw the dynamic immediately. This woman probably lived down the road in the Mexicantown section of Detroit, came up here every day to take care of the white people's big house. She probably thought it was a great job. All things considered, it probably was.

She led us through the living room and the dining room. It was all a bit too stuffy for my taste, with too many glass cabinets filled with little figurines and crystal goblets, but I couldn't argue with how immaculate everything was. This woman obviously did her job well. There was a sunroom in the back of the house. That's where Mr. and Mrs. Grayson were waiting for us.

It had been three days since their daughter had been murdered.

They both looked like they had aged ten years. Mr. Grayson stood up and shook our hands, his eyes red, his grip weak. Mrs. Grayson stayed put in her chair. She was wearing sunglasses.

"Mr. and Mrs. Grayson," Bateman said, "I'm so sorry to see you again under these circumstances."

Coffee was offered and declined. We were finally all seated. Mrs. Grayson looked down at her hands. Even with the sunglasses, I could tell she was crying. Mr. Grayson slid over a box of tissues on the glass table. I wondered how many boxes they'd already gone through.

"We asked you to come here," Mr. Grayson said, "so you could share any progress you might have made at this point."

"You know you can call me at any time," Bateman said. "Day or night."

"I wanted to hear it in person. I wanted you to see how important this is to us."

The detective started to say something, then stopped himself.

"We've thought of nothing else since it happened," I said. "Literally nothing else, night and day. I know we can't even imagine what you're going through . . ."

"No," Mr. Grayson said. "I don't think you can."

"Granted," I said. "But you have to know, this is our only mission in life right now. Both of us."

Bateman looked over at me and gave me a quick nod. "Officer McKnight speaks the truth," he said. "Every waking hour, it's all we're doing."

"Okay, fair enough," Mr. Grayson said. "So how far have you gotten?"

"We've been running down many leads," Bateman said. "We still don't have anything solid. But I'm confident we will."

"As I understand it, the first forty-eight hours are crucial in an investigation like this. When someone is . . ."

He paused, took a breath, gathered himself, and continued.

"When something like this happens," he said. "The trail gets cold very fast after that. Am I correct?"

"In most cases, you want to develop your information quickly, yes. That's always going to be the best way to go. But we're confident that if we keep doing what we're doing . . ."

"You seem to have a lot of confidence," Mr. Grayson said. "You had confidence that first night, too. Just how long is that going to last?"

"Until we find out who's responsible," Bateman said. "That's how long."

"I understand that a reward can be helpful in a case like this. Has that been your experience?"

"It's often helpful, yes. Were you considering—"

"A hundred thousand dollars," Mr. Grayson said. "To whoever provides information leading to the apprehension of the animal who took away our Elana."

Mrs. Grayson stood up at that point, knocking her shin on the coffee table. Without saying a word, she left the room.

"She'll be okay," her husband said. "I'll go see her in a moment. I just want to know what else I need to do to make the reward happen."

"That's a lot of money," Bateman said. "You probably don't need to—"

"It's nothing, Detective. Now that our daughter is gone . . . it's literally nothing to us."

"Well, I'll get right to our PIO. Sorry, that's the public information officer. He'll make the arrangements, and we'll make sure it's publicized."

"Today?"

"Yes, today. We can make sure it's on the news this evening."

"Okay, good. Let's make that happen. Now, if you'll excuse me, I need to go see how my wife is doing."

He left us there. The maid reappeared and showed us out the front door.

"I don't know how Mister and Missus are going to survive this," she said to us. Her eyes were red, too. "Elana meant everything to them."

"I understand," Bateman said. There wasn't much else to say.

"You're going to find out who did this, right?"

"Yes," he said. "Yes, we are."

"Okay, thank you."

Then she closed the door. The detective closed his eyes and let out a long breath.

"That's a big reward," I said. "It has to help, right?"

"Yes and no. It'll get us more calls, but if we get a thousand of them all at once . . ."

His thought was interrupted by a car coming up the driveway. It was a silver Jaguar. The driver pulled up alongside the detective's car. The door opened and out stepped Ryan Grayson. Elana Paige's brother.

"Sorry, we were just leaving," Bateman said to him.

"You came with news?" The man was a bit of a mess. More red eyes. I'd pulled over enough DUIs to recognize the loose way he was walking and talking.

"No, we came to talk to your parents about a reward."

"As opposed to just doing your job and catching this guy. It's been what, four days now?'

"Hey, let's not get on the wrong track here," Bateman said. "We all want the same thing, as soon as possible."

"Yeah, sure," the man said. He came up to the front door, took a wrong step, and launched himself right into me. Fortunately, I caught him.

"Easy," I said. "Come on, you know you shouldn't be driving that vehicle if you're impaired. You get in an accident, that's not going to help anybody."

"So arrest me." His face was close to mine, and his breath took away any reasonable doubt.

"I'm not going to do that," I said. "I'm going to let you go inside and sleep it off."

"Do you have any idea . . ." Then he trailed off. He would have sagged to the ground if I hadn't been holding him up.

"We're doing everything we can," I said. "I promise."

"You want to know what happened to my sister?"

I looked over at the detective.

"What are you talking about?" I said.

"I'll tell you what happened to her. She married the wrong guy. Kinda guy who would let her walk around by herself in goddamned downtown Detroit. He's out playing golf while she's being . . ."

That's the same line he had the first time I met him, I thought. He'd probably take it with him for the rest of his life, never letting his brother-in-law off the hook.

"I was going to be a fireman, you know that? You know why I'm not?"

"No, why?" I said, wondering just where this drunken conversation might go next.

"Because I'm white. Because I took the test and aced it and had to wait in line so they could hire a bunch of black guys and fill their quota."

This is going downhill fast, I thought. I really don't need to hear this, no matter how broken up he is.

But before he could take it any further, his eyes rolled back in his head and then he threw up all over the front porch. I dodged most of it. When he was done doing that, he started crying. We opened the door and walked him back inside. The maid took him into the kitchen to clean him up. We could still hear him sobbing as we left.

When we were back in the car, I found some takeout napkins in the detective's center console. I used those to wipe off my pant leg.

"Thanks for your help," he said. "You handled all of that pretty well."

"It's all right."

"You know how to talk to people. It's something they can't teach at the academy."

"There was a lot of anger in him. Not that I can blame him for most of it."

"I'd stay away from him if I were the husband. At least for a while."

"I wasn't about to tell him my wife's going to Wayne State, too. Which I guess would make me just as bad."

Bateman shook his head. "You can't blame the whole city. It's a good school."

"Yeah, tell that to him."

He pulled out onto Twelve Mile Road, heading west. Away from the freeway that would take us back to the precinct.

"Where are we going now?" I said.

"I'll give you one guess."

All we had to do was cut down Orchard Lake Road to Eleven Mile and we were at the town house owned by Tanner Paige and the late Elana Paige. It was nothing near as impressive as the Grayson house, but what the hell, they were still relatively young, only married a few years, no kids yet. A little town house in Farmington Hills was all they needed.

"I actually tried to call him," Bateman said as we pulled into the lot. "Yesterday. Then today. I haven't gotten an answer yet."

We went to the front door and rang the bell. It was one those places with four separate town houses in one building. Then another building next to it, looking exactly the same. Then another and another.

Nobody answered the door. Bateman rang the bell again. After a few seconds passed, we both looked at each other, and I could tell the same thought was hitting us at the same time.

"You don't suppose . . ." he said.

"Wouldn't be the first time."

He stepped back and looked up at the second-story windows. "I think the lights are on up there. It's hard to tell in the daylight."

I was picturing our grieving husband either hanging in the closet or else lying face up on the bed, an empty pill bottle on the floor beside him. I was wondering if that was a suspicion I should be calling in to the station immediately, so we could get someone out here to open the door. Or better yet, at least find out what kind of vehicle he was driving, so we could check the parking lot before doing anything else.

Then the front door opened.

Tanner Paige stood there in the doorway. We'd already seen some red eyes that morning. Tanner's set a new standard. He was wearing a robe, sweatpants, and slippers. He obviously hadn't shaved, showered, or done anything else for himself since that first evening we saw him. You couldn't have drawn a better portrait of a man who'd given up on everything.

"Mr. Paige," Bateman said. "We're sorry to bother you. Are you okay?"

He just looked at us like he'd forgotten the English language.

"Mr. Paige, can we do anything for you? Come on, let's go inside."

He pushed the man backward, into the town house. Mr. Paige didn't offer any resistance. He let himself be led to the couch in the living room. He let himself be lowered into a sitting position.

"Have you been eating?" Bateman said. "What can we get you?"

He gave me a quick nod, and I went into the kitchen. The whole town house was just as much a wreck as the owner. He didn't have a maid to keep things in order, like his in-laws.

"Mr. Paige," I heard Bateman say, "you need to have someone here to help you. Is there somebody you can call?"

"My wife," the man said, finally speaking. "You can call my wife."

A warm half gallon of milk was sitting on the counter. I opened it and poured it right down the sink. Then I heated up some water and found some tea bags. I wasn't sure what else to do.

The in-laws all have each other, I thought. I didn't know why this man was left alone like this. It was clearly driving him insane.

When the tea was ready, I brought it into the living room and put it on the table in front of the couch. Mr. Paige looked at it like he wasn't quite sure what it was.

"Here, drink this," Bateman said, picking up the mug. "This might help you feel better."

Mr. Paige took the mug. He gave it an experimental sip. Then he closed his eyes and began to drink. I knew it was a little too hot to drink this fast, but I wasn't about to stop him.

When he was done, he took a few deep breaths. Then he opened his eyes and looked back and forth between us.

"Detective Bateman," he said. "Officer McKnight, was it?"

I nodded.

"You'll have to excuse me. It's been a rough couple of days. I haven't slept at all since . . . I mean, if I do I just have these nightmares where she's . . ."

"It's okay," Bateman said. "We understand."

"I assume you have news," he said, putting the mug down. "Have you caught him yet?"

"I'm afraid not," Bateman said. "But we were down the road at the Graysons'. So I thought we'd stop by."

"I don't understand. Why come out here if there's nothing to tell us?"

"Your father-in-law asked us to come out. He's going to put together a reward for any information leading to an arrest."

"Is that going to make any difference?"

"It usually does, yes. A large sum of money tends to make people get over their reluctance to call the police."

"Okay," Mr. Paige said, nodding slowly. "Okay. So that's good. That should do it, right?"

"We hope so."

"Detective Bateman," he said. "That first night . . . I think you promised us that you'd catch this guy. Didn't you?"

"I'm sure I promised you that I'd do everything I can to catch him, yes."

"No, no. You said, 'I promise you, we'll catch this guy.' Or words to that effect. But that was the message. We'll catch him."

"I don't remember exactly what my words were," Bateman said, hesitating. "You understand, we can only do what we can do. Some things are out of our control."

"All right, so if you said that and you don't really mean it, then promise me something else."

Bateman looked over at me.

"What is it you want us to promise you?" I said.

"Promise me that if you catch this guy, you won't take him right to the station."

"I don't understand. Where else would we—"

"Bring him here," Mr. Paige said, grabbing my arm. "That's all I ask. Bring him here for one hour. So I can have him first."

Bateman dropped his head and rubbed his forehead. Mr. Paige kept his eye contact with me, his grip still tight on my arm.

"You have to promise me," he said. "I'm not letting you go until you do."

"Mr. Paige," I said. "You know we can't bring him here. That's not how it works."

He kept squeezing my arm, with surprising force for a man who probably hadn't eaten a real meal in three days. Then he let go.

"God, listen to me," he said. "I'm so sorry, guys. I'm just . . ."

"It's all right," I said. "I'd probably be thinking the same thing, believe me."

"I don't know what to do," he said. "What *thing* do I do next?"

"Maybe we can send somebody over to talk to you," Bateman said. "I'll give you a call tomorrow, too. And the day after that. Okay? We're not going to let you face this alone."

"I appreciate that," he said. "But at the end of the day, I'm the one who has to try to sleep in that empty bed."

"You should get out of this place," I said. "Go somewhere else for a while."

He nodded.

"It's a great idea," Bateman said. "Is there someplace you can go?"

"I'll find a place. You're right. I'll just go crazy here."

He stood up then. He went into the bathroom and slapped some water on his face, tried to do something with his hair. When he came back out, he looked like he remembered how to be a human being, at least.

"I appreciate you guys coming over," he said. "I guess I needed somebody to knock some sense back into me."

We left him with a promise to get back to work and to let him know the second we had a break. The detective and I walked back to the car in silence. We got in, he started it, and we headed back to the freeway. Back to work.

"Grief's a bitch," Bateman finally said.

I nodded my head once and watched the other cars as we blew by them.

"So that reward . . ." I said, a few miles later.

"Yeah, I hope you're ready," he said. "We'll get a thousand calls by the end of the night."

We got the calls. Maybe not a literal thousand, but our phone did not stop ringing for more than a few minutes at a time. Most of them were fishing expeditions. A young man down the street who always acted suspicious. He kind of looked like that portrait in the newspaper.

Some of the calls were more specific. This young man next door, he came running home that same evening as the murder. I haven't even seen him since then, which is weird because he's always hanging around front with his no-good friends. Now it's like he disappeared off the face of the earth.

Those were the calls we followed up on, right away. A drive out to the house in question, a knock on the door. A quick census of everyone who lived there. Your older son, ma'am, where might he be? Oh, there he is right now. Okay, that's not who we were looking for. Sorry to disturb you. Have a good night.

Then back to the car, trying not to let the disappointment build when it was one dead end after another. We worked every lead we could that night. We picked up more leads in the morning. The photograph I had in my mind was still *right there*. I knew I'd recognize him the second I saw him. That was the frustrating part. All those doors opening, all those young faces looking up at me. Not one of them was the face I was looking for.

Other murders kept occurring in the city. They weren't going to stop just because we had one particular case we wanted to solve. They weren't even going to slow down. It was a hot summer, and there were wars going on over the crack business. The casualties would get rolled into the hospitals every night. Literally every night without fail that summer. You didn't say it loud, that one drug dealer shooting another was not something that was going to make you lose any sleep. An innocent bystander was another matter altogether. Someone just standing there on the street when a car comes by and the bullets start flying as randomly as raindrops.

The Uzi was big that summer. A compact little machine pistol from Israel, not much louder than a sewing machine. It was the perfect weapon for making a point about who owned a particular corner, and making it dramatically.

Five days after the murder of Elana Paige, we had another high-profile case in our precinct, this time an eighteen-year-old kid from Allen Park who was shot dead over a ticket-scalping dispute outside the Masonic Temple. He'd come down to attend a rock concert, ended up bleeding out on the sidewalk. His assailant had disappeared into the crowd, this time with no police officer around to serve as an eyewitness. Another news story, another grieving family. Another case to eat up some of Bateman's workday, because there were only so many homicide detectives to go around.

At the end of the week, Sergeant Grimaldi called me aside and told me that the approved overtime for my double shifts could not last forever, and that I'd end up killing myself if I didn't go back to a normal schedule anyway.

By the start of the next week, it was official. The case wasn't closed, of course. It would remain open until it was solved, whenever that might be. But there were other crimes to solve, too, and resources had to be put back into balance. Priorities adjusted for maximum effectiveness. Or some words like that. Whatever they were, I didn't really hear them. Because to me they meant we were all but giving up on ever putting away the man who killed Elana Paige.

I was back on patrol, but I still checked in with Detective Bateman every day. He was usually sitting at his desk, a pile of paperwork in front of him. Often on the phone. Never a smile on his face. Not his usual flashy self at all. Not that month.

"I had to call the family today," he said one morning. "The Graysons first, then the husband. Naturally, they all wanted to know what the hell was going on. All these days gone by, still nothing."

He stopped to beat the edge of his desk with a pen.

"I'm not a good liar," he said. "I'm sure they could hear it in my voice. Everything I was saying was just so useless."

Later that same morning, he received what he thought might be a solid lead. He called me in from the beat, and we went out together to chase it down. Once again, it turned into nothing. Once again, we were no closer to breaking the case.

So aside from those occasional futile morning trips with the detective, it was back to the squad car for me. Back with my partner, Franklin. He took it easy on me for a while. He could tell I was still wearing the case around my neck.

I kept watching as we drove, of course. Every young black man on the street, that could have been the man I was looking for. One day, I was driving through a neighborhood when I suddenly stopped dead, sending Franklin's coffee onto his shoes.

"What the hell!" he said.

I was looking at a woman hanging up her laundry in her backyard.

"That's what made you stop?" Franklin said. "Because all I see is a woman putting out her family's clothes to dry. Probably doesn't have a working dryer in the house."

Out of all of her laundry, the shirts, the pants, the dresses, the towels, it was the one combination that had caught my eye.

"Wait, is it because she's got some blue jeans on the line?" Franklin said. "Along with that gray shirt? Because I hate to break it to you, but those aren't exactly exotic items of clothing. I'm pretty sure we could both go home and find that particular outfit for ourselves right now."

I got out of the squad car and went to talk to her. A minute later, I came back and got behind the wheel. Franklin was still looking around for something in the car to wipe his shoes with.

"Those clothes are hers," I said. "There are no men in the house."

"You're going to drive yourself crazy. You're going to ruin all of my shoes, too."

He was right, of course. At night, after a full shift of driving around with my eyes wide open, I'd always make a point of taking the long way home. North from the precinct, through those same neighborhoods in Detective Bateman's "horseshoe." Or even east or west, because there was no guarantee that we were one hundred percent right in our initial assumptions about where he was running to. In fact, I was becoming more and more convinced that I didn't see him running up Trumbull at all. Or if I did, that he took a last-second turn and didn't cross that bridge over the freeway. He could have doubled back and gone toward one of the neighborhoods next to Mexicantown. So that's where I drove, down one street after another. Then I'd finally go home to Jeannie.

I wasn't talking to her enough that month. With everything else that was going on, I should have reached out to her. But I have to admit, I just didn't do it. I had no idea what to say. I kept it all inside me, and the next day I'd get up and do it all over again.

Two more weeks passed. The kids were all out of school, running around on the streets. I was still on the day shift until the end of June. The days were hot, and the nights seemed even hotter. For the first time, Sergeant Grimaldi did not so much as mention the Elana Paige case during roll call.

I was out in the car with Franklin. I was driving that day. There's a place called Covenant House, up on Martin Luther King Jr. Boulevard. They take care of young people who have nowhere else to go, and this wasn't the first time we'd taken some kid up there with the vague hope it would be the right place for him or her. If it's that or prison for some girl who's shoplifting food from the 7-Eleven, we'd rather give the House a try first.

When we had dropped her off, I was driving back east on the boulevard. I was looking at every young face on the sidewalk, something I'd probably never stop doing for the rest of my life, especially when I was in this part of town.

"How hard did you hit this street?" Franklin said. "This was still in the target area, wasn't it?"

"We drew a line here, actually. This is about as far north as we thought our man would come."

"All these apartment complexes," he said, looking out the window as we rolled past them. "That's a lot of doors to knock on."

"We knocked on every one. Probably twice."

When I got to Wabash Street, I turned right and headed south.

"Where are we going? Oh, don't tell me . . ."

It was late in the day, time to get back to the precinct. But there was no rule about taking the most direct route.

"You must have covered all of these neighborhoods," he said. "This was right in the middle of the detective's golden triangle, or whatever he called it."

"The horseshoe. Between the freeways."

"The horseshoe, that's right. You must know every house by now."

"Pretty sure I do."

"And yet here we are."

I came up to the first intersection. Ash Street. I slowed down, thinking to myself, the man is right, we worked the hell out of each one of these streets. This is just a waste of time.

I turned anyway.

We passed Fourteenth Street and the little corner store. Three young men were hanging around out front. I looked them over and then kept going.

We passed Fifteenth Street and then Sixteenth Street. The elementary school was closed up tight for the summer. Some more kids were hanging out on the playground equipment, violating a minor rule but nothing I was going to stop for. I looked them over and kept going.

I came to Seventeenth Street and was about to make the turn. There was only a block more, with just a few houses. Then the street dead-ended at a locked gate, with a parking lot on the other side.

I kept going straight.

"Oh, come on," Franklin said. "You're driving yourself crazy. You're also going to make me late for dinner."

He was right. I had no argument. But I kept going down that last block, already figuring I'd loop back and then head down to Butternut Street, maybe check those houses on the way because what the hell, as long as I'm there, and why did I even bother because I don't see a soul on this street now anyway, except for that one woman hanging out the laundry.

I was two houses past before I even realized what I'd seen. I stopped the car.

"What is it?" Franklin said.

"Probably nothing," I said, swinging the car around. "At least I didn't ruin your shoes this time."

I rolled back down the road slowly, the house on our left now, out my driver's side window. It was a white two-story house with a little porch on the front. A woman was out in the side yard, hanging clothes from a line she had strung from the side of the house.

"Oh, come on," Franklin said. "Not this game again."

I watched her take out another pair of jeans and hang it on the line. Next to the other jeans, and the gray shirt.

"I told you," he said. "You're going to drive yourself crazy."

I looked more closely at the shirt. Plain gray. Yes. But the sleeves . . .

No. There was no tear. Both short sleeves were perfectly intact.

"I'm sorry," I said, rubbing my eyes. "I guess I'll never look at a gray shirt again without doing a double take. I'll go my whole life just waiting to see that one torn sleeve."

I took my foot off the brake and aimed the car dead ahead. To the precinct, to civilian clothes, to dinner.

"Alex, hold up!"

I stopped the car again and looked out the window, just as the woman was pinning another gray shirt to the line. A gray shirt with one ragged short sleeve.

CHAPTER THIRTEEN

I went back to the Soo the next day. I needed to try out this idea, to say it out loud, hear myself saying it, see someone else's reaction to it. Someone I could trust.

I parked on Portage Avenue, a busy street on this day, one of the last days of the tourist season. The freighters would keep running until the weather closed them down for the winter, but today was one last chance to walk through the Locks Park without a warm coat. I knew people came from all over to see these seven-hundred-footers go through the locks. I don't totally understand the attraction, but then I live just up the bay, so I see these boats all the time.

I walked into the Soo Brewing Company. The air was heavy and the front window was steamed up, but enough light came through to make the furniture in the seating area look even further past its prime. Although I suppose the lingering aroma of the hops more than made up for it.

Leon appeared from the back room, dragging a large metal trash can. "Alex," he said when he saw me, "two visits in two days. I knew this beer would win you over."

"You need help with that?"

"I got it. But I bet you can't guess where it's going."

I looked into the trash can and saw nothing but a soggy mass of grain. "I'm guessing the Dumpster out back?"

"Hell no. This is from the mash tun. It's going to the buffalo ranch so they can feed it to the herd."

"The buffalo ranch."

"Down toward Pickford, yeah. You've seen them."

"If you say so," I said. Then I saw his coffee on the counter and realized I desperately needed one myself.

"I've got a pot going," he said, before I could even ask. "I'll get you a cup."

A couple of minutes later, we were sitting in the front room on the beat-up couch. The cushions were shot, and I knew it would be a battle to get back on my feet, but for now I was comfortable. I took a sip of coffee.

"You don't look like you slept a whole lot," he said to me.

I shook my head.

"I imagine the story you told me last night has something to do with that."

"I'm not exactly sure how I know this," I said. "Or why I didn't know it until now. All these years later. But I believe we put away an innocent man."

"You believe this based on what?"

"Well, based at least partly on something I thought of in the middle of the night. You're the one I always come to when I need help seeing something clearly, right?"

"I try."

"You do more than try. You have a gift for it. You cut through all the clutter that gets in the way and you go right to the *one thing* that makes it all fit together. I've seen you do it over and over again."

"You're flattering me now. But go ahead."

"When I was telling you what happened at the train station, when I was chasing Darryl King down the tracks, you stopped me and you asked me a question. Do you remember what it was?"

He thought about it for a few seconds.

"I asked you," he said, "why the young man threw away the bracelet and not the knife."

"Right. Which is exactly the same question I asked Detective Bateman, when he told me the story."

"What was his answer?"

"His answer was the kid threw away the knife later, after he got home. Or he just wasn't thinking straight at the moment. Or whatever. It really doesn't matter, because the whole question is just one of those things that gets in the way of us seeing the situation clearly."

He nodded his head slowly. "Okay . . ."

"So that's what I realized last night. I was asking that question when I should have been asking something else."

He raised his eyebrows, waiting for it.

"Why throw away *anything*?" I said. "What good does it do?"

"It's incriminating. It's a natural reaction to throw it away. When you were chasing somebody with drugs, you must have seen—"

"Them throw away bags of crack. Yes, I saw that all the time. We'd go pick it up after the arrest, and inevitably they'd say, 'Oh, no, Officer, that's not mine. I don't know where that came from.'"

"So it's the same idea here," he said. "The kid had the bracelet, so while you were chasing him he threw it away."

"Exactly. Now you've got it."

"Got what? We're back where we started, aren't we?"

"No," I said. "Now we're somewhere else. Look . . ."

I noticed that he had his cell phone clipped to his belt, so I reached over and grabbed it from him.

"I just took your cell phone," I said. "It's much nicer than mine, after all. It probably even works up here sometimes. So now I'm going to leave before I get caught, right?"

"Yeah?"

"But wait, here comes a cop, so I'm going to throw it away."

I tossed it onto the table.

"It wasn't me, Officer. I have no idea how that cell phone got on that table."

He looked at the phone, then at me.

"Now let's say I just killed you," I said. "And I happened to take your cell phone while I was at it. Here comes that cop. What am I going to do? If I'm still carrying around the freaking *murder weapon,* do you think I'm even *thinking* about the stupid cell phone at that point?"

"No," he said, grabbing his phone from the table. "No, you're not."

"Darryl King threw away that bracelet because he had just committed the crime of taking it, so when I was chasing him he naturally threw it away. He was disassociating himself from the crime. Which I realize sounds like something you would say. Maybe you're rubbing off on me."

"If you look at it as a simple robbery, you mean . . ."

"Then it all makes sense, yes. He does exactly what you'd expect him to do."

"So he doesn't throw away the knife . . ."

"Because he doesn't have a knife."

Leon sat back on the couch and thought about this. I could tell he was really working it over. He started to say something, stopped himself. Started again, then stopped.

"But it is *possible* . . ."

"If you make up that story in your head, you can make him throw away the bracelet and keep the knife, yes. I suppose in some cases, somewhere, it's actually happened that way. People do things that don't make any sense."

"But in this case . . ."

"In this case, I think he found a dead body. She wasn't dead for long, because we know from the forensics that she was killed right around that same time. But he goes up there and he sees the bracelet and he takes it. Because at that point, why not? Then he leaves, and I show up and start chasing him."

"So he throws it away," Leon said, still thinking it over. "'Not me. I didn't do it. I didn't take this from that dead woman up there . . .'"

I just sat there and watched him as he seemed to reenact the whole scene in his head.

"Damn," he finally said, "that feels right. It really does."

"I'm glad to hear you say that."

"It's completely unprovable, of course. Just one of those things you know in your gut. But now you try to put that up against the fact that he confessed . . ."

"We go back to that, yeah. Why he would just roll over and give up."

"Instead of swearing up and down that he didn't kill her."

"Well, he's getting out soon," I said. "Maybe I can ask him."

Leon looked at me. "You're really thinking of doing that?"

"I might. I don't know. It'll probably bug me forever if I don't."

"That'll be one interesting conversation," he said. "But wait a minute. Hold the phone . . ."

"What is it?"

"Alex, if this Darryl King of yours didn't kill that woman . . ."

"Then someone else did," I said. "I realize that."

"I would think *that* would keep me up at night, just as much as the thought of sending the wrong man to prison."

"Well, thanks. Tonight I'm sure it will."

"Seriously, what are you going to do about this? Somebody killed her and just walked away."

I didn't have an answer for that. Leon didn't have an answer, either. Not a real answer. I thanked him for listening to me. Then I let him get back to work.

When I was outside again, I found myself walking through the iron gate to Locks Park. Another freighter was coming through the locks. People were standing around watching it, but it barely registered for me. I was too busy thinking about that dead woman left on that balcony in that train station, and a murderer with no face and no name, who never paid the price for his crime.

My honeymooners were gone from the last cabin, so I spent a couple of hours closing that up. Vinnie came by for a few minutes, then left for his shift at the casino. The sun went down, and it started to get cold. The wind was blowing hard by the time I got to the Glasgow Inn. It was just me and Jackie and a few stragglers wandering in on their way up to the Shipwreck Museum. Jackie could tell something was bothering me. He put a cold Canadian on the table next to my chair and left me alone.

I knew Leon was right about not being able to sleep, no matter how tired I was. But when I got back to my cabin, I gave it a try anyway. It was midnight and I was just starting to doze off when I heard a loud knock on my door.

I got up and opened it. It was Leon.

"I'm sorry," he said. "I had to come over. This can't wait."

"Leon, what is it? What the hell's going on?"

I invited him in. He sat down at my table. He had a folder of papers with him. As he opened it I saw notes and copies of news items.

"I kept thinking about what you told me today," he said. "I've been on the Internet, looking up some stuff."

"Like what?" I sat down next to him.

"I got thinking," he said, shuffling through his papers, "that a murder like this is just so brutal . . . So extreme . . ."

"Yes?"

"Here's one," he said, holding up a printout from a newspaper Web site. "Just read it."

I took it from him. From the *Cleveland Plain Dealer,* an interview with the chief of police. The man was talking about an unsolved murder in his city. A woman who had been stabbed seventeen times in a hotel stairwell.

I checked the date. Five years after the murder of Elana Paige.

"I know every murder doesn't get solved, and stabbings aren't that uncommon. But look at these, too."

He handed me two more news items. One from the *Chicago Sun-Times,* another follow-up on a case that was still unsolved six months after it happened. A woman stabbed to death in a parking structure next to a mall, just outside Chicago. Then the other one, from the *Milwaukee Journal Sentinel.* Yet another unsolved case. Yet another woman stabbed multiple times. This time left outside, in a park overlooking Lake Michigan.

So Cleveland five years after Elana Paige, then Chicago four years after that. Then Milwaukee three years later. Each one of these crimes represented by a single sheet of paper on my table, here in this small cabin hundreds of miles away from any of these crimes, and yet I knew all too well what lay behind the simple facts recited in the news stories. The terrible last moments of an innocent person's life. Then families torn apart by grief.

"It's possible there are more," Leon said. "These are just the obvious ones I found in five minutes."

"This doesn't have to be the same person," I said, spreading the pages back out on the table. "Or if it was for *these* murders, it doesn't necessarily have to include Elana Paige."

"It doesn't have to, no. But what does your gut tell you right now?"

"I'm tired of my gut telling me things," I said. "It's not always right, you know."

"Sure, maybe it's wrong this time. Maybe there's no connection. Hell, if Darryl King really did kill Elana Paige, then you *know* there's no connection. Because he was in prison when these other murders were committed."

"That's right," I said, honestly trying to convince myself. Outside, I could hear the cold wind still blowing, driving the last day of summer into oblivion.

"So what are you going to do?" he said.

"I'm going to try to sleep a few hours," I said, knowing it probably wouldn't happen. I was already starting to feel sick to my stomach. "Then first thing tomorrow morning, I'm going to call the one person who might have some answers."

CHAPTER FOURTEEN

I put the car in park. I sat there watching the woman hanging up the shirts and pants and dresses on the clothesline. It was a good day for letting the late-afternoon sun dry your clothes.

"How do we play this?" Franklin said. "Should I call it in?"

"In a minute," I said. "Let's just make sure we've got something here."

I turned the car off and got out. Franklin followed me as I walked over to the woman by the laundry basket. She was an attractive woman, maybe pushing forty but obviously not letting it slow her down. She moved with a brisk economy, like a woman who worked hard every day. She probably didn't have much choice, not with a house and a family that needed food and clean clothes.

She stopped hanging another shirt when she spotted us walking across her yard. It was mostly weeds and crabgrass, but somebody was obviously keeping it all mowed.

"Can I help you?" she said.

"Sorry to bother you, ma'am. We're just taking one more trip through this neighborhood. I'm sure someone else was here before?"

"Looking for someone who killed that white woman." Here's where she could have added her own comment about how black men get shot down every single day and nobody canvasses her neighborhood for them, but she didn't.

"Yes, ma'am." Just as I was thinking about what to say next, the back door opened. A young man stepped out of the house. The hair, the high cheekbones. For one tenth of a second my brain was already sending a signal to my right hand, to reach for my service revolver. But then the spell was broken as I put everything else together. This kid was a couple of years younger. Twenty pounds lighter. He didn't have the muscular swagger of the kid I chased down the railroad tracks. Not even close. This was the kid who got his lunch money taken at recess, not the kid doing the taking.

"What's going on, Mom?" the kid asked.

"It's nothing, Tremont. These police officers are just making the rounds again. Like they did the other day."

The kid named Tremont gave me a shy look and a quick nod of his head.

"How are you?" Franklin said. "You like being out of school for the summer?"

"Yes, sir."

"Don't know a kid who doesn't," the woman said.

How to ask this next question, I thought, without giving myself away . . .

"Looks like a lot of mowing you gotta do here," I said to her, nodding at her backyard. It wasn't real grass, but every square foot was mowed down to something that looked neat and trim anyway. "You got anybody else living here who can help you out?"

"It's just me and my two kids these past few years now. Please don't even ask about their daddy, because I try not to use profanity if I don't have to."

"Oh, two kids?" I tried to keep my voice even. No big deal, just passing time here. You've got two kids, do tell.

That's when the back door opened again. A little girl came out. She was ten years old, maybe eleven.

"That's Naima," the woman said. "Why they need to spend half the day inside watching television, on a nice day like this . . ."

The girl came over and started picking through the clothes in the basket. She didn't so much as look in my direction.

"Well," I said, already feeling deflated, "okay, a boy and a girl. It looks like you've got your hands full here."

"No complaints, Officer. We're doing just fine. God provides and we are thankful."

I looked around at what she was thankful for. The house seemed to be in decent shape, but I could see water damage around the top-floor windows. It needed new siding, too. I spotted the lawn mower beneath the one large tree at the back of the property. There was no shed to store it in, so it was rusted out and I couldn't even imagine it starting, let alone cutting through all of these weeds. Next to that was a weight bench that had probably once belonged to the father, before he ran off. On the other side of the tree a swing hung haphazardly from a thick branch. Not a tire, but a plank of wood tilting a few degrees past level. Tremont jumped up onto it and began to swing back and forth slowly.

Something. There was something in that scene.

Wait a minute. Wait one goddamned minute . . .

"All right," I said. "Again, sorry to bother you. We'll let you finish up with your laundry."

"No bother at all," she said. "You gentlemen have a good rest of the day."

"Thank you," Franklin said. "It was very nice to meet all of you."

We went back to the patrol car.

"That obviously wasn't the kid you were looking for," Franklin said as he sat down beside me. "I'm glad we didn't call it in. Get everybody out here, make us look like fools."

I picked up the radio and hit the transmitter. "This is Unit Forty-one. Is Detective Bateman still in the precinct?"

A few seconds of radio silence, with my partner looking at me, waiting for an explanation.

"Affirmative, Forty-one. Detective Bateman is at his desk."

"Ask him to wait for me," I said. "We'll be there in a few minutes."

"Okay," Franklin said when I put the transmitter back, "are you planning on telling me what the hell is going on at some point?"

"That woman was lying. I'm trying not to take it personally, because I'm sure she thinks she's doing the right thing."

"How do you know she's lying?"

"You saw that weight bench in the backyard?"

"Yes."

"Do you think our little friend Tremont pumps a lot of iron?"

"I'm guessing it would kill him if he tried."

"So who uses those weights?"

"The father," he said. "He didn't take it all with him. So—"

"So yeah, that's what I thought, too. Then I noticed something."

"What?"

"There were weight plates stacked on the ground."

"Yeah? You got a weight bench, you're gonna have plates."

"Did you also notice how well-mowed that backyard was?"

"I did," he said. "Are you approaching the point here, or are we gonna keep playing 'I Spy'?"

"If the weightlifter in your family left, would you still keep picking up the plates, mowing under them, and then putting them back on the ground? Every time you mowed? For *years*?"

He thought about it for a moment.

"Of course not," he said. "I'd leave them stacked on the bench."

"There you go. Meaning that there's someone else living at that house. Somebody who keeps himself in shape."

He sat there looking at me as I drove back to the precinct.

"Hot damn, Alex," he finally said. "Just when I thought you took too many foul balls off your mask."

The mother's name was Jamilah King. The son named Tremont was in the public school system. So was the daughter, Naima.

So was the other son, at least until recently. He was two years older than Tremont. His name was Darryl. He hadn't been in school since turning sixteen. He didn't have a driver's license. There was no employment record for Darryl King, or any other public record at all, but then that wasn't unusual for a young black male in Detroit, where it's so easy to just disappear into the streets.

Detective Bateman looked at the name on the high school transcript, the last official documentation of his existence before he dropped out.

"Darryl King," he said. "Pleased to meet you, young man. I'd like to introduce you to our SWAT team."

"I don't think that's the right play," I said. "It's possible that this kid is inside that house right now, but it's just as possible he's somewhere else. If there's a record for him at that address, it wouldn't be smart to be there."

"Look at this transcript and tell me this kid is smart."

"You know there's more than one brand of smart, Detective. He's done a great job of staying off the radar, and obviously he has his mother working hard to keep it that way. You try to flush him out now and he might disappear for good."

"So what do we do? Watch the house? Wait him out?"

"That's how I'd approach it, yes."

"Yeah, okay," he said. "That's the way we do it. Did you see a good spot to park a van?"

"The street comes to a dead end, just a block away. Actually, there's a locked gate there. On the other side is the back of the parking lot for one of those apartment complexes on MLK."

"Perfect," he said. "We put our van in that lot. Use the plumbing and heating sign. Or the cable sign, either one. Have that gate unlocked so we can move through it quickly."

He picked up the phone to make the arrangements. At one point while he was on hold, he looked up at me with a smile on his face.

"What is it?" I said.

"It's my new mission in life. Once we catch this guy."

"Yeah? What's that?"

"Get you your gold shield. You said you're taking the test, right?"

"Eventually."

"Next test, you're taking it. You'll do great, of course. The rest is politics. That's where I come in."

"Tell you what," I said. "Let's just catch this guy. Then we can talk about gold shields."

They rolled the van over that very evening. They parked it in the back of the parking lot, with a direct sight line to the house. We were lucky to have a streetlight on the corner as well, so there was no problem watching for people going in or out.

I was immediately approved for overtime duty again. I spent the evening shift in the van with Detective Bateman. We didn't see anything happening at the house.

We turned it over to a single night-shift officer while we went home to sleep. Nothing happened. The detective and I were back in the van the next morning, holding large cups of coffee. We'd arranged with the apartment complex to use one of the empty units for bathroom breaks.

It was the first time I'd ever done several consecutive hours of surveillance. My first experience with such a new level of how to do absolutely nothing, with a single thread of anxiousness running through it so that you're never completely comfortable in your boredom.

The day shift passed. The woman had come and gone, with the daughter, Naima. The son Tremont had come and gone. That was it.

It was evening now. I was going on fourteen straight hours of this, wondering if my sanity would hold if I had to come right back here the next day. They could have done this without me, theoretically. Just wait for a stranger to show his face and then call out the dogs, drag him in and bring me down to identify him. But I was the one person who could pick out this kid before blowing our cover. That was an advantage nobody else could bring to the van.

"I'm gonna be pissed if that kid's been inside the house this whole time," Bateman said. "He could be eating pizza and watching television."

"I admit," I said, "I'm starting to rethink my original idea. Even if he's not there, the mother would have to give him up eventually, wouldn't she?"

The detective looked away from the little observation window. "The long hours are making you delirious, Alex. Like she'd ever do that in a million years."

I took my turn at the window. It was getting close to midnight. Time for the night-shift officer to relieve us.

Then I saw the headlights.

A beat-up old car came rolling down the street, slowly. It stopped in front of the house. The headlights were turned off.

The driver waited a full minute to get out. When he did, he was just a shadow in the darkness, backlit by the streetlight behind him. But I recognized the body type. I recognized the way he moved.

"Hey, Detective," I said, not taking my eyes off him. "I thought you said this kid didn't have a driver's license."

"He doesn't."

"Well, then we'll have something else to charge him with."

He came over to the window and looked out at the house. "Is that our man?"

"He must have missed his mother's home cooking," I said. "Let's go get him."

We called for backup first. No sense doing anything stupid, now that we had him pinned in the house. As soon as the squad cars rolled up, Bateman dispatched units to all four sides of the house. Then he went up on the front porch and banged on the door.

"Open up! Police!"

Silence.

"Darryl, we can do this the easy way or the hard way! Just come on out and nobody will get hurt!"

The door opened. A figure stood in the doorway.

"Get on the ground!" Bateman yelled, his gun pointed right at the kid's chest. "Turn around and lie face down! Right now!"

I don't know if you can give the kid credit for this or not, but he kept standing there, calling the detective's bluff. Like he was saying, go ahead and shoot me.

In the end, the detective walked right up to him and tackled him. A dozen other officers swarmed the house then, guns drawn. A police dog was barking. The radios were all squawking in unison. I stood back by the sidewalk, watching the pandemonium, feeling oddly out of place. All of these officers belonged to another squad, after all. They were virtual strangers to me. Now they were all working together to back up Detective Bateman on the big arrest.

I was finally called inside to make the official ID. I walked up the porch steps and looked down at the young man lying on the floor. His hands were cuffed behind his back. There was a fresh scrape on his forehead from where he'd been pushed down onto the hardwood floor. He looked up at me.

It was him. This was the man I'd chased down the tracks.

The mother was screaming. The little sister was crying. I saw the brother running down the hallway into the bathroom. If you had anything resembling a human heart, you knew that this was another family devastated by the crime.

Darryl King was picked up off the floor and taken away.

I filled out some paperwork while Darryl King was booked, finger-printed, and put in a holding cell. He hadn't said a word yet, not to anybody. Not even to his mother. She had been brought down to the station with her son, because of course you can't interrogate a minor without a parent or guardian in the room.

I waited around for a couple more hours. The mother was doing all of the talking, telling us all we had made a big mistake. She didn't want a lawyer for her son. She said Darryl didn't *need* a law-yer because he hadn't done anything. It was a mistake I'd seen play out again and again over the years, and it never stopped surprising me. If the police arrest you, put you in a room, then ask you if you know anything about anything, don't say a word until you have a lawyer at your side. Even if you *know* you haven't done anything wrong.

But with Darryl not talking and his mother playing the same tape over and over again, there didn't seem to be much hope of a confession before we had to formally charge him based only on my ID and the fingerprints on the bracelet. The sergeant on duty pat-ted me on the back and sent me home.

Jeannie was asleep when I got home. She was gone the next morn-ing when I woke up. It was late. But I had been given that day off.

I made dinner reservations. I was looking forward to having a normal life again. Maybe recapturing something with Jeannie, before it was too late. That's what I was thinking.

But then it turned out she had a late class that evening. I had totally forgotten about it, and she didn't want to skip it. I told her I understood. We made a makeup date for that weekend. She told me she was proud of me. She told me that she loved me. That was the last time she'd ever say that.

That was the last day of June, meaning I was rolling over to nights. At least this time I wasn't doing it coming off a short shift. But when I got to the precinct for the midnight roll call, there was a little surprise waiting for me.

"Bateman got it," Sergeant Grimaldi said to me. "He got the confession."

"What are you talking about?" I said. "I thought we had given up."

"What can I tell you? He took one more shot at it."

"Did somebody think maybe they should call me and let me know?"

"If Bateman didn't do that," he said, "then I should have. I apologize."

"It's all right. Can I see the confession, at least?"

"Sure thing. You know what? Detective Bateman will be here when you get back from your shift. So go find him and make him play the tape for you. I don't think you'll have much problem getting him to relive his big moment of glory."

I could tell Sergeant Grimaldi was still feeling bad about how I'd been left out of the loop when the case was closed. So he made sure I got a big round of applause at the roll call. I tried to wave it off, and then I stood up and told everyone that Franklin deserved some of the credit. Which was the absolute truth. I had driven us there, but I was just about to drive away. Then Franklin saw the shirt with the torn sleeve being put on the clothesline.

"You didn't have to do that," he said to me when we got in the car.

"Yes, I did. Maybe it's about time for you to get a gold shield, too."

He smiled and shook that off. As we rolled out, we knew we had a long eight hours ahead of us. That first night was always the hardest, whether you were short-shifting or not. You're trying to fool your body into staying awake and alert through eight hours in the dark. Your body knows a lie when it hears one. So you just try to pace yourself, deal with everything that comes up, talk to the knuckleheads, try to keep a lid on things and have as peaceful a night as you can possibly manage.

It was yet another hot summer night. There would be nothing peaceful about it.

There was a disturbance at the hospital on Woodward Avenue. The place was already the epicenter of that city's hot summer, with gunshot victims being wheeled into the ER every night. It was a job I couldn't even imagine, dealing with that over and over. Now there was apparently a Code 35 wandering around the ER waiting room. A Code 35 is a mentally disturbed person.

What happened next is a story that changes a little bit every time I tell it. It was all too much to take in when it was actually happening. Years go by and I'll remember little details for the first time.

We went into the lobby. We talked to the receptionist. She told us that the man had been bothering the inpatients all night. At one point he had tried to hide behind the plants.

She had heard this man lived down the street, in a high-rise apartment building. It was a building Franklin and I had visited, more than once. It was one of those addresses you knew immediately, as soon as you heard it on the radio. Oh great, this place again.

The elevator was broken. We had to take the stairs. Franklin complained with every step. His knee was hurting. We had gone back to the sports banter that night, everything back to normal. Football versus baseball, the endless argument.

The man was named Rose. We went into his apartment and sat him down at his kitchen table. There was aluminum foil on the walls.

In the middle of our pleas for him to stop bothering the people at the hospital, he took out the Uzi from beneath the table. It had been taped to the underside. In that endless minute he had the gun pointed at us, ready to shoot the second either of us moved, he told us he had found it in a Dumpster. Not an unusual find in a summer filled with gun battles over the crack trade.

I hate thinking about what comes next. It's something I replay in my head and I always try to make turn out differently. But of course it never does.

He shot Franklin five times. He shot me three times. That's what you can do with an Uzi, before either one of us could even get our revolvers out of their holsters. I lay on the floor, looking up at the ceiling, which Rose had neglected to line with aluminum foil. I can still see that ceiling when I close my eyes at night.

Franklin died on the floor next to me. He left behind a wife and two daughters. I was still in the hospital when they held the service for him, then put him in the ground.

Jeannie told me she would stick it out, but the wife-of-a-cop thing had already been wearing her down. This was much worse, and I can still remember that expression on her face as she looked down at me in my hospital bed. Like this was all just too much. When I finally got back on my feet, I spent a lost year drinking and taking painkillers, and one day, a few weeks into that dark period, Jeannie left me. Although I suppose you could argue that I had already left her, in my own way. I guess it doesn't really matter in the end.

I was off the police force on two-thirds disability. I never went back.

When I was pulling myself back together after that year, I came up to Paradise to sell off the cabins my father had built. I've been up here ever since. But if I thought I could run away from my past, I was sorely mistaken. It always finds you, even in the most remote little town you can imagine. Even in a town called Paradise.

Even now, when I think I've finally come to terms with everything that happened in my life, I find something new. I can look back on that last summer in Detroit, past the shooting, to that one last big case I helped solve. All these years later, and somehow it's just coming to me that I never did get the chance to see that confession, and that this young man may have been innocent of the crime for which he was charged. And worse, that the real killer walked free. Possibly to kill again. Possibly all because we missed something that would have pointed to him.

We could have stopped him then. That was the one thing I couldn't get over. If we were so goddamned smart, we could have charged Darryl King with robbery and maybe tampering with a crime scene, put him on probation, given him back to his mother, and then gone out and found the man who really killed Elana Paige.

I was cut down by a madman myself, after all. A madman who got caught just a few days later and put away forever. So how could I live with myself now, knowing that in that same hot summer, I may have missed my chance to catch an even bigger monster?

PART TWO

THE FALL

CHAPTER FIFTEEN

My first call that morning was to FBI Agent Janet Long. When she picked up, I was smart enough to thank her one more time for dinner before launching into my question.

"This is going to sound a little strange," I said, "but bear with me."

"I'm listening."

"Somewhere in your bureau, there's an agent or two who are aware of several unsolved homicides throughout the Midwest."

There was a brief silence on the line.

"Yes," she said. "More than one or two agents, actually. What about it?"

"All women, all multiple stabbings. I know of cold cases in Cleveland, Metro Chicago, and Milwaukee. Are there more?"

"Alex, what are you getting at?"

"Look, you know I was involved in that case in Detroit. The woman who was stabbed in the train station."

"That's the case you were telling me about at dinner. With the killer who's getting out soon."

"Right. But let's just suppose for a minute that he didn't really do it. If you happened to add Elana Paige to that list of unsolved stabbings . . . I mean, I can't help thinking that would be something useful to whoever's tracking those other cases."

"If it's the same killer, yes. Of course it would. It's usually one case that breaks the whole thing. That one time he makes a mistake of some kind."

"That's exactly what I was thinking."

"Just to get it straight," she said, "you're talking about the man who was convicted of killing that woman in the train station, right here in Detroit. The man who confessed to the crime. That's the case you're talking about."

"Yes."

She stopped talking again. I could hear her tapping away at her keyboard.

"Elana Paige," she finally said. "In Detroit. That was before the other murders."

"I was wondering if that was the case. So yes, maybe that's the one time he made a mistake. If it was his very first time."

"But just because it was a multiple stabbing, that doesn't necessarily connect it with the others. Especially with a confession and a man in prison. Who obviously couldn't have killed anyone else while he was in there."

"That's my point, Janet. If Darryl King confessed to a crime he didn't commit . . ."

"I'll pass this along to the right person," she said. "If there's an angle here and it helps break these other cases, then everybody will be happy. But you have to promise me something right now."

"What's that?"

"By giving it to me, you let it go. Are we clear?"

"Even if I wanted to," I said, "what could I do? These are major cases in other states, going back years."

"Something tells me you'd find a way. So promise me."

"I promise. I just wanted to let you know. That's all."

"Okay," she said. "I appreciate it."

"Will you at least let me know if you guys find something?"

"Yes. You'll be the first person to know, outside the bureau."

One more silence. Maybe both of us realizing that there wasn't much else to say. We didn't make another dinner date. We didn't even say "See you soon." I just thanked her and told her to take care of herself.

As soon as I ended the call, I had a brief debate with myself. Then I dialed Detective Bateman. I wasn't breaking my promise to Janet. I was simply following up on the conversation we had on his boat.

Bateman answered the phone.

"Arnie," I said, "this is Alex McKnight."

"Alex, good to hear from you again. Good seeing you the other day, too. We should do that again sometime."

"I'd love to. But that's not why I was calling. Actually, I just wanted to ask you one question."

"Shoot."

"Is there any chance I could finally see that confession some time?"

Nothing for a long moment. Phone silences were apparently going to be the theme for the day.

"You know, I had this feeling when you were here, and I was telling you about it . . . You were doubting even before you got here, weren't you?"

"I admit, I may have been."

"Hearing me tell you how it all broke down, that didn't settle it for you?"

"It's one thing to hear about it after the fact," I said. "It's another thing to see it and hear it yourself."

"Well, first of all, why are you thinking about this now? It was a long time ago. If you had any doubts . . ."

"I honestly haven't thought about it at all," I said. "Not until I got the call about him getting out."

"So now, looking back, even though you weren't there to see it, you feel like you need to tell me it wasn't a clean confession. Is that what I'm hearing?"

"Look, I know it was a big case for you. We *all* wanted it to be solved, but—"

"We all wanted it to be solved," he said. "So we solved it. You were the one who ID'd him, for crying out loud. How can you even be saying this now?"

This is going beautifully, I thought. This was such a great idea.

"I know this is out of the blue," I said. "Let me try to explain why I'm thinking this way."

"I told you I was sorry, Alex. You should have made the arrest. You should have gotten the big award, too. We both should have been up there. Even if I had to wait for you to get back on your feet."

"Wait a minute," I said. "Stop right there. This has nothing to do with who got credit. Will you please give me one minute to explain?"

"Yeah, sure. You just came up with some new evidence that would overturn a conviction based on a *sworn confession.*"

"Arnie, come on."

"I'll call the prosecutor. We can schedule the hearing. I'll get up there myself and tell everyone it was all bogus. Then I'll give back the award. Would that do it for you?"

"Listen to me . . ."

"No, thanks. I've heard enough. Have a nice life, and maybe get some help, huh? I think you got a real problem letting go of old grudges."

I didn't get in another word before he hung up. I stood there looking at the phone, too stunned to even be mad. Then I got over it.

"If you weren't already half crippled," I said to the phone, "I'd come down there and kick your ass."

The next couple of days were tough for me. I don't have much of a talent for putting things out of my mind. I just tried to stay busy. The cold weather was right around the corner, so I started getting cabins ready. There were windows to seal up. One of the woodstoves was on its last legs, so I spent an afternoon with Vinnie, putting in a new one.

"You've been thinking about something else all day," he said when we went down to the Glasgow Inn. "It's a good thing I helped you with the stove. You probably would have installed it backwards."

"I'm trying to keep my head here in Paradise," I said. "I'm really trying."

But it was getting harder with each passing hour, not easier. I'd be doing something around one of the cabins and I'd suddenly have this vision of a woman lying on a cold floor, all of the blood drained from her body. I hadn't seen any of these other crime scenes, of course. Not in Cleveland or Chicago or Milwaukee, or wherever else this same killer may have struck. So some part of my mind would make up the details and all of a sudden it would be *right there,* right in front of me. I was starting to wonder if I'd keep seeing them for the rest of my life. That would surely drive me insane.

Leon was no help, because he was just as compulsive as I was. Maybe even more so, if that were possible. I went down to the Soo Brewing Company a couple of days after his late-night visit. He was standing behind the counter, looking like a man who hadn't slept much.

When he had a break, he came over and sat down next to me on the old couch. He was carrying a folder. I didn't have to ask him what was inside.

"I suppose you can guess what I've been doing," he said.

"I probably can."

"I found a couple more cases."

"More stabbings?"

"Yes."

"In the Midwest?"

"No, that's the thing. See, if you look at the dates for those first three cases I found, they happen anywhere from May to September."

"Okay . . ."

He opened the folder and took out the news stories.

"So I looked a little further," he said. "Here are three more open cases. All three are women, all three were stabbed to death. Nobody arrested in any of them yet."

"Janet told me they have an active profile," I said. "She didn't say there were this many."

"Savannah, Georgia. Mobile, Alabama. Jacksonville, Florida. The years are mixed in with the others, the difference being that these three all occurred from November to March."

"You're telling me we've got a fair-weather murderer here. He goes south for the winter, and if he sees his opportunity down there . . ."

"That's about the size of it, yes. So what are we going to do?"

"Well, the FBI already knows everything you're telling me. It's the Detroit angle that's new. If that can be tied in, I mean, maybe it helps. Especially if it was earlier than the others."

"Assuming they buy your idea that it was a false confession," Leon said, shaking his head. "Assuming they can do anything with that case, even if they do believe it. All these years later."

"I officially have never felt so useless," I said. "How about you?"

"I'm with you, buddy."

"Let me give her another call," I said, taking the folder from him. "I'll make up some excuse. But really I just want to find out if anything new has happened."

"Let me know, okay?"

"I will. Thanks for doing this. Now you should probably try to put it out of your head before it makes you crazy."

"I'll do that as soon as you do."

I had no comeback. I left him there to his beer brewing. I went back to Paradise.

My call to Janet went about as expected. She listened to me read off the other cases Leon had dug up. She already knew about all of them. Not only that, she had one more to add to the list.

"Indianapolis," she said. "Two years after Milwaukee. So that's seven unsolved murders, all multiple stabbings. All with the same kind of knife, by the way. I don't know if I mentioned that before."

"You didn't, but what about the Detroit case?" I said. "Have you heard anything about how that might be connected?"

"You know I can't say anything, but I also know you're not going to sleep until I do. So here's what I can tell you . . ."

"Go ahead."

"It turns out they did look at that case. It was three or four murders in, when they were first trying to establish the pattern. They couldn't help but notice the similarities to the murder in Detroit."

"Okay . . ."

"So they checked it out. They called the detective who was in charge of that case."

"That was Arnie Bateman."

"I don't know the name. Just some guy who was kind of a blow-hard, I guess."

"That's him. So what happened?"

"Not much," she said. "It was a sworn confession, with a man sitting in prison. If there was something more concrete to tie this murder to the others . . ."

"He gave you the stiff-arm. Isn't that obvious? He didn't want to reopen the case that made his career."

"I asked the agent to look at it again, okay? What else can I do?"

"That sounds like all I can ask for," I said. "Thanks for doing that."

"If this takes him down a rat hole, it's not going to make me look good. You realize that."

"That's impossible. You always look good."

"Don't even try that," she said. "Unless you've thought some more about moving down here."

I wasn't about to lie to her. So we left it at that. I thanked her and let her go back to work. Then I tried to do the same, even though I had a whole new set of dead bodies to think about. I knew it would be a long night.

Maybe I'll call the detective again, I thought. That would *really* make the day.

I didn't, of course. I didn't have to. All I had to do was wait until that night.

The phone rang just after nine o'clock. I picked up the receiver, thinking it would be Leon, or maybe Janet. I got neither.

"Alex, this is Arnie Bateman. I'm sorry to call so late."

"Detective, what's going on?"

"Don't call me detective. I'm not sure I deserve the title right now."

"I don't understand. What are you talking about?"

"Darryl King got out today," he said. "He's out of prison."

"Okay, I knew it was coming up pretty soon, but—"

"You want to know what I did to mark the occasion?"

"I'm guessing you didn't go down and throw him a party."

"I watched the tape, Alex. I watched the world-famous confession."

"What, you have a copy of it?"

"No, no. I had to call down to the old precinct, the district now, find somebody who still remembered me. I asked if I could see it and they said sure, if we can even find it. It got moved over to the records building. Some old VHS tape in a dusty old box. They finally found it, and this sergeant calls me back, tells me he can't let it leave the premises, but I could see it if I came down there."

"So you did."

"Yeah. I don't drive much anymore on account of the leg. Hurts too much to sit that long. But I figured this was worth it."

"Why did you think that? You sounded pretty sure when I called you that it was all a big—"

"Okay, just stop," he said. "I'm sorry. All right? Will you accept my apology before we go any further? I was totally out of line."

"Accepted," I said. "Now tell me about the tape."

"Well, I guess the surprising thing is that it went pretty much exactly how I remembered it. There wasn't one thing he said that didn't match my memory."

"So you're just calling me to confirm it was a good confession. That I was totally wrong to even question it. Is that what you're saying?"

"No, Alex. I'm calling you to tell you he didn't confess at all."

He let that one hang for a moment, just the faraway buzzing of the telephone line as I tried to process the words.

"You're going to have to explain," I said. "I'm afraid you lost me."

"I watched it three times. At no point does he ever say, 'Yes, I killed that woman.' He says, 'I'm a man, and if there's something I need to do, I do it.' That's what he says."

"I remember you telling me that, yes. You said those were his exact words."

"Yes."

"But then you said he went on to explain exactly what happened. How he saw her up at the station, how he got her up to the balcony . . ."

"He didn't do that, Alex. He didn't explain it. It was *me* doing all the explaining at that point."

"How do you mean?"

"It was just a classic dumb mistake in interviewing. Everything I had been trained to do, just right out the window. Because after I got what I thought was the initial confession, I should have made him describe everything in detail from the beginning. But instead I jumped right ahead and said, 'Okay, so you saw her at the station, right? You thought she'd be an easy mark?' And so on, right down the line. I led him into it, and all he had to do was keep agreeing with me."

"Okay . . ."

"He never said he did it, Alex. Not in a real way. Not one goddamned time. But I was so anxious to solve the case. Hell, we all were. I just heard what I wanted to hear and I rammed the rest right down his throat."

"I think I see what you're saying. But that still doesn't explain why he went along with it. Even if you were leading him."

"Well, that's what I'm going to find out. I'm going to go down and ask him myself. Tomorrow."

"Are you serious?"

"It's the only way I can know for sure. You want to come with me?"

"Again . . . are you serious?"

"We can ask him together. Maybe it would be a good idea, too, just in case he's got some . . . you know, anger that he might not be able to control. I'm not exactly the physical specimen I once was, if I have to defend myself."

"Did you contact him? Does he know you've got this in mind?"

"Nope. I figure it's better to just go down there. Let him have tonight to get settled. Then knock on his door in the morning. 'Did you do it, Darryl? If not, why did you confess to it?' Maybe we'll get a genuine, spontaneous answer if he doesn't have time to prepare for it."

"You're really going to do this."

"Hell, yes. I think you want to, too. Am I wrong?"

I thought about it for all of a second and a half. "No," I said. "You're not wrong. How about I come down in the morning and pick you up? You said you're not great on driving these days."

"That would be fantastic. It'll be just like old times."

"Yeah, something like that," I said. "Listen, can I ask you about something else? I was talking to an FBI agent today, and—"

"Oh God, so you already know."

"About the other cases?"

"It was a few years later, yes. They contacted me and said they were looking at the Paige case, on account of certain similarities. Same kind of knife, all women, all stabbed approximately two dozen times. No other evidence on the scene, so the killer was being careful. It all makes sense now, looking back at it, but I'm afraid at the time I was less than accommodating."

"As I recall, nobody had much love for the FBI back then."

"Then or ever. But I should have at least looked at it, right? I couldn't take one day out of my life to go down there and work with them?"

I wasn't sure how to answer that. Or if I should even try.

"If I find out there was really a connection . . ." he said. "Hell, how will I ever forgive myself for being such an idiot?"

"Well, let's just find out first," I said. "Don't forget, I was part of this case, too."

"I tell you one thing, this'll be a big shock to the brother and the husband."

"Wait, do you still stay in touch with them?"

"I talk to them all the time. Both Ryan Grayson and Tanner Paige. I've even had them up to the lake. Took them out on the boat."

"Really?" I had a hard time picturing it.

"Sure, why not?"

"What about Elana's parents?"

"Oh, they both died a while ago," he said. "One right after the other. That kind of grief is a heavy load. But yeah, Ryan got married, had a couple of kids. If you remember, he had a lot of anger toward his brother-in-law."

"I remember."

"He's got over that, I'm happy to say. He knows it was misplaced."

"You must have talked to them this past week," I said, "when they found out about Darryl King's release?"

"A few times, yes. It really got to them. Sort of brought it all back, you know? Just thinking about your sister's murderer walking around free. Or your wife's murderer."

"They're not going to do anything stupid, are they?"

"I'd like to think they both have the sense not to. But if this new angle is true . . . I mean, that puts it all in a different place, doesn't it? I'm not sure it's better, but at least they don't have to think about Darryl King walking around in the sunshine on a nice summer day."

"I don't think that's better."

"No, you're right. If this is the same guy, he's been walking around all this time. Nobody's even touched him yet."

"Well, the FBI's still on this," I said. "Now they know about this new possibility, at least."

"I kept copies of the old files, you know. I've been going over them all day, looking for what I might have missed. In fact, you should work with me on this, Alex. It'll be just like old times, you know? Except maybe we'll get it right this time."

"Okay, one thing at a time. Let's start with talking to Darryl King, like you said."

"All right, fair enough. We'll do that."

"I'll see you in the morning, Arnie. Try to get some sleep."

"Yeah, sure. You, too."

Of course, we both knew that would be impossible. I was ready to hit the road right then, drive all night if I had to. I didn't want to wait for the daylight.

I didn't want to wait to finally hear our answer from Darryl King himself.

CHAPTER SIXTEEN

It was my second trip down to the Lower Peninsula in a week. The first time I'd been on my way down to have a drink with my old sergeant and dinner with Janet. The trip had turned into something else, of course. Now I was heading back down that same road, once again crossing the Mackinac Bridge just as the sun was coming up. Once again it felt like I was leaving a world of stark simplicity and entering another world where I had grown up and become a baseball player and later a cop. Where in one hot summer I had seen the horror of a murdered woman, just days before seeing my own partner die as I lay bleeding on the floor next to him. This world was always there waiting for me, this world of my past on the other side of that bridge. No matter how hard the wind blew off the lake, I would never stop hearing its call.

I made the Houghton Lake exit by eight o'clock in the morning. I drove around the lake to the detective's cabin, down that same driveway. I pulled in behind his Jeep and got out.

I knocked on the door. Nothing. But then I knew he wasn't exactly jumping over the furniture to answer the door. I knocked again.

After a full minute, I took out my cell phone and dialed his number. It rang a few times and went to voice mail. I called the number again, but this time I put my head against his door. I could just barely hear the faintest ringtone from somewhere inside.

I knocked on the door again, really banging on it. Then I tried turning the knob. It was locked.

I went around to the back of the cabin. There was a raised deck where the ground sloped away from the house, and there were sliding glass doors on either side of a central fireplace made of stone. I put my face against the glass. I couldn't see anything inside.

He's in the shower, I thought. He can't hear me knocking. He can't hear his phone. I'll wait two more minutes and knock again.

I sat down on one of the patio chairs and looked out at the lake. I couldn't imagine living here and looking out at that calm, flat water every day. Not after living on a lake that sees twenty-foot waves and higher, every fall.

Of course, it would be suicide to take the detective's pontoon boat out on Lake Superior, so to each his own.

I got up and rapped on the window a few times. I made that glass rattle. No way he couldn't hear that.

Then it occurred to me to actually try sliding open the glass door.

I pushed the door open, hearing it grind on the tracks. It needed some oil. I was reminding myself to suggest that to Detective Bateman.

Then I stopped dead.

In the deepest, reptile part of my brain, I knew something was terribly wrong. It was probably just the smell in the air. That's the thing that plugs right into that part of your brain, after all—but it invades every other sense, and all of a sudden you feel like the air itself *looks* wrong. It *feels* wrong against your skin. And even though the house was silent, the silence itself seemed to be spiked with one single high note of wrongness.

"Detective," I said. "Are you there?"

I walked through the cabin. There were stairs leading up to a loft. There were books piled on the coffee table. I went toward the side door and found the short hallway that led to a bathroom on one side and a half-closed door on the other. Probably the bedroom.

I put my hand on the door and slowly pushed it open.

The detective was lying in his bed. He was tangled in the covers. The fabric was soaked through with blood. His face was destroyed. Utterly destroyed beyond recognition. His head was caved in like a goddamned pumpkin.

I looked away. I made myself breathe.

I looked one more time. At the obscenity of what had happened to this man. There was a pipe on the floor, next to the bed. A heavy steel pipe, maybe two and a half feet long. It was covered with blood, and in the blood there were clumps of hair and other material I didn't want to think about.

I had spoken to this man the night before. Just a matter of hours before this moment. My voice may have been the last he ever heard.

Unless whoever killed him had something to say to him before swinging this pipe.

Unless whoever killed him had a special message for him, something he'd been preparing in his mind for years.

Because you know exactly who did this, I thought. He got out last night. He came here.

You know who did this.

I had to close my eyes again. I had to stand there and command the room to stop spinning. Then, when I could finally open my eyes, I took my phone out of my pocket and dialed 911.

I had been through this routine before. It's a testament to my willingness to go looking for trouble, or to my bad luck, or to *something,* I don't even know what, that I'd had a lot of prior experiences with reporting homicides, even now that I wasn't carrying a badge anymore. I stayed on the line with the 911 operator. While I waited, I told her that they needed to go find Darryl King, very recently released from prison, living with his mother on Ash Street in Detroit. It felt strange to be dropping the dime on him now, after everything that had happened in the past few days to lead me here. But they had to start with him. *They had to.*

There was a Michigan State Police post right in Houghton Lake, just minutes away from where I was standing. I had passed it on the way here. So I figured they'd be responding. I had gone outside to get a better cell signal, and to get away from the air in that cabin. I waited by my truck, leaning against it, knowing that I was already on my way to a very long day.

The cruiser pulled into the driveway. One of the boxy old "Blue Goose" cars with the single red flasher on top. Two troopers hopped out and came right over to me. Both of them had freshly buzzed heads under their trooper hats. I hung up the phone and told them where they could find the dead detective. One of the troopers went inside while the other kept an eye on me. He went back to his car and talked to someone on his radio. I knew there'd be more troopers coming down the driveway soon. Eventually there'd be a state homicide detective on the scene. That might take a while, because he might have to come over from one of the other posts. A homicide detective who would investigate the homicide of a retired homicide detective.

The trooper who went inside came out. He wasn't looking so happy with his career choice.

I kept waiting, just standing there by my truck, feeling the morning sun on my face. When the detective finally got there, he came up to me first. As he shook my hand, he introduced himself as Detective Gruley. Then he asked me politely to stay put while he went inside. When he came back out, he started asking me the basic questions. Name, address, phone number. He looked me in the eye as I answered, like listening to every word was the most important thing in the world to him.

"So tell me what happened," he said. "Start at the beginning."

I gave him the rundown. My background first, then the current timeline from the moment I had heard Darryl King was getting out of prison to my discovery of Detective Bateman's body.

He listened intently, writing down only the occasional word in his notepad. When I was done, he stood there nodding to himself. Then he took a step closer to me.

"Let me get this straight," he said in a low voice. "The two of you were going down to Detroit this morning to confront the man you put away for murder, back when you were both on active duty?"

"We weren't going to *confront* him," I said. "We were going to ask him if he really did it. Seeing as how we've both developed some doubts about his confession."

Gruley kept nodding. "Did he know you were coming down to ask him this?"

"No, he didn't."

"Are you sure?"

"I'm positive. I mean, I know I didn't say anything to him. I've had no communication with him at all."

"Since back in the day, you mean. When you arrested him."

"The detective made the actual arrest. But yes. No contact since then."

"So it would seem," Gruley said, "that Mr. King had already made plans for his first day out of prison, independent of this little mission of yours."

"I guess it looks that way," I said. "May I ask if you've located him yet? I gave his name and address to the 911 operator."

"No, I don't think he's been located yet. Detroit PD is helping us out on that one."

I might have caught just a hint of the patented Michigan State Police superiority complex as he said that. Like this part of the operation is out of our hands, so God only knows if it'll get done correctly.

"This is a former Detroit cop we're talking about," I said. "I'm sure they'll be all over it."

"I'm sure they will be, yes."

"Look, Detective, I know this whole thing sounds crazy. For it to turn out this way . . . I still can't believe this happened."

"You see the irony," he said. "You thought maybe this man was innocent of murder, yet he ends up killing someone within hours of getting out."

"If it was him."

"If it was him, yes. By the way, you see where he might logically take this next, right?"

I looked at the detective. My stomach hurt and I was starting to feel a little light-headed.

"You were also closely involved with his conviction," the detective said. "Surely you must understand the stakes here."

I put my hand out to the hood of my truck.

"Mr. McKnight, are you okay?"

"Yes," I said. "It's been a rough morning."

"No doubt. But I hope you understand what I'm trying to tell you. If this man made a list of people to get back at, the minute he got out of prison . . . Well, yours may be the second name on his list."

Yeah, no kidding, I thought. I never would have made that connection on my own.

"You don't look so good," he said. "I think we should get you out of the sun. Get you some water."

He took me over to his car and opened up the passenger's-side door. He started the car and turned the air on. Then he pulled out a bottle of water from a cooler in the backseat. I took a long drink and started to feel better.

"You never get used to seeing something like that," he said. "I don't know how the crime scene guys do it."

"I never did get those guys. They were a breed apart."

"When you're up to it, I'd like to take you back to the post and get an official statement."

I took one more drink and felt the cold air from the dashboard vent on my face.

"Ready when you are," I said, "but I'm not sure this story is going to look any more sane on paper."

I spent a good part of the day there. I knew I would. You get into a police station, or a state police post, or any law enforcement building in the world probably, and time stands still. Sometimes they make you wait for a reason. To soften you up, to let you stew in your own guilt, whatever mind games they feel will help their cause. Other times it's just a matter of them doing things their own way, one slow step at a time. They'll apologize at every turn, tell you you'll be on your way in just a few more minutes. But then the wheels keep grinding away, as slow as the hour hand on the clock.

I sat in their interview room. I answered some more questions. I wrote out my statement. I sat some more. I had some coffee. I declined the offer of lunch, because I couldn't stand even the thought of eating. I had some more coffee. It was late afternoon by the time Detective Gruley finally drove me back to my truck. By that time, the crime scene unit had descended upon Detective Bateman's property. I took one more look around the place, including the pontoon boat docked on the lake. Then I left.

I had Detective Gruley's card in my pocket, with his cell phone number and a polite request to let him know if I was going to leave the state. To be available for more questions, and yes, I knew the drill.

When I was almost back to the freeway, I pulled the truck over in a gas station and just sat there for a while with my eyes closed. Then I picked up my cell phone and called Leon. As soon as he answered, I let him have it.

"He's dead," I said. "Detective Bateman was murdered."

"Alex, slow down and tell me what happened."

I took a breath and gave him the whole story. When I was done, there was a long silence on the line. I thought the call might have dropped.

"Leon, are you there?"

"I want you to listen to me very carefully," he said. "You really need to hear this."

"What is it?"

"Are you listening?"

"I'm listening. What is it?"

"This was not your fault."

"I know that."

"Like hell you do. I know exactly what you're thinking right now, and you need to stop. Because it's going to drive you insane. If this was Darryl King getting revenge, then he was plotting this for years. *For years,* Alex. It was set in motion long before you even started thinking about this case again. No matter what you did or didn't do or were planning on doing today, it wouldn't have mattered. This thing happened, and it had nothing to do with you."

"Okay," I said. "I hear what you're saying."

"I take that back. It *does* have something to do with you. Because you might be next. In fact, King could be on his way up to Paradise right now."

"Or in Paradise," I said, looking at my watch. "He'd have had plenty of time to get up there. Hell, if I hadn't left this morning, I could already be dead by now."

"I'm about to get off work. Let me go over and just check out your place. I'll give Jackie and Vinnie a heads-up, too."

"Okay, but be careful."

"I will, don't worry. I might take my Ruger, though. Just don't tell my wife."

"I promise," I said. "And thank you."

"What are you going to do now?"

I looked out at the road. The entrance to the freeway had two arrows. One for I-75 North, and the bridge to the Upper Peninsula. Another for I-75 South, and Detroit.

"I have absolutely no idea what to do next," I said. Then my phone made a beeping noise I'd hardly ever heard it make before. I looked at the little screen. There was another call coming in.

"Somebody's calling me," I said, reading the caller ID. A 313 area code. "I should take this."

I ended the call with Leon and answered a call from the last person in the world I would have expected.

Darryl King's mother.

CHAPTER SEVENTEEN

It took me a moment to remember. I had given Mrs. King my card, on that surreal afternoon I'd sat with her in her living room, eating her chocolate cake. Now, as I answered her call, I could barely make sense of what she was saying. All I could make out was that Darryl was gone, after just one night in the house, and the police had been tearing the place apart and asking ridiculous questions. I told her to sit tight, that I'd be there in less than three hours. A crazy thing to do on a day that had already gotten turned upside down. But what else was I going to say to her?

While I was driving down I-75, I gave Sergeant Grimaldi a call, just to let him know what had happened. Then I called Janet to do the same. They were both shocked. They were both worried about me. They both wanted to know what I was going to do next. I didn't tell either one of them the truth.

I stopped for some gas. I hit a drive-through just so I'd have something in my stomach. I kept driving. Two and a half hours later, I crossed under Eight Mile Road. I was back in Detroit.

I cut over to the west side of town. I went to Ash Street. I parked the truck in front of that house. I sat there for a moment to get my bearings and to shake out the sound of the road from my ears. Then I got out and looked at the house. I could see where the weeds had all been trampled down by the police officers' boots. The trail circled the house, and there were dirty footprints on the sidewalk.

Okay, I thought, so they were here looking for him. They probably turned this place upside down. But why aren't they still here now? If they don't have him in custody yet, surely somebody's keeping an eye on the place.

That made me remember, of course. My own time watching this very house, all those years ago. Even with some of the houses gone, and the weeds grown up, there was still probably one prime spot for surreptitious surveillance, as they call it. I stepped back from the far side of my truck and looked down the street. Sure enough, there was the vehicle, right in that same spot on the other side of the fence, in the parking lot behind that apartment complex. It was a green minivan, not the panel truck we had used back in the day. I thought I spotted a little lens flash, probably from binoculars. I almost waved to him, whoever the lucky sap was who had drawn this duty, but I thought better of it.

I went up on the leaning front porch and was about to knock on the screen door. Then I looked inside and saw Mrs. King kneeling on the floor, her head on the seat of her chair.

I opened the door and went to her. "Mrs. King," I said. "Are you all right?"

She looked up at me. Her face was wet.

"Oh, thank God, you came, Mr. McKnight. Thank you so much."

"Do you need help? Here, let me help you to your feet."

"It's okay, I was just praying."

She let me help her to a sitting position on her chair. I took the other chair.

"It was so good to have him home," she said, wringing a handkerchief in her hands. "But it all went wrong so quickly. He didn't even have one piece of his cake yet."

"Tell me what happened. Tell me everything."

She wiped her face, then took a moment to compose her gray hair.

"I waited all day for him," she said. "I thought he'd be out in the morning, but by the time he did all his processing and such, it was nearly dinnertime when I finally got to see him. He looked so . . ."

She stopped and worked at her handkerchief again.

"He looked so tired, I guess. So used up by all those years in prison. He was so happy to be out, but I could tell he was feeling a little lost, too. Which I guess is understandable. All these years and suddenly you're standing outside that prison, with no idea what you're going to do with the rest of your life. Anyway, I had my sister's car. I don't drive that much anymore, but I still have a license. So I went to get him, and after all that waiting, I finally got to bring him home."

"Did he say anything? About what he was going to do?"

"No, he didn't. Not at all. He didn't say much of anything. He apologized, said he was still just taking it all in, trying to get his feet under him. He wasn't very hungry. He had a little dinner, but like I said, he didn't even have any cake. He said he'd have some today."

"Okay . . ."

"He sat with me for a while, then when it got dark, I asked him if he was going to go to bed. Up in his old room, just like old times. I thought he must have been pretty tired after the big day, but he said he wanted to go out for a little bit. I got kinda upset about that, because I know he's on parole, for one thing, and they have all sorts of rules about where you can go and how late you can stay out at night. Then he asked me if he could borrow my sister's car for a little bit, and I got *really* upset. Because I knew he still has to go down and get his license. But he insisted on going out. He just said, 'I gotta do it, Mama. I've been cooped up all these years. I just gotta get some air in my lungs and move around a little bit.' So eventually I just let him take the car for a while, as long as he promised to come right back."

She stopped again. She smoothed the fabric of her dress over her knees.

"He never came back?"

She shook her head. A fresh tear ran down her cheek.

"So what happened today? The police came?"

"They rushed right in and started looking for him. Going up the stairs. I told them they had no right to do that, but they said on account of Darryl being on parole, they can do whatever they want. Go in anywhere and just drag him out."

"I'm afraid that's true," I said. "You give up certain rights if you're on parole."

"Yeah, well, I never gave up my rights. They had no cause to do that."

I looked around the room. "It doesn't look bad right now. Did you have to clean things up?"

She dismissed that with one wave of her hand. "I don't care about mud in the house. Not with Darryl in trouble again. If I cleaned today, it was just to keep my mind busy. I didn't know what to do, Mr. McKnight. If I didn't have your number to call, I don't know who I would have turned to."

"Mrs. King . . ."

"Thank you, by the way. Did I say thank you yet?"

"Yes, you did. It's okay. But tell me exactly what the police said to you."

She shook her head, like she didn't even want to think about it. "Just nonsense, they were saying. They wanted to know where he was. They kept telling me I must know and that I'd better tell them or I'd get in trouble."

"But you didn't know? You had no idea?"

"Of course not," she said, giving me a sharp look. "Do you think I'd be sitting here if I had any idea where he's at right now?"

"Mrs. King," I said, knowing this next part would be tough. "Did they say anything to you about what they thought Darryl had done?"

"Yes." Her voice was dead calm. "They said some foolishness about an old retired detective being killed. Way up north. Like a three-hour drive. I told them Darryl couldn't have had anything to do with that."

"Did they mention that that old retired detective was the man who arrested your son?"

She looked away from me, shaking her head. She can't handle this, I thought. She can't let herself even think about what this might mean.

"He didn't do it," she said, looking back at me. "Whoever got killed, wherever it was, up north or just down the street, I don't care. Darryl's spent half his life in prison and he's not about to throw away whatever time he has left. It's that simple."

"Okay, I understand." What could I even say?

"You have to help me, Mr. McKnight. I know I have no right to ask, but I don't know who else to turn to. Will you please go find my son and bring him back to me so we can get this whole mess straightened out?"

"Mrs. King . . ."

I may not have to look for him, I thought. He might end up finding me first.

"Please, Mr. McKnight. Alex. I'm begging you."

On the other hand . . . Given the choice between waiting for him to show up on my doorstep and actually doing something . . .

I didn't get the chance to say anything else, because at that moment I glanced out the front window and saw the Detroit police car pulling up behind my truck. There were two officers in the car. One was looking at my license plate and talking on the radio. The other was opening his door to get out. He looked both confused and unhappy, never a good combination in a cop.

"This is going to sound a little strange," I said to Mrs. King, "but do you have a dollar?"

"I do, yes . . ."

"Can you give it to me?"

"Right now?"

"Yes, please."

She reached into the waist pocket of her dress and pulled out a dollar bill. She gave it to me.

"You just hired me as a private investigator," I said. "I now have the right to be here, no matter what the police say. And anything we say to each other is protected by client privilege. Do you understand?"

"I think so."

"Good, it's nice to be working for you. Stay right here a minute, okay?"

I left her there in the house and walked out the front door to meet the officer.

"Stop right there," he said. "I'm going to need some ID."

"You just ran my plate," I said. "You already know who I am."

"Some ID, please. Right now."

I took out my driver's license and handed it to him.

"What precinct are you guys from?" I said. "Oh no, wait, you don't even have precincts anymore, right? It's all districts now?"

"Can I ask what you're doing here?"

"Look, I'm a former Detroit cop myself. So can we start over?"

He gave me back my license. "I just need to know why you're here. I also need to know if you have any connection to Darryl King."

"No, I don't. I'll be honest and tell you that I'm looking for him, too."

"Mr. King is the subject of a murder investigation, Mr. McKnight. Not to mention the fact that he's already violated his parole. We're going to need to know any information you might have in regards to his current whereabouts."

I dug around in my wallet, thankful that I hadn't cleaned it out in a while, and found another of my old PI cards. "I'm currently a licensed private investigator. I've been hired by Mrs. King."

"You're supposed to let the police know if you're working in our jurisdiction," he said, looking at the card with a frown. "You know that."

"I do know that. I was just hired thirty seconds ago. So consider this your heads-up."

The other officer, done with whatever he was doing on the radio, got out of his car and joined us.

"Mr. McKnight," he said, "I just talked to a Detective Gruley from the Michigan State Police. Is it true you're the one who found Detective Bateman's body this morning?"

"Yes," I said, looking back at the house. "It's been a hell of a day."

"The detective has a message for you," the cop said. "He wants to know, with all due respect, if you've lost your mind."

"I wouldn't bet against it," I said. "But let me ask you guys something."

"What's that?"

"Don't take this the wrong way, but who's coordinating your surveillance these days?"

The two officers looked at each other. They clearly had no idea what I was talking about.

"You can't pull up in a squad car," I said, "and announce to the world that you're here, while at the same time you've got your other man down the street . . ."

"What man is that, Mr. McKnight?"

I pushed past them and went to the sidewalk. I looked down to the parking lot, to where I had seen the man with the binoculars, in the green minivan.

He was gone.

CHAPTER EIGHTEEN

When the two police officers drove off, I walked down to the end of the block. The street had fed into the parking lot behind the apartment complex, once upon a time, but someone had decided there needed to be a gate here to secure the lot. It had obviously been decided long ago, because I remembered this gate being here back in the day, when I was sitting in that panel truck watching the house. The weeds had grown up on both sides of the gate now. I would have bet anything it hadn't been touched since the last time I was this close to it.

I looked over the gate, into the parking lot. I didn't see the green minivan.

"If you're not the police," I said to the spot where the minivan had been parked, "then who the hell are you?"

When I went back to the house, once again I saw something inside that made me go right in. This time it was Mrs. King standing in the middle of her living room, holding her cell phone to her ear, her free hand against her chest. A fresh batch of tears was running down her face.

"Darryl, honey, please!" she said into the phone. "You have to come home! We'll get this all straightened out, I promise you!"

I gestured for her to give me the phone. Not a polite move on my part—in fact, it was downright rude—but I wanted to talk to him.

She started to hand me the phone, then hesitated. I took it from her and put it to my ear, just in time to hear the faraway voice of Darryl King.

"It's no good, Mama. It's no good. Whatever they think I did this time . . ."

"Darryl," I said. "Is that you?"

"Who is this?"

"My name's Alex. I need to talk to you."

"Where's my mother? Put her back on the phone right now."

"She's okay, Darryl. She wants me to talk to you."

I stepped closer to her, wrapped my arm around her, and held the phone between us so we could both talk into it.

"Tell him it's okay to talk to me," I said to her. "Please. Tell him it's okay."

"It's okay, Darryl!" she said. "He's a good man. You can talk to him."

"See, it's all good," I said. "So tell me where you are."

"I'm not telling you nothing. Who are you, really?"

"I told you. My name is Alex. You probably even remember me."

"From where?"

"I was once a police officer," I said, looking at Mrs. King. This was officially the strangest phone conversation I'd ever been part of. "I was one of the officers who was here the day you were arrested."

He didn't say anything.

"I was the one who chased you at the train station. You remember me now?"

"What's your name again?"

"Alex. Alex McKnight."

"I don't remember you."

I stood there in Mrs. King's living room, looking down at her wet face. I was talking to her son, the convicted murderer, and now I was trying to decide just how good a liar he could be.

"Are you seriously trying to tell me that you don't remember me at all?"

"You're white, right?"

"Yes."

"That's all I remember. A white cop chased me. Another white cop arrested me."

"That was Detective Arnie Bateman."

"Yeah, that name sounds right. I remember him. What's the point, man?"

"He was killed sometime last night."

He took a moment before responding. That said something important, if you believe the guy who wrote the book on interrogating suspects. If he denies it right away, that means he already knows it, and he's got his story ready. If he takes a while to think about it, then it might be news to him, and he won't respond until he's had some time to think it over.

Of course, a really good liar has probably read the same book, and he knows how to beat that game.

"Are you telling me," Darryl finally said, "that all of those cop cars were on my street because . . ." He trailed off into a mumbled string of every obscenity ever invented.

"Darryl, where did you go last night?"

"I went out."

"Where did you go?"

"Where do you think I went, man? I was in prison for a *long time*."

"Okay, so you were with somebody?"

He hesitated. "No, I wasn't. I drove around looking to pick up someone. But I just couldn't go that way. I guess I really am getting old or something."

"So you didn't go to Houghton Lake?"

"What lake? What the hell are you talking about?"

"That's where the detective lives."

"Well, I sure as hell didn't go there. And I sure as hell didn't kill nobody. That's the craziest thing I ever heard."

"It's not so crazy if you were looking for revenge."

I heard him let out a long breath. "Look, man. I just got out of the joint, okay? You really think I want to go right back in? So I what, went and killed some old detective who was doing his job? Do you really think I'm that kind of man, Mr. McWho, whatever your name was?"

"If you didn't do it," I said, "and I guess I'm at least prepared to believe that you didn't, then you need to turn yourself in. Your mother and I will both go with you."

"Okay, first of all, my mother and you are not going to do anything, because you're going to leave that house right now, do you hear me? And second of all, I'm not turning my black ass in to nobody, because I know how that will go. I've been down that road before, believe me."

"The last time, you confessed," I said, looking at his mother again, wishing that I could just talk to this man for one minute without her watching. "Which is the reason I came down here in the first place. I was hoping you could tell me why."

"I was convicted of that crime and I served my sentence. That's all I have to say. You got no business asking me anything else."

"You didn't do it," I said. "You confessed to a crime you didn't commit."

"I was convicted of that crime," he said, slowly this time, "and I served my sentence. Now give my mother back her phone."

"Not until you tell me, Darryl. I want to know why you confessed."

"Give her a message," he said. "Tell her I've gotta go try to make things right first, while I still have a chance. Then I'll come home."

"Darryl—"

"And tell her she shouldn't be inviting white cops into the house."

He ended the call before I could say another word.

Mrs. King looked up at me, like she expected me to tell her everything was all right. Darryl was on his way home, and everything would be good again.

"He said he was calling on a pay phone," she said. "He wanted to know why all the cops were here. When he saw them, he just panicked and drove off."

"He said to give you a message. He has to make things right while he still can. Then he'll come home."

"He's going to go back to prison," she said, looking away from me. "I only had him home for a couple of hours."

I wasn't sure what to say to her. I certainly had nothing that would contradict her prediction. So when all else fails . . . you go do something. Even if it's stupid.

"Mrs. King," I said, "do you know where he might have been calling from? I'd like to go look for him."

She looked back up at me. A small glimpse of hope there, in the face of this woman who should have given up hope long ago.

"He said he was calling from a pay phone. I didn't think they even had those anymore."

"You make a good point," I said. "That might make it easier to find him. Just find the one working pay phone left in the entire city."

I knew it wouldn't be that easy, but I figured it was worth a shot. I had no idea whether Darryl King was telling me the truth or not, but either way I wanted to find him.

Mrs. King gave me a photograph of a grown-up Darryl. It was a few years old, she told me, and it wasn't a great photograph at all, but it gave me a fair idea of what he would look like if I were to run into him. The high cheekbones were still there, but his face was much fuller now. He was probably seventy pounds heavier, and it didn't look like prison muscle. He had a little gut on him now, and his hairline was receding. He was photographed sitting in the visiting room at either Jackson or Harrison, and he was wearing a thin smile that he probably didn't get to use much in prison.

I put that photograph in my back pocket, along with the description of Mrs. King's sister's car, and I went out into the fading light. Another strange twist on an already strange journey, that now I was driving down these same streets, looking for the same person. Only now I knew his name, and I had a photograph to show people.

But I wasn't wearing a badge.

I tried to think where I would go if I were in Darryl King's shoes and I'd just seen a swarm of police cars around my house. He was driving his aunt's car, and if he had a brain in his head he'd have to assume they'd found out and broadcast the description and plate number. So every minute on the road would be dangerous. He'd want to get away from the house, but off the road as soon as possible.

This was all assuming, of course, that I believed him and that he didn't drive up to Houghton Lake. Which would mean he was set up, and that raised a whole new set of questions.

But one thing at a time.

I started out at the end of the street. It was long and straight, so you'd be able to see the police cars from a few blocks away. Arguably a misplay by my alma mater officers, but I wasn't about to fault them for it. He was right here at this corner, I thought, starting down on Wabash. He's about to turn, he sees the cops, he panics, he keeps driving.

Why did he panic, by the way? If he's just coming back from a night driving around looking for company, why not just come home and face the music?

Because he's been out of the joint for less than twenty-four hours. He knows he's not supposed to be out unaccounted for, well after dark, and on top of that driving without a license. He sees himself sitting in front of the parole officer's desk, sees himself getting taken right back to prison. True or not, it's an understandable reaction on the spur of the moment.

Okay, so assume he's coming north, coming from downtown and everything that downtown has to offer. He bails out, he keeps going north to MLK. Does he turn? No, not if he has any sense. He stays off the main road, works over to where, Rosa Parks? Grand River?

This is hopeless, I thought. If you gave me one city in the country to hide out in, this would be the one. Too much area, not enough cops. A thousand streets. So many abandoned buildings.

"The pay phone," I said out loud to myself. "Look for the pay phone, then go from there."

I thought back to the conversation with Darryl King, tried to remember if I had heard any kind of specific noise in the background. It would have been much more considerate of the man to call from a bowling alley, say, because then I would have heard the rattling of the pins and I'd be heading over to the old Garden Bowl on Woodward. But no, I couldn't remember anything that distinctive, so every bar, restaurant, liquor store, or anywhere that might still have an old pay phone hanging on the wall was fair game.

I started with the first bar I could find, up by Adams Field, where all of the sports teams from Wayne State came up to play. There was a pay phone by the front door, so I went to the bartender and pulled out the photograph. Here's where that old badge of mine would have come in real handy, because a random white guy off the street is not automatically going to get every ounce of cooperation. I'd find that out as I left the bar empty-handed, then went down Warren Avenue and hit the pizza place and the next bar and then the next restaurant, and so on. If I found a pay phone, I asked whoever was working there if they had seen a man looking like the man in the photograph. I'd get a little resistance, or a lot of resistance. Or occasionally I'd be stonewalled completely. "If you're not a cop, then why do I have to say anything to you?" I was asked some variation of that question a few times, and I never had a good answer. Because I'm looking for him. Because I'm a human being and you're a human being and we don't have to play this game.

In the end, it didn't matter. With or without cooperation, I didn't find anyone who had seen Darryl King that night.

After a few hours of this, I called Mrs. King to let her know I had come up empty. I promised her I'd try again the next day.

"You must have been thinking about this," I said. "Is there anywhere in this city where you think he might have gone? Somewhere he'd know he was safe?"

"He hasn't lived in this city for a long time," she said. "Everything he once knew is gone now."

"Oh, one more thing," I said. "I almost forgot. There was a green minivan parked at the end of the street today. Do you know who that might have been?"

"No, I don't know nobody with a green minivan."

"Just keep an eye out. Let me know if you see it around."

"Okay, if you say so . . ."

One more thing for her to worry about. I was sorry I brought it up.

"Good night," I said. "Try to get some sleep."

Then I drove over to my favorite little cheap motel on Michigan Avenue.

"Hold on to something, Leon, because this is going to be the craziest thing you've ever heard."

That was my first line when Leon picked up the phone. I was sitting in that same motel room, not just the same motel across from the Tiger Stadium site, but the very same room I had stayed in the last time I spent the night in Detroit. The night air was cooler now, but it didn't feel like fall yet. Not like back home in Paradise.

When I told him who had hired me that day, and why, he took a moment to process it.

"Okay, so you're following your gut," Leon finally said. "Like you always do. I wish I was down there to help you."

"Yeah, well, consider us both hired. Remind me to give you your half of the retainer."

"She actually hired you to find her son."

"Her son who, on paper, wants to kill me, yes."

"But then you talked to him, you said. Did you believe what he told you?"

"If I'm really following my gut, like you say, then yes. I believed him."

"For what it's worth, I talked to Vinnie and Jackie today. Neither of them have seen a stranger around."

"See, that's the part that never added up," I said. "If he was going to take his revenge on both of us, he should have come right up to my place after he killed the detective. It's only three more hours."

"Maybe you just missed him. Or maybe he was only going after the detective who put him away. It would have been easy to find him, you realize that. With the Internet, you can find anybody. And he had years to do it."

"Maybe," I said. "Or maybe the detective was killed for another reason entirely. Maybe having Darryl King around for a likely scapegoat was just a happy accident."

"If it was someone else, you mean."

"Someone who had reason to believe that Arnie Bateman might be on his trail now."

"You've got to be careful, Alex. Whether it's Darryl or somebody else . . . He's obviously capable of anything at this point."

"I always wondered if following my gut would get me killed one day."

He took a moment to think that one over.

"Tell me again why you're doing this, Alex. Instead of just coming home."

"Because I was there at the beginning," I said. "I helped put all of this in motion. I just want to understand what really happened. Besides, I really, really like Mrs. King."

He gave me a little laugh on that one. I thanked him and ended the call. I knew I should try to sleep a few hours. I'd been running on reserve power for way too long.

As I lay there, listening to the traffic rumbling by on Michigan Avenue, I took out the photograph of Darryl King and looked at it one more time.

"I still have no idea what's going on here," I said to that face, "but I do know one thing. Wherever you are, no matter what you really did or didn't do . . . I'm going to find you."

CHAPTER NINETEEN

Detective Gruley called me the next morning. He wanted to follow up with me on just what I might have been doing at the home of Darryl King, a fugitive currently unaccounted for, and also the lead suspect in the murder of Arnie Bateman.

"I'm sorry," I told him. "My services have been retained by Mrs. King, so by law I am not allowed to divulge any information."

He expressed a colorful opinion or two on that subject. I promised him I'd call him back as soon as I was in a position to talk more freely.

After another colorful opinion, I ended the call and drove to my client's house. I didn't think I'd want to do much more driving around the city, looking for her son. In the light of day that seemed like a waste of time. But I was wondering if he'd contacted her again. Getting him back on the phone, trying to break through and get some answers . . . That seemed like my best shot.

I pulled up in front of the house. I sat there in my truck for a moment, looking down Ash Street. There was no green minivan parked on the other side of the gate. In its place was another vehicle altogether, a cream-colored SUV of some sort. I wasn't that interested in the exact make and model. I was more interested in the lens flash I was once again picking up through the windshield. Somebody obviously didn't realize that you can pick up a pair of binoculars from several blocks way, especially in bright sunlight. But now the question was, what was I going to do about it?

I knew that rusted old gate was locked, and that I'd never be able to get through it before he got clean away. I also knew that if I tried to circle around to MLK Boulevard and the entrance to the apartment complex, he'd still have plenty of time to escape.

I could disguise the fact that I was trying to catch him, but I couldn't do that if I pulled away right now. I just got here. Cranking the truck around in a U-turn would spook him, and he'd be taking off himself in two seconds.

If I waited, I'd have a better chance. But then I'd have to wait— and hope that he was still parked there when I came back out.

Which left one option.

I got out of the truck. I didn't look down the street. I went right to the front door of the house and knocked. Mrs. King opened the door, and I went inside.

"Good morning," she said, looking tired and despondent. I was already moving past her.

"Pardon me," I said. "I need to use your back door."

"What's going on, Alex?"

"Just me doing something stupid. As always."

I went through the kitchen and out the back door. There were two steps down to the backyard, which ran through the weeds to the far edge of the property. I looked to my left and didn't see a line of sight to the parked car. So he probably didn't see me coming out the back. So far so good.

Where the yard had once been neatly mowed, now it was just an unbroken expanse of knee-high weeds, going back to the property line and into the empty lots behind it. I made my way through and eventually hooked a left, fighting my way over some fencing that had fallen down and now was almost completely grown over.

There were six or seven more lots to get through. In one I could see the old foundation of a house that had once stood a couple of doors down from Mrs. King. I saw the remains of a pile of charred wood, now almost completely reclaimed by the earth. The weeds grew taller and thicker as I got closer to the fence that marked the end of the street and the beginning of the parking lot. I had already scraped myself against the thorns of a dozen plants, but now I was faced with the final challenge—how to get through the last thick barrier of foliage on this side of the fence, without going down toward the street, where I'd surely be seen.

I walked a few yards deeper into the field, thinking it might be slightly easier to get to the fence if I got closer to the apartment building. There were abandoned tires and cinder blocks that I wouldn't see until I was just about to break my ankles on them, but I kept making my slow progress until finally I could see the fence.

I put my head down and pushed myself through the thicket. I felt a hundred pinpricks from the wild raspberry plants. I tried to keep them off of my face, at the very least, but I knew I was destined to donate a pint of blood or two. I thrashed my way to the fence and grabbed it and finally hauled myself over.

When I got to my feet, I was pulling thorns out of my arms and looking down the fence line to where the SUV was still standing. Thank God, because to go through that and see that it was all for nothing would have been too much to bear.

Of course, now I had an even bigger problem. I was about to go roust someone I knew nothing about. Someone who could be armed. Someone who could quite possibly be the same person who killed Detective Bateman in cold blood. Someone who could quite possibly be the serial killer who killed all of those women. And here I was, unarmed and scratched all to hell. My only defense would be bleeding on him.

Something I could have thought about before that moment, of course, but what else was new? I made my way to the SUV, trying to stay low and out of sight. There were a few other vehicles to hide behind on this far side of the lot, so I made my way from one to the other. I was trying to see through the side windows of the SUV, but from this angle I was getting too much glare off the glass.

There was only one thing left to do at that point. I had to commit.

I stepped out from the last vehicle in the line and walked right to the driver's side door. No hesitation, but no rush either. I went right to the door and grabbed the handle. I pulled. It was unlocked. The door swung open.

I was already reaching inside for the driver's neck. My surprise was that there were actually two men in the front seat of the car. Their surprise was even bigger, as the man in the passenger's seat dropped the binoculars and they both looked up at me with wide eyes.

"Out," I said, pulling the driver from the vehicle. He was a big man, and I was already getting ready for a fight. But when I finally got a good look at his face, I stopped myself.

He looked familiar.

"Who are you?" I said, holding on tight to the front of his shirt. My right hand was ready to hit him if I had to. If they had guns, I was already dead, of course. The second man could have dropped me at any moment.

"Who are *you*?" the man said, trying to get free. "Let go of me."

That's when I finally recognized him. His hair was streaked with gray now. He wore glasses, and he had put on the inevitable few extra pounds. Otherwise he had aged well.

"Mr. Paige? Tanner Paige?"

"How do you know who I am?"

"I'm Alex McKnight," I said, letting go of him. "I was one of the officers who worked on your wife's case."

"I'll be damned," he said. "It *is* you. What are you doing here?"

"I was going to ask you the same thing."

The other man opened his door and got out. When he came around the vehicle, I had to take an extra beat to figure out who he was. He hadn't aged nearly as well. His face had filled in more, and he was sporting the signature red nose of a man who's spent a few too many hours on a bar stool. But then it came to me.

"Mr. Grayson," I said. "Ryan Grayson."

"I remember you," he said, then he looked down at my arms. "You're all scratched to hell."

I tried to wipe away some of the blood but only succeeded in smearing it through the hairs on my forearms.

"Not a bright move on my part," I said. "I just wanted to see who was watching the house."

"Here," Paige said, reaching into the car and bringing out a wad of fast-food napkins. I took them and started dabbing at the worst of my cuts.

"I assume you guys were here yesterday?" I said. "In the green minivan?"

"That was mine," Grayson said. "We figured it would be a good idea to switch vehicles today. Obviously, that didn't work so well."

"It's not exactly something we're in the habit of doing," Paige said. "Either of us."

"Are you guys going to tell me why you're here," I said, "watching that house?"

"We know who lives there," Grayson said. "We know it's only a matter of time until he shows up."

"And then what?" I said.

The two men looked at each other.

"Listen," Paige said. "Can we go somewhere and talk about this?"

"Sure," I said, "but I should tell you one thing right now. You remember Detective Bateman?"

"Of course," Grayson said. "We both just talked to him this week."

"He was murdered yesterday morning," I said. "The cops are looking for Darryl King."

I waited for them to absorb that.

"That would explain all the squad cars yesterday," Paige said.

"We figured he did *something*," Grayson said. "But we had no idea . . ."

"I'll tell you something else," I said. Then I stopped myself. "Actually, is there someplace we can go and sit down? This is going to take a little explanation."

They put me in the backseat of the SUV and drove me to a little corner bar on Grand River. There was an abandoned industrial building next door to the bar, and vacant lots on the other three corners. Ryan Grayson's green minivan was parked in the lot. There were only three other cars there. Tanner Paige suggested that we go inside for a drink, and I could see Ryan Grayson looking around at the neighborhood and getting ready to object. In the end we went inside and sat down at a table. There were the usual accoutrements for a bar in Detroit, with the Tigers schedule on the wall and all of the other posters for the Red Wings, Pistons, and Lions. As well as both the Michigan Wolverines and Michigan State Spartans, just to be fair to both sides. I excused myself for a minute and went into the bathroom to wash off my arms. When I came back to the table, I didn't look so much like a human pincushion anymore. Someone had ordered three beers.

"I was sorry to hear about your parents," I said to Ryan Grayson. "The detective told me they both passed on a while back."

"They never really recovered from that day," he said. "Either of them."

"I also have to say I'm a little surprised seeing the two of you working together," I said. "I didn't think you guys got along all that well."

"The blame for that is all on me," Grayson said. "I had a lot of anger, and I didn't know where to direct it. I always regret not being a better brother-in-law."

"It's all good now," Paige said, waving it away. "We were all hurting."

"So all these years later," I said, "what in God's name are you two doing watching that house? Surely you weren't thinking of doing something that would get you both thrown in prison yourselves."

They both looked at each other.

"You have to understand something," Grayson said. "It's not like we've both been sitting around every day, thinking about some lowlife who killed my sister. You have to move on. Obviously. Or you'll go insane. But when we got the call . . . When we found out that he would be getting out of prison . . ."

He looked down at his beer.

"It's amazing how it can all come back. All at once. One minute you're not thinking about it, and then bam! Guess what, the man who did this thing will be out walking around by the end of the week."

"So what were you going to do?" I said. "You weren't spending all that time watching for him just so you could see him in your binoculars, a block away."

They looked at each other again.

"Honestly," Paige said, "I don't think we really—"

"We were going to follow him," Grayson said. "At least that was *my* idea. Follow him and wait for him to go into a bar or something. Someplace like this . . ."

He looked over at the empty corner of the bar, like he was imagining Darryl King sitting there at that very moment.

"Then, when he got up to go use the bathroom, I just had this little fantasy, I guess you'd call it. That we'd follow him in there. Lock the door. Wait for him to realize who we were. Then we'd just start beating the hell out of him. Just grab him by the hair and . . ."

He held his hand up to demonstrate, making a claw where he was clutching the hair on the back of the imaginary Darryl King's head.

"And just start beating his face against the edge of the sink. Over and over again. Just . . ."

He stopped abruptly and wiped at his eyes.

"I'm sorry," he said. "I know I sound a little crazy."

"It's okay," Paige said, grabbing his arm. "I get the same thoughts, all the time."

"Mr. McKnight," Grayson said, looking up at me, "I was her brother. Older than me or not, it doesn't matter. She was my sister and I was supposed to protect her. You understand what I'm saying?"

"Yes," I said. "I understand, but there's no way you could have—"

"That was my job. To protect her. If my father were still alive, you could ask him, because he's the one who told me. Until you get married and have a family of your own, being a good brother is the most important job in the world."

"It was my job, too," Paige said. "Being a good husband, I mean."

"I'll be right back," Grayson said, pulling his arm away from Paige. He got up and went into the bathroom. That empty bathroom where there'd be no Darryl King waiting to receive his punishment.

"It should come as no surprise," Paige said to me, as soon as his brother-in-law was out of earshot, "that this whole crazy thing was Ryan's idea. Sitting around and watching for him. I tried to talk him out of it, but I knew he'd do it alone if he had to. So I agreed to come along so I could keep an eye on him."

"Arnie said he's got kids now? Surely he can see that this is a horrible idea."

"See, that's the thing. He was engaged to be married when Elana was killed. I don't know if you knew that. They went ahead with the wedding, even though maybe they should have waited a little bit. Let everybody heal a little more. But that's all hindsight, I guess. Anyway, he went right from being a grieving brother to a husband to a father, and it seemed like he was doing okay for a long time. Taking over the business from his father and everything, but then when his second kid went away to college . . ."

"It's been that long?"

"They had their two kids pretty quickly. Within two or three years of Elana's death. So yes, it was all kind of a blur to him, I think. Until all of a sudden his kids are gone and he breaks up with his wife and he's all alone for the first time. It's like he never really dealt with it until now. Obviously, it hasn't gone well."

"It seems like you've dealt with it a lot better."

"I had a lot more time to myself to deal with it. But that first year or two, God, I was a mess. In fact, now that I think of it, didn't you and the detective come to the house?"

"We did."

"So wait a minute," he said. "I know you already said this, but I still can't believe it. Arnie Bateman is really dead right now?"

Ryan Grayson came back to the table then. He had washed his face and put himself back together. I was glad to see him, because I didn't want to have to explain this part twice.

"He is," I said, "and they're looking for King right now."

"He was out of prison one day," Grayson said. "Not even twenty-four hours and he's killing again. What the hell were they thinking letting him out?"

"You have to hear me out," I said, "but I don't believe that Darryl King killed the detective."

"Are you serious?"

"Furthermore, and here's the part where I know you're really going to need some explanation . . . Because I know this was your sister we're talking about, Mr. Grayson. And Mr. Paige, I know Elana was your wife. I wouldn't say this if I didn't have good reason."

They both sat there listening to me. They didn't move. I don't think they were even breathing at that point.

"But I don't think Darryl King killed her, either."

They both just looked at me.

"What are you talking about?" Grayson said. "Have you seriously lost your mind?"

"That's the second time I've been asked that," I said. "But no."

"He confessed," Paige said. "He confessed to the crime and then he signed it and then he went to prison. Where he should have stayed."

"I know he confessed," I said, "but I think there's something else going on here. I'm still not sure what."

They both leaned back in their chairs. The body language was clear. They wanted nothing to do with this. I spent the next solid hour trying to explain it to them. All of my gut instincts coming together, the questions I had asked, the way the story fit together if you could just believe that Darryl King had confessed to a crime he didn't really commit. How if you were willing to go that far, the next step would be to look at all of the other murders that had been occurring over the years, murders with the exact same characteristics. All of them unsolved.

"What you're really saying," Paige said, when I was finally done, "is that Elana was really murdered by a mass murderer?"

"By definition, he would be a serial killer," I said. "Someone who kills one person at a time. From what I can tell, Elana might have been his first victim."

"How many others?" Paige said.

"Maybe seven, that we know of. Four women in the Midwest, three more down south during the winter months. And now Detective Bateman, which is different from his pattern, of course. Although I think Arnie might have been killed for a whole different reason."

"Is this supposed to make us feel better?" Grayson asked. "This idea that Elana might have been the first of many? Because if it is, I'd really like to know how."

"I don't imagine it will make you feel better, no. All I'm asking at this point is that you keep an open mind. That you not destroy your life going after someone who may ultimately be an innocent man."

"Wow," Grayson said, shaking his head. "That's all I can say. Just, wow."

"I know it's a lot to take in all at once."

"So why are you here?" Paige said. "Are you trying to prove this wild theory of yours?"

I raised both hands in surrender. "Look," I said, "the FBI is already on these other murders. I heard that from an agent myself. If Elana's case can give them a new angle, then maybe they can all—"

"Stop," Paige said. "Just stop. I apologize. This has obviously shaken us both up, but we shouldn't take it out on you. If there's something to this idea, then we should both want to learn the truth just as much as you, right?"

"Yes."

"So okay. Please accept my apology."

"Accepted. No problem."

We all settled back for a few moments and finished our beers.

"So," Grayson finally said, "this is what you do nowadays? Go dig up old cases?"

"I don't make a habit of it," I said. "But I was part of this case, back in the day. And now, especially with Arnie getting killed . . . Well, I guess I'm just trying to help make things right."

Darryl's own words, from our brief conversation on the phone.

It was my own version of making things right, while I had the chance.

"Does that mean you're going to go look for this serial killer?"

"Hell, no," I said. "I'll let the FBI do that, thank you. If I can just help out Mrs. King, I'll be happy."

"But what if that means you run into the killer?"

"Then I'll probably wish I had brought my gun with me."

"I think you're probably crazy," he said. "Where are you staying, anyway? Is it someplace safe, at least?"

"I'm in a motel down on Michigan Avenue. I'm fine."

"I've still got the house in Southfield. You were there, you know how big it is. Now that it's empty . . ."

"I appreciate the offer, but I'm fine, really."

"Well, let me know if you change your mind. You'd have a whole room to yourself. Hell, half the house."

"I'll keep that in mind. Thanks."

I was glad we left that bar on good terms, at least. I promised them both that I would call them immediately if I found out anything concrete. They both promised me that they would stop watching the house. I guess that's all any of us could have hoped for.

Grayson got in his minivan and drove home. Tanner Paige gave me a ride back to Mrs. King's house. He looked tired and more than a little shell-shocked. Not that I could blame him.

When he pulled up in front of the house, he looked out at the sagging porch. "You're seriously telling me that the man who lived here is maybe not the same man who killed my Elana."

"I'm going to try to find that out," I said. "By the way, I never got the chance to tell you this before. Back when I was a cop trying to solve that case. But I was married then, too, and my wife was taking classes at Wayne State."

"Really? Did she know Elana?"

"No, she didn't. I'm just saying, I realized it just as easily could have been my wife and not yours. If it had been, I'm not even sure what I would have done. But I know I can't blame you or your brother-in-law for whatever crazy things you might have come up with over the years, even sitting down there at the end of the street like a couple of undercover cops."

He shook his head.

"If the sun's in front of you," I said, "make sure you don't flash your binoculars. A little tip for next time."

"There won't be a next time," he said. "But hey, thanks for everything you told us today. Even if it didn't seem like we wanted to hear it. Please be careful."

"You, too. Keep an eye on that brother-in-law of yours."

He said he would. I watched him drive away, wondering what other surprises this day would have in store for me. When I went back into the house, Mrs. King took one look at me, sat me down at the kitchen table, then went to get the first aid supplies.

"What in heaven's name did you ever do to your arms?" she said as she pulled her chair up to mine and started dabbing me with disinfectant. This close to her I could see how hard the years had been on her. She wore it on her face, around her eyes that had seen too much. She wore it in her hands, that had worked too hard for her to be sitting every night in an empty house.

"What were you doing running around in that back field, anyway?"

"I thought there might be somebody watching your house," I said. "So I wanted to see who."

"Did you catch them?"

"I did, but they won't be coming around anymore. You've got nothing to worry about."

"They were looking for Darryl," she said. Not a question.

I looked out the back window, toward the back edge of the property, where I had just recently gone stumbling through the weeds. There was something missing.

The big tree.

I could see the stump. I flashed back to that day, when I spotted the gray shirt on the clothesline and came wandering back here to talk to Mrs. King. The tree gave shade to the whole backyard. A makeshift swing hung from the low branch.

There was a girl who came out the back door to stand by her mother.

There was a boy on the swing.

There was a boy on the swing.

My God, I said to myself, if you are not the biggest idiot who ever lived on this earth. It was just like Ryan Grayson said . . .

Being a good brother is the most important job in the world.

CHAPTER TWENTY

"Mrs. King," I said, trying to stay cool and even. "Can I ask you something?"

"Of course," she said. She kept finding new cuts on my arms. She'd shake her head in disapproval as she squeezed out more disinfectant on her cotton ball.

"Tell me about your family."

She looked up at me for a moment, then went back to her work. "What do you want to know about them?"

"I know you had two other children. I saw them that first day I was here, when I was a police officer. They were in the backyard with you."

"I remember, yes."

"When I came back here the other day, the day we had the chocolate cake . . ."

I paused for a moment, like a man taking a deep breath before going underwater.

"You told me a couple of very sad things," I said. "You said that your daughter was gone, first of all . . ."

"The drugs, yes. The drugs took my Naima from me."

"I'm very sorry. But as far as your other son goes, I think you said he was homeless?"

"He's been away for a long time, yes. It wasn't long after Darryl went to prison. With him gone and no other man in the house . . . Tremont didn't have anybody to look up to."

"Tremont," I said. "That's right. That was his name. I think my partner asked him if he liked being on summer vacation. Then he went over and sat on the swing you had hanging from that tree . . ."

"Darryl was always hard on his little brother. But I know he loved him. He looked after him, because all the other kids would tease him. He was a little different."

"How was he different?"

"He was just more sensitive than other children. He didn't talk a whole lot. Whenever he'd get picked on, Darryl would be there to make things right."

To make things right. Those same words yet again.

"How did he make things right?" I said.

"He'd go after any of those kids who picked on Tremont. Didn't matter how big they were. Darryl wasn't that big himself, but he was strong. He worked out all the time."

"Yes," I said, remembering that weight bench in the backyard. "But what else would he do to make things right?"

"Tremont was always running off somewhere. I'd be worried sick because he'd be out at all hours of the night, even though he was only fourteen years old, understand. But Darryl'd always say, 'I got him, Mama. I'll go find him.' He always would. He might whip his ass a little bit on the way home, but he'd always find him."

"Where would Tremont go when he ran away?"

"Oh, just about anywhere. Darryl would have to go all over the place to find him. But he'd always bring him home in the end."

That's when the question came to me. The one question I should have asked a lot sooner.

"Mrs. King, did Darryl ever go looking for Tremont at the train station?"

"No, Tremont knew he wasn't allowed to go there."

"Why is that?"

"It's way down by the river," she said. "That's too far away for a fourteen-year-old boy to be going all by himself. And besides . . ."

I took her hands then. I made her stop her work and I sat there holding her hands and looking into her eyes.

"Besides what?" I said. "Why was he not allowed to go to the train station?"

"Because it was a bad place, Alex. People sold drugs in that park in front of the station, and men would go down there if they were looking for young boys."

"If he *was* there . . ."

"He loved his trains, Tremont did. Ever since he was little. But he knew he wasn't supposed to go to that place."

"I'll ask you again," I said, holding her hands tighter. "The things that went on at that station . . . If Tremont *was* there, is it possible that's why?"

She looked away.

"Mrs. King, please answer me, no matter how painful this might be. It's important."

"If he was," she said, "then I wasn't able to see it. I'm ashamed to say that now, but it's true. I just couldn't imagine my boy doing something like that."

"What about Darryl? Did he know?"

"I don't know. Maybe. Maybe that's why he was so hard on him."

"As far as I know, Darryl never said anything about this to the police. Not when the detective was questioning him."

"I don't suppose that's surprising," she said. "I don't suppose he'd be real proud to tell people why he was down at the station, if he was looking for his brother, and thought that he was . . ."

"Is it possible," I said, thinking here was where I had to choose my words carefully, "that Darryl may have thought he was protecting Tremont when he confessed to that crime?"

"If he really confessed, then yes, I'd say that's the most likely reason he'd do something so foolish. If he came back home and got his hands on Tremont, and asked him if he was down at that station on the same day that woman was murdered, and Tremont said yes, he was . . . Then by the time those police showed up to arrest Darryl, I can see him having it in his head that they were going to send *somebody* away, no matter what, so it should be him instead of his brother. I can see that all day, yes."

No mention of taking the diamond bracelet while he happened to be there, I thought. No mention of the possibility that Tremont may have been involved in the murder of Elana Paige.

But no, I can't even ask her this. I can't say the words out loud, not in this kitchen.

"I'll tell you this," she said. "When Darryl got taken away to prison, sometime I'd think to myself, there's a reason for this, Jamilah. In your darkest hour, this is a small blessing, that it's Darryl in that prison instead of Tremont. Because Darryl's a strong boy. Real strong. While Tremont wouldn't last a day in that place. Not one single day. I know that sounds like a bad way to see it."

"You never said anything about this before," I said. "When you told me that you knew Darryl was innocent . . ."

"I didn't say anything about Darryl saying the wrong thing to the wrong person, no. Or why he might have said it. Because I don't care about that. I only care about the fact that *neither* of my two boys would kill anybody."

"Okay, I understand. But tell me more about what happened to Tremont after Darryl went to prison. You said he ran away for good?"

"Yes, because Darryl wasn't here anymore to go fetch him. Tremont just ran away and he never came back."

"You never heard from him?"

"Oh, he'd call me sometimes. Those first few years, anyway. I'd wire him some money sometimes, but he always said he was fine. He said he was riding the rails, like he always wanted to. He got hooked up with some people who would hitch rides on freight trains, go all over the place, do some work if they could find it, or else just panhandle. Then hitch another freight train and do it all over again. I guess they've got this whole way of life."

"Like hobos, you mean. Like modern-day hobos."

"Doesn't sound like any kind of life to me. But he said he was finally happy, riding the freight trains and never knowing where he'd end up next."

She stopped. She finally took her hands from mine. She smoothed her dress over her knees and raised her head high.

"It was something else I just had to accept, Alex. One boy in prison, the other a homeless wanderer out on a freight train somewhere. My daughter in a grave. None of them going to school. None of them sleeping in their room at night."

"When's the last time you heard from Tremont?"

"It's been a long time. I couldn't even tell you if he's alive or dead right now. I know a mother's supposed to know such things. I'm supposed to *feel* if he's still out there somewhere, but I guess I'm not feeling much of anything anymore."

"But when you did hear from him," I said, already dreading the answer, "you say he'd be in a new place every time?"

"Cincinnati, if I recall once. Somewhere in Pennsylvania. Chicago."

"What about during the winter?"

"That's when he'd head south. Hitch a train to someplace warm. That's what he told me, anyway."

I closed my eyes. It all fit together now. Including why Darryl said he had to try to make things right, while he had the chance.

He was going to go try to find his brother, one last time.

I went outside to make the call, pacing back and forth on the grown-over sidewalk in front of Mrs. King's house. If I felt any sense of betrayal, I got over it in about two seconds, imagining all of the women who'd been killed across the country. Not to mention Detective Bateman.

When Janet Long answered, she didn't waste any time.

"Let me guess," she said. "You're not calling me from Paradise."

"I need to tell you something. It's very important."

"Okay, I'm listening."

"You need to find Darryl King's brother. Tremont."

A long silence.

"Where are you?" she said.

"I'm still in Detroit."

"Where in Detroit?"

"At Mrs. King's house."

"Can you come down to our office?"

"And have your partner get hold of me? I'll be there all day."

"Come and talk to me in person," she said. "I'll meet you downstairs."

"Okay, I'll see you in a few minutes."

I ended the call, took one more look at the house, and got in the truck. I drove down to Michigan Avenue, then headed east, past my luxurious little motel, toward downtown. I pulled into the lot next to the federal building. It hadn't been that long since I was last here. That night when I took Janet to dinner and I actually thought that's why I had come down to Detroit. How different things can look in just one week.

I saw Janet standing outside the main entrance. When I got out of the truck, she came over and gave me a quick hug.

"Let's go take a walk," she said. "Are you hungry?"

"We don't have to do that. I just wanted to tell you what I know."

"I need to get away from this place for a minute. Come on."

She took me by the arm and pointed me down Cass Avenue. With everything else on my mind, it was still good to see her. We walked down past the Free Press Building, toward the river.

"Where are we going?" I said.

"I've got a craving for a Coney, and only Zef's will do."

"Is that place still there? My partner used to drag me there all the time."

"Well, now it's my turn."

We looped around by Hart Plaza, where the great sculpture of Joe Louis's fist hung in its triangle. Then back up Woodward, into the heart of my old precinct. We passed the Municipal Center with the famous *Spirit of Detroit* statue out front. The big green bronze man holding the sun in his left hand and a family in his right. That got me thinking of the building itself, renamed to honor Coleman Young, who was mayor when I was a cop. His hand-picked police chief would be convicted of stealing over two million dollars of undercover funds, a few years after I left the force. That's always a fun conversation, getting ex-cops to talk about our beloved mayor and our beloved police chief.

A conversation I never got to have with Arnie Bateman.

"This is nice," I said. "It's like a little time-out before life gets crazy again. But now you really need to get back and do something about this new information."

"Are you that sure about what you're telling me?"

"I think I am."

"So Darryl King's brother, you say. What was his name? Tremont?"

"Yes. Tremont King."

"Tell me what you know about him."

"Well, he's a couple of years younger. Very different kind of kid. He ran away from home, right after Darryl got put away. He's hasn't been back since. He rides on freight trains."

"Say that again?"

"He rides on freight trains, all over the country. He goes south when it's cold."

I could see her working this over in her head. The list of cities, north at certain times of the year, south at others.

"What about Detective Bateman?" she said. "Do you think he killed him, too?"

"I don't know for sure. Maybe. Tremont's a total mystery to me, but somehow I think he found out that Bateman was looking into the case again. Hell, for all I know, Bateman knew exactly where to find him. Which reminds me . . ."

"What?"

"Bateman said he had a copy of the case files. You should take a look at those. I didn't see the case at the very end, so maybe he turned up something else. I don't know. But you should also find out if he made any phone calls in those couple days before he was murdered. Besides to me, I mean."

"Okay," she said. "I'm on it. Suddenly I'm not so hungry anymore."

We started walking back to the office.

"I'm officially no longer surprised by anything you do," she said. "Although I will remind you, not that it will do any good, that you promised me you were going to let this go."

"I thought I was."

"You promised me you were going home. Do you remember?"

"I didn't go out looking for a serial killer. I just stumbled into this. You should be happy I'm bringing it to you. You've got a solid lead now. You can watch the rails and pick this guy up."

"If this pans out," she said, "then yes. You're right. It'll break this case wide open. After all of those man-hours, we'll finally have this guy."

"He won't kill anyone else. That's all that really matters."

She looked at me and shook her head. "I don't even know what to do with you. I'd tell you to go home now, but clearly you're not going to listen to me."

"This time," I said, "I think I will."

When we got back to her building, she thanked me and gave me another little kiss on the cheek. She told me to drive safely. I told her I'd see her again soon.

I got in my truck and drove back to Mrs. King's house. I debated with myself all the way there. How much was I going to tell her? In the end, I decided to just tell her I didn't think I could find Darryl. It hit her hard, I could see that, but she let me off the hook. She thanked me and gave me a kiss on the cheek. The same cheek that Janet had kissed.

"I'll be in touch," I said to her. "The second you hear from him, give me a call, okay? When he comes back, you let me know and I'll come right back down here. Whoever I need to talk to, I'll do everything I can to make sure he doesn't get in big trouble over his parole violation."

I didn't say anything about Tremont. I didn't say, oh, by the way, your other son might be a psychopathic serial killer, and the FBI is out looking for him right now. I figured she'd find out all about that soon enough. At that point, just having Darryl back home would be all either of us could ever hope for.

I drove away in my truck, knowing that she'd be in tears as soon as I left the street. She'd be back down on her knees praying. I knew I'd feel that in my gut, all the way home.

As I drove back to the motel to check out, I decided to take one last detour. I turned the other way on Michigan Avenue and went west, to the train station. I wanted to see that towering wreck one more time.

I stopped by Roosevelt Park. I got out and walked around the Cyclone fence. Maybe they'll really fix this place someday, I thought. Maybe then I'll be able to come back and marvel at just how beautiful this building is. Maybe I won't think about what happened inside on that abandoned balcony.

Yeah, maybe, but I kinda doubt it.

As I stood there, a freight train came by on the tracks. It was going west, so that meant it had come out of that long tunnel from Canada. From here it would keep going west to Chicago, or else turn south into Ohio. You could get anywhere in the country by hopping aboard, as long as you knew where the train was going. As long as you didn't kill yourself in the attempt.

Fate couldn't be more obvious, I thought. What a heavy-handed touch, to see this freight train going by, just as I'm about to leave the city behind.

He could be on this train right now, I thought. This very train going by.

He's not on this train. There are thousands of freight trains moving all over the country at any moment. He could be on any one of them. That's why you need the FBI to throw a blanket over the whole thing.

You're not looking for a serial killer. You're looking for Darryl.

Who, in turn, might be looking for a serial killer. So no, thanks.

You promised her you'd find him, Alex.

That was before.

Since when do you walk away like this? No matter how futile this may seem, you never, ever walk away.

"Okay, just stop," I said out loud. An actual argument with myself, maybe the product of living alone for too long. "There is nothing else you can do here. So you have to go home now. You have to go back to Paradise."

The train kept rumbling by.

"There's nothing you can do," I said to myself, "that they can't do better."

Car after car after car.

"You've got no angle that they don't."

The last car passed by.

"Except . . ."

The train disappeared down the tracks.

"Maybe one."

I took out my phone and called Leon.

"I've got a question for you," I said as soon as he picked up. "I know it'll take you all of five minutes to look up the answer."

"Yeah? What's that?"

"How many rail yards are there around Metro Detroit?"

CHAPTER TWENTY-ONE

If you look at a map of Michigan, and you look at those railroad lines that people usually ignore, you'll see that they all converge on the southwest corner of Detroit. It took Leon all of twenty seconds to see this, and another twenty seconds to figure out that this was the CSX Livernois Yard, the biggest rail yard in the state of Michigan. It felt like something beyond a shot in the dark, but I figured I had to try it.

I headed down to Livernois Avenue. A few more blocks south and the road dipped below the tracks. As soon as I emerged on the other side I could see the northeast corner of the yard on my right. The tracks split apart like an unraveling rope, going from four tracks to a dozen to a dozen more. There were long lines of freight cars waiting to be pulled somewhere. Just more and more cars, as far as the eye could see.

I saw a line of semis turning into the yard, each one of them carrying one of those containers you see rolling along on the open flatbed cars. As I looked toward the service entrance, I saw a pair of gates, and I knew there'd be a man or two standing in each one. I pictured them holding clipboards. I also pictured them less than amused if a pickup truck driven by a curious ex-cop got in line with the semis, so I kept driving, figuring I'd eventually find the main office.

There was a high fence running all along the edge of the yard, topped with razor wire. On the other side of the fence were the same kind of closed freight boxes I'd see on some of the freighters going through the locks. Or on the long freight trains I'd see coming over the railroad bridge from Canada. Here there were more of them in one place than I'd ever seen before, stacked two and three high for a good half a mile. I made the turn on Vernor and came around the southern edge of the yard. At last, there was a sign there, CSX INTERNATIONAL, with another service road. This one ran into more gates, but there was a building near the gates and maybe a better chance of someone there in a mood to humor me.

I saw an opportunity to pull off the service road even before I got to the gates. I parked in the lot and went in through the front door. There was a woman sitting behind thick glass. She looked up at me and hit a button on her desk. Her voice sounded like something half metal as it came through the speaker mounted in the glass.

"Can I help you, sir?"

"I'm wondering if I can speak to the head of security," I said, figuring that was as good a line as any. "I just have a couple of questions."

"Can I ask what this is in regards to?"

"I'm a private investigator," I said. "I just want a minute of his time to ask about unauthorized people who ride on the freight trains."

I saw her frown at that, and it occurred to me that I probably could have phrased that better. You could hear that and think I was there to accuse someone of letting riders on the trains, like maybe one of them got run over and now here I am representing a lawyer looking to make a big payday, but before I could clarify, she was already on her old-school stand-up microphone.

"Mr. Maglie will be out in a minute," she said. "He'll meet you just outside the door."

I stepped outside to prepare myself for Mr. Maglie. About a minute later, a gleaming white pickup came roaring out of the yard, passing through the gate without slowing down. It came to an abrupt halt a few yards away from me. Naturally it raised a cloud of dust that I had to shield my eyes from.

"I'm Maglie," he said as he got out of the truck. He was wearing a dark blue uniform with short sleeves, the better to show off his forearms. Pushing sixty, once a tough guy, I could tell. Now even tougher with age.

"My name is Alex McKnight." I didn't bother reaching out my right hand to shake his.

"What's your business here, sir?"

I took out one of my cards and handed it to him. He read it with obvious skepticism, then handed it back to me.

"I just wanted to ask you a couple of questions," I said. "Let me just say, I don't represent anyone who's out to make a buck or anything."

"Who *do* you represent?"

"I'm not allowed to disclose that, but it really doesn't matter. I'm just looking for somebody who rides on the freight trains."

"Does this person work for the railroad?"

"No, I'm sure he doesn't."

"Then he doesn't ride these trains. Not in this yard."

"This is the biggest rail yard I've ever seen," I said. "How many hundreds of trains do you have coming through here every day?"

"You want an exact number?"

"No, I'm just saying. I know that people hitch rides on trains. They've been doing it for years."

"Look," he said. "I know you probably have this image in your head. Hobos riding the rails, all over the country, sitting in empty boxcars, playing the guitar, all their belongings tied up in a handkerchief and hanging from a stick . . ."

"I'm sure it's not that way anymore, but—"

"Do you see all those boxes?" he said, gesturing at the stacks behind him. "That's what we pull nowadays. It's all closed up. It comes off the truck, we load it, we move it down the line, unload it at the destination. Do you see a place for some hobo to hitch a ride?"

"No, I honestly don't."

"That's right. If they did try to hitch a ride, you know where they'd have to go? They'd have to break into one of the helping engines and ride in the empty cab. Do you think that would be a good idea?"

"I'm guessing no."

"If we were at a construction site, would you want some vagrant to wander off the street and go climb into the cab of a big crane? Some drug addict sitting behind the controls of a twenty-ton machine?"

"Of course not."

"That's what we're talking about here. A high-risk industrial environment where people can get themselves killed in about two seconds if they don't know what they're doing, and get other people killed, too. So unless you have some specific reason to believe that somebody is breaking into my trains . . ."

My trains. He actually said that.

"No," I said. "I don't. I just know that one person rides them somewhere. Obviously he doesn't ride them here."

"Obviously not. Are we done?"

"I believe we are. Thank you for your time."

"Exit's that away," he said, pointing back toward Vernor. He got back into his white pickup and took off. Probably to go wash the dust off the bumpers.

"Okay," I said. "I'm so glad I decided to stay in Detroit today."

I got back in my own truck and sat there for a moment, trying to figure out where to go next. If there had been any justice in the world, here's where a long line of hobos would have come skulking through the parking lot and then hopped onto the nearest train.

I was about to put the truck in gear when I noticed another man coming out of the front entrance. He held the door open for a moment, long enough to finish some joke to the receptionist. He was still laughing as he walked to his car.

He's about my age, I thought. Better yet, he appears to be a genuine human being. I wonder if . . .

He went right to a perfectly restored mint green midsixties Mustang. This was my chance. I got out of the truck.

"Hey, excuse me!" I said. "Is that a 1965?"

He looked at me and smiled. "Actually, it's 1964."

"I can't believe it," I said, bending down to give it a closer look. "This is maybe the most beautiful car I've ever seen. Did you do the work yourself?"

"My son and I did. You want to see inside?"

"I'd love to."

He opened the passenger's-side door so I could make a big fuss over the interior, right down to the original gearshift knob.

"You're not selling this," I said, "are you?"

"Not unless you've got a million dollars on you."

"If only I did," I said, shaking my head, "but hey, you work here at the yard, right?"

"I do."

"Cars and trains. My two passions. Would you mind if I ask you a couple of questions?"

"Sure, go ahead."

"Is there someplace around here I can buy you a beer?"

I followed him to a place two blocks down the street. It was a workingman's bar, for the rail workers and for the men who worked at the city's truck garage right next door, too. A lot of steel-toed work boots had come through these doors.

"So let me ask you something," I said, when I'd set us both up. "What's with your man, Mr. Maglie?"

"Oh, he's always been like that," the man said. I hadn't gotten his name yet. "You should have seen him before his wife came back."

"Someone came *back* to that?"

"Imagine being that lonely, yeah."

"The people who ride the trains," I said. "I was just wondering how that works, and I guess I must have hit a nerve."

"Yeah, I'd hate to be hitching a ride and run into Maglie, but you're really not gonna see that kind of thing here anyway."

"Why not?"

"It just doesn't make sense. Trying to get through that fence, then pick out the right train . . . There's too much going on here.

Much better to let the train get on its way, so you know which direction it's going in, then hop on later."

"So you're saying you could hop on just about anywhere."

"No, that wouldn't make any sense, either. Depending on what kind of load they're carrying, these trains will get up to seventy miles an hour. You feel like trying to jump onto that?"

"So where do they get on?"

"They call it 'catching out,' by the way, but usually one of the small stations is your best bet. The trains will still come in slow. Sometimes they'll even stop to switch out the crew or take on a new car or two. There's a lot less security, plus you already know pretty much where the train is heading, because there's not that much traffic. Hell, sometimes the crew will even tell you if you catch the right guy on the right day."

"Have you been that guy before?"

"Maybe. Once upon a time. When I was working down the line."

"Maglie said these guys have to break into the helper locomotives now. That that's the only way they can ride."

"He's an idiot. It's true there aren't that many open boxcars anymore, but you've got the rear platforms of grain cars, you've got your empty slots in a car carrier. You can even lie down under a semi if it's getting piggybacked. There's all sorts of places you can ride, believe me. I admit, even though I've worked around trains all my life, I've often thought it might be a blast to just hop on and ride someday. See where I end up."

"Okay," I said, "so here's the big question. If I wanted to find someone who's riding the rails, where would I go?"

He looked at me. "You're not really a train geek at all. This is why you're buying me this beer."

"I think you got me," I said, "but I did love your car."

That made him smile. "You could have asked me that from the beginning," he said. "Because the answer is pretty simple. If someone is riding the rails, the only person in the world who'll be able to find them is another person who's also riding the rails. You'd be surprised at how fast word can get around. Especially if you put a little money behind it."

"So how do I find someone like that?"

"Go to one of the smaller stations, like I said. Probably River Rouge is your best bet. Lots of trains, pretty much anything going south or east has to go through there. You should be able to find a rider if you look hard enough. Or find a worker who looks like he's an easy touch. Like me. He'll know where to send you."

"River Rouge," I said. "I got it. Here's the last question, I promise. This one's the hardest yet."

"Shoot."

"Say I don't want to get the word out. Say I want to find out what the word is that's already gotten out."

"Come again?"

"My guess is that somebody's already done exactly what you've just described to me. He's found out how to get a message down the line to someone on the rails."

"So you want to know what that message is. Even though it's not a message for you."

"That's about the size of it, yes."

"Well, remember how I said a little money would help?"

"Yes."

"Just bring more. That's the one thing these guys will always respond to."

I reached out and shook his hand.

"Can't tell you how much I appreciate it," I said. "My name's Alex, by the way."

"Jerry, and I wish you good luck. It sounds like you could use some."

"You can say that again."

I thanked him one more time. Then I went out, got in my truck, and headed downriver.

It's called downriver, naturally, because the Detroit River flows south between Michigan and Canada, all the way to Lake Erie, and on the Michigan side you'll find a set of suburbs that probably aren't going to rival the French Riviera. The River Rouge cuts inland from the Detroit River, and it was once so polluted it caught on fire. I hear it's a lot cleaner now, but as you cross the River Rouge you'll still pick up the heavy smell of pig iron from the blast furnaces on Zug Island.

I found the rail yard. My new friend was right—it was a lot smaller than Livernois. There were maybe a dozen tracks at its widest point, all running north and south, with plenty of freight cars standing by. Probably just enough to give a rider a little cover, without being an overwhelming jumble. The fence that ran along Haltiner Street had a token string of barbed wire on top, but I'm pretty sure I could have gotten over it myself if I had to.

I knew better than to march through the front entrance and ask to see the head of security. Even if he didn't turn out to be another Maglie, I had already learned my lesson about who to talk to. I found the main parking lot, across the street from the yard. A sign let me know that I'd be towed if I wasn't there on official yard business, but I figured I could take my chances. I parked the truck and waited.

Another human being, I thought. That's all I need here. Funny how that's a real commodity these days, no matter where you go.

It was still the middle of the afternoon. Not exactly prime time for the men who worked in this yard to be coming out to their vehicles. Eventually, I did see two men walking across the street to the parking lot, but I didn't get the right vibe from them. They both looked unhappy, like maybe they'd both just gotten fired. So I let them go without a word. About a half hour later, I saw another man. He looked a little happier, so I figured he was worth a shot.

"Hey, hold up," I said as I got out of the truck. "Can I ask you a quick question?"

"Who are you?" He didn't stop moving.

"I just want to ask you a question. I'm a private investigator."

That usually gets people interested, at least, but this guy put it into a higher gear and practically jumped into his car. He sped off without so much as another glance in my direction.

"Now that," I said to myself, "is a man who's expecting to be served with a summons any day now. Either that, or I'm a lot scarier than I think."

I got back in my truck and sat there for another hour. I had the windows rolled down and there was a nice breeze, but it was still my own version of hell, just sitting there and not accomplishing anything. Finally, I saw a car pull into the lot. A man got out. He didn't look particularly unfriendly. As he was about to walk across the street, I got out to intercept him.

"Hey there," I said. "Sorry to bother you. Can I ask you something?"

"I'm in a hurry here."

"Just one quick question?"

"Sorry, pal."

"I'm a private investigator," I said, deciding it was time to pull out all the stops if I didn't want to spend the rest of the day sitting here. "And I've got fifty bucks right here if you'll answer one question."

That stopped him dead. He turned around.

"What's this about, pal?"

I stepped closer to him. I opened my wallet and took out a fresh fifty-dollar bill.

"One question," I said, "and then I'll let you go."

He looked at the fifty. I could tell he didn't mind the sight of it.

"I'm told that certain people hitch a ride on freight trains here," I said. "I think they call it 'catching out,' right?"

"That's right."

A good sign, that he recognized the term.

"Any chance you know where I could find these people?"

"Anyone in particular?"

"Well, I'm looking for one person, but I'd settle for anybody who could tell me if a message got sent down the line recently."

He nodded his head, then sneaked a look at the front entrance to the yard.

"You know, catching a ride is trespassing," he said, "and helping anyone catch a ride is grounds for getting your ass fired."

"Sounds like that's none of my business," I said. "None of Mr. Grant's business, either."

He looked a little confused about that one, until he looked at the face on the bill.

"Well, I may be able to put you in contact with someone," he said. "If you give me a little while."

"How long's a little while?"

"There's a train going out at nine thirty tonight. I'm guessing you might be able to talk to a couple of guys who just might be hitching a ride."

"That's a long time to wait."

"That's their train," he said. "This isn't Amtrak, in case you didn't notice."

"I appreciate the help," I said, giving him the bill. "Where do I meet these guys?"

"Be back here in the lot at nine. I'll set it up."

"I'll be here."

"Oh," he said, "and you might want to bring some more of those fifties."

I grabbed something to eat. I sat in my truck and read the paper. I found a bar and watched the first two innings of the Tigers game. When I looked at my watch for the five hundredth time, I figured it was finally time to head back to the rail yard.

The sun was down. It was a cool night, almost cold. I knew it was probably below freezing up in Paradise. A good night to be sitting by the fireplace at the Glasgow. So of course here I was, waiting to meet a couple of vagrants in River Rouge.

I pulled into the lot. I sat there and waited for a while. The lights were on in the yard, and I could see a long train coming through. It didn't stop. Not the train these guys were waiting for, I thought. It was only eight thirty.

At eight forty-five, I saw my new friend walking across the street to the lot. He looked both ways on the street and then came over to my truck. I rolled down my window.

"Evening, pal," he said. "You got another fifty for me?"

"I thought I already paid you."

"You paid me for the front end of the deal. I made the contact and arranged the meet. Now I need the back end."

"That doesn't sound like two ends of anything," I said, but I was already pulling out my wallet. I wasn't about to see the whole day go down the drain over another fifty bucks.

"You go down this street," he said as he pocketed the bill. "Toward the southern end of the yard. There's a street there called Emiline. On your right, you'll see a boarded-up house. The guys hang out there until it's time to jump the fence and get on board."

"How do I know you're not just sending me down a dead end and pocketing a hundred dollars?"

"You don't," he said. "Have a good night."

He left me and walked back across the road. I shook my head and started up the truck. When I pulled out and hit my lights, he gave me a little wave over his shoulder.

I drove down the street, parallel to the fence line. I found Emiline Street about a quarter mile down. There was a boarded-up house on the corner, just as advertised. I pulled up in front and turned off the truck. I wasn't sure what I was supposed to do next. Eventually, I got out and wandered around to the backyard of the house. I knew I was just over the Detroit line, but here was yet another house that had once held a family, with kids playing in the yard and a dad going off to work every day. The job disappeared and then so did the family. They couldn't sell this house, because it's one of a million other houses for sale. So now it's just a boarded-up wreck.

I heard a scraping noise. Then I realized one of the boards was moving. Two men emerged from the house and came toward me. As they got closer I could smell cigarettes and cheap liquor, sweat, and maybe a few other things that they probably wouldn't be bottling as perfume anytime soon. They were both wearing dark clothing, the better to blend into the darkness, I'm sure. One had his hair tied in a ponytail. The other's was wrapped up in a bandanna.

"You the guy with the fifties?" one of them said.

"Apparently I am."

"Let's see 'em."

I let out a long breath as I took out my poor wallet again. I didn't even bother asking if they'd be willing to split one bill.

"I've got a hundred right here," I said, "but first tell me what you know."

"Guy said you're looking for a message that got sent down the line. Maybe we heard something."

"When did you hear it?"

"Two nights ago."

I worked that out in my mind. Two nights ago was the night Darryl King took his aunt's car and disappeared. So far, it was checking out.

"What was the message?" I said.

The two of them looked at each other. "It's gonna sound a little fuzzy," the one said. Apparently he'd been elected to do all of the talking.

"I'm all ears," I said.

"The message was 'Meet me in the breadbox. At midnight.'"

"That's it?"

"That's the message."

"Meet me in the breadbox. Whatever that is. At midnight, when? What night?"

"Whatever night," he said. "Guy's probably just going there every midnight until the man he wants to see shows up."

It occurred to me as I gave them their money that they could have just made up this message. They might be hopping on the train and laughing about it for the next few hundred miles, but then the silent partner finally spoke up.

"The message was for TK," he said. "If that's any help."

"Oh yeah," the other one said. "For TK."

TK. Tremont King.

I thanked the two of them and wished them well. I was tempted to ask them a lot more questions about life on the rails, but they had a train to catch, and I had to go figure out just what the hell the breadbox was, so I could be there at midnight.

CHAPTER TWENTY-TWO

It was going on ten o'clock at night when I pulled up at Mrs. King's house. Too late for polite company to knock on her door, but I figured this was important enough to bend the rules.

Then I stopped myself, just as I was about to get out of the truck. I was working with the gut feeling that one of her sons might be a killer, after all. I was still trying to find her other son, but in doing that it felt more and more like I might eventually end up finding them both. Could I really ask her to help me do that?

I thought about it for a few seconds. That's really all it took. Then I got out and went to knock on the door.

"Alex!" she said as she opened it. "I thought you were going back home!"

"Yeah, I thought so, too, but then I thought better of it."

"I don't understand. You said there was nothing left for you to do."

"There really isn't," I said, "but there is something for *you* to do."

"What's that?"

"Tell me where the breadbox is."

She looked at me for a long moment.

"It's in the kitchen," she finally said. "Where else would a bread-box be?"

"I don't think that's the breadbox I'm looking for."

"Come sit down," she said. "I'll make some coffee. You can tell me what in heaven's name you're talking about."

I was about to protest, but a cup of coffee sounded perfect at that point. I sat in the kitchen and watched her make it. I tried not to show my disappointment, because I had just seen my angle disappear. Her intimate knowledge of her two sons, that was my advantage, after all. My *only* advantage. The FBI had a national organization with agents spread out across the country. They had the technology. They had satellites in space, for God's sake. All I had was Mrs. King.

"You're the only one who can figure this out," I said to her. "If Darryl wanted to meet Tremont at the breadbox, where would that be?"

She put the two mugs of coffee on the table and sat down.

"I never heard them use that term before," she said. "Neither one of them."

"Are you sure? Think back."

She sat there and worked it over.

"No, Alex, I'm sorry. I've never heard either one of my boys call anything a breadbox, except the one we've got right here in the kitchen."

"Well, I suppose they could always meet here," I said, looking over at the wooden box on the counter, "but that just doesn't make sense. Why would you say it that way? You might as well say, 'Meet me at the toaster.'"

"Maybe they're going to meet at a bakery," she said. "Somewhere they make bread."

"Do you know of a place like that? Maybe even called the Bread-box?"

"No, I don't, but that bakery where they made the Wonder Bread, that was just a few blocks over."

"Wait a minute," I said. "Was that still open when Darryl was still . . ."

I did the math in my head.

"I think it was," I said. "The big Wagner Bakery, with the WON-DER BREAD sign out front. On Grand River."

"Which isn't there anymore."

"He has to know it's not there anymore, right? It's been closed for years. In fact . . ."

"The casino," she said. "They used that building for the casino."

I tried to imagine Darryl King meeting his brother at the Motor City Casino. Maybe the most camera-dense environment in the entire city. He'd be a fool to show his face there.

Yet what if he sent that message down the line without thinking about what that building had become? He could be sitting outside that casino, watching for his brother to appear, cursing himself for not doing a better job in his planning, but sitting there just the same because the message had been sent and now he had to play out his hand.

"I should go over there and check it out," I said. "Lacking any better idea."

"I'll keep thinking," she said. "If I remember another kind of breadbox, I'll give you a call."

"All right, please do. I'm gonna get going."

I was half out of my chair when she stopped me.

"It was really him? Darryl's really looking for his brother?"

"Somebody's looking for TK," I said. "As of two nights ago."

"That has to be Darryl," she said. "After all this time, he's looking for his brother."

That much was true, I thought. As for what he'd do with him when he found him . . . I wondered if I'd end up being there when it happened.

It was a short drive to the Motor City Casino. Of course, that was the general idea behind the message. Pick a spot they both knew, a spot both could have walked to, back in the day. Pick a spot that would mean something to the two of them, but nobody else.

But if you were looking for the old bakery where they made the Wonder Bread, dominating the corner of Grand River and Temple Street, your only clue would be the WAGNER BAKING CO. sign high on the original brick walls. The rest of the corner was taken over by the gleaming metal facade of the casino, with the new hotel looming right behind it.

It lit up the night sky, of course, as all non-Indian casinos do. There was a parking structure next door that took up a good city block. It was already feeling like a lost cause, but I drove up through the structure, all the way to the top level. I parked near the edge overlooking the casino, and I went and stood there and looked down at the people all dressed up for the evening, going into the casino to lose their money.

I looked at my watch. It was pushing eleven o'clock.

"One hour," I said to the night. "What are the odds it'll be anywhere around here?"

I went down to the street and walked around the casino. I tried to look like I was on my way somewhere at all times. I figured the security guys probably wouldn't look kindly on a man just standing outside, scoping out the building for an hour.

Midnight came and I had my answer. If Darryl was going somewhere every night at midnight, hoping to meet his brother, I was pretty sure it wasn't here. My biggest worry was that the meeting had already happened. I just had to hope that a few days would pass before Tremont got the message and made his way up here, assuming he felt like coming at all.

I gave Mrs. King a call, apologizing for the late hour, but of course I knew she'd be up. I told her I had come up empty. That we would regroup tomorrow and try to think up a new plan.

"Put it in your head," I said to her. "Right as you're going to sleep. Ask yourself where the breadbox is. Maybe in the morning it'll come to you."

I wished her a good night. Then I went back to my motel.

When I went back to see her the next morning, she didn't have an answer for me.

"I did like you suggested," she said. "I told myself that I'd remember some reference to the breadbox by the time I woke up, but it didn't happen."

We had coffee in her kitchen. I had brought along my map of Detroit, and I spent a good part of the morning figuring out just how far a young Tremont would venture from his mother's house, and where Darryl would go to find him.

I shook my head and drew a big circle, with Ash Street at the center. It was a good-sized piece of the city, from downtown all the way up to Wayne State. It was basically the western half of my old precinct.

"I know these streets," I said. "I drove on them every day. That same summer he went away. So where the *hell* is the breadbox?"

She got up and grabbed the phone book. Then she sat back down and looked up "Bakery" in the Yellow Pages.

"There's a bakery over on Cass," she said. "Kinda far, but no, this is one of those organic places. I don't think that was around then."

"I imagine not."

"Here's a bagel place by the college. Did they even have bagels back then?"

"In New York, yes. Michigan, I'm pretty sure, no."

She went through the rest of the listings.

"There's just no other bakery in the area anymore," she said. "Of course, I'm not surprised. Most of the businesses are gone now."

I looked at her. "Say that again."

"Most of the business are gone now."

"So we need to go back in time," I said. "Look up bakeries in old phone books."

"Where are we going to find those?"

"Where do you think?" I said, getting up from the table. "You feel like taking a ride with me?"

I held open the passenger door for her. My truck was a little high off the ground, but she hauled herself up with no problem.

"I can't remember the last time I rode in a truck," she said. "Not since my man ran off."

"Sounds like the worst move any man ever made."

She smiled at that. "You got that right, Mister."

She put her seat belt on, then sat with her purse in her lap as I drove us over to the Detroit Library. We parked and went inside, found the reference desk, and asked for the old editions of the Yellow Pages. I remembered being here once before, at this very desk, asking to see the old city directories. I was hoping that once again the trusty reference librarian would come through for me. Ten minutes later, Mrs. King and I were sitting at one of the big tables, looking back in time.

"There was so much more of everything," she said as she took a quick run through the book at random. "Even back then, when it felt like we were already hurting."

There wasn't much to say to that. So I asked her to go to "Bakery" and start reading off the entries. I had a pad of paper to write down any that sounded promising. There was the Wagner Baking Company, of course. We'd already been down that road. We found another old bakery that had been on Michigan Avenue, and another that had been up on Warren Avenue. There was nothing else within reasonable walking distance from Ash Street.

We thanked the reference librarian and got back in my truck. Then we went and searched for the address of the old bakery on Michigan Avenue. It was west of the stadium site, on a block where someone had been taking old abandoned storefronts and painting them bright colors.

"Someone's going to town here," she said. She nodded her head toward the building in the center of the block. "That one's got the windows you'd expect to see for a bakery, huh? Put those nice cakes right out front for people to see?"

"Did you ever come here to buy bread? Or anything else?"

"Not that I can remember."

As we sat there pulled up against the curb, I couldn't help but look out across the opposite side of the street, where the old train station rose a few blocks away from us, high above everything else.

"All right, let's check out the other one," I said, pulling back into traffic. We turned on Rosa Parks and went up to Grand River. It was the one diagonal street in a neighborhood full of east-west and north-south. When we got to the intersection with Warren Avenue, it was yet another illustration of just how badly this city had fallen apart.

"I remember this," she said, pointing to the southwest corner, where there was now nothing but a buckled slab of concrete in the ground. "There was an auction house here, and a place to buy tents and awnings and things."

"I think the bakery was half a block this way." I took the turn around a great brick building that had probably once been a manufacturing site. The sign on the top of the building now advertised ARCHITECTURAL SALVAGE. At ground level someone had spent many hours spray-painting an elaborate set of graffiti and garish cartoons.

I couldn't find the actual address for the bakery. Whatever building it had once lived in was now long gone.

"No breadbox here," Mrs. King said as she looked at the empty lot. "There's nothing here at all."

"We've got a couple of possibilities now," I said. "Although that last one down by the station feels a little more promising. Coming up here, that's the opposite direction entirely."

"What are we going to do next?"

"You're going to go back home. You never know when Darryl might just show up there."

"What are *you* going to do?"

"I'm going to do my favorite thing in the world," I said. "Sit around and wait."

I took her back to her house. Then I went back to the Michigan Avenue site by myself to scout it out. There was a pawnshop on one corner, then the old storefronts, then a bar on the other corner. There were two more bars across the street. It was quiet now in the afternoon, but I had to figure this block would really pick up after dark.

I circled around the block. There was parking behind the buildings. I could keep making a loop around the block, watching for Darryl King, or for the car he was driving, assuming he was still in his aunt's car, a ten-year-old powder blue Pontiac Bonneville with a big dent in the front right quarter panel. Or else I could get out and walk around on foot. Either way, I'd have to keep my eyes open.

If it was later in the day, I would have just stayed there and gotten ready for my midnight watch. But I still had hours to kill, so I ended up going back up to the other location. I still wasn't feeling like this was nearly as promising, but I parked my truck anyway and walked around on the empty streets. There was an auto parts store next to the old empty bakery site. Next to that was one of those "wholesale distributors" where you can buy office furniture, light fixtures, refrigerators, probably even a kidney if you hit them on the right day.

This can't be the place, I thought. I turned to go back, already thinking about when I would grab something to eat. Then I saw the railroad bridge.

It was a block to the north, down a little one-way side street. As I walked closer, I saw that it was actually two separate bridges for two separate, parallel sets of tracks, about thirty feet apart. There was a sidewalk that ran under the bridges, and as I walked along it I found what seemed like a decade's worth of trash and dirt and a few halfhearted attempts at graffiti.

There was a thin trail that sloped up from the sidewalk into the gap between the two bridges, where it disappeared into a thick mass of sumac trees. It was the last thing I wanted to do at that point, but the train tracks were here, *right here* behind the site of an old bakery, and I couldn't make myself ignore that fact. So I bent down to clear the lowest branches and pushed myself through the underbrush, following the trail as it led up a short slope to the higher ground between the tracks. This little sumac forest was protected on either side by the tracks, and it ran from this street all the way to the next street a block away, where the train tracks crossed over another set of bridges. It wasn't a place you'd expect to find any people, not in this forgotten strip of real estate, yet the ground was littered with candy wrappers and condoms and hypodermic needles and God knows what else. I was just about to turn around and get the hell of there. That's when I saw the remains of a little shed at the end of the trail.

"Oh, no way," I said to myself. "This can't be it." Yet as I moved closer I saw that it had been here for a long, long time and, while empty at the moment, had been used by a thousand drug addicts and vagrants and probably a few animals.

A low rumbling had been building all the while I was up there. Now as it broke through to my consciousness, I knew exactly what it was. I stood there next to the shed and watched the freight approaching on the northernmost tracks. It didn't seem to be going that fast, but as it came upon me I felt the push of the air around me and the earthquake under my feet from the ten thousand tons of iron. It was close enough that I could reach out and touch it if I wanted to. I could imagine grabbing a handle as it passed by, letting it lift me off my feet with a great jerk. The moment of sheer terror as I trusted all of my weight to the strength of one hand, with failure meaning that I'd surely fall under the wheels and feel my legs sliced cleanly from my body.

You might come here, I thought, if you were a fourteen-year-old boy with nowhere else to go. No friends to hang out with. If you loved trains and dreamed about hitching a ride on them someday, you might come here to this little shed in the right-of-way between the railroad tracks, behind the bakery.

You might even call it the breadbox.

I wasn't sure how much I wanted to come back here at midnight, but I knew that was exactly what I had to do.

CHAPTER TWENTY-THREE

When the night came, I rolled into the lot by the auto parts store. There was a service center built into the store, with a dozen cars all parked outside waiting for new brakes, a muffler, or whatever else. I lined my truck up between two of those cars and turned off my ignition and lights.

I had gone to a hardware store and bought a strong flashlight, the kind with a long, heavy handle that could double as a club if it had to. That was the only preparation I had done.

Now that I was finally here, sitting in my truck and waiting for midnight to come, I had a couple of hard questions to ask myself. Questions that I had been doing a good job of avoiding. I was there to find Darryl King. That's the only thing I knew for sure, but once I found him, then what?

Try to talk to him. Find out what he knew about his brother. Find out what he planned on doing with his brother, once he found him.

So you're looking for a man, I told myself, who is himself looking for another man. So what happens if you find them both tonight?

Then maybe I find out if my gut feeling about Tremont is right after all, and maybe I finally learn that I should think these things through a little better, before I start wandering down dark streets at midnight all by myself.

There were a few cars going by. I watched them stop at the intersection, waiting for their green light. Midnight was coming fast. I got out of the truck and headed down the street. I had my light jacket on, with the flashlight tucked inside. I couldn't help but wonder if I'd be feeling better with a gun tucked in there as well. Or if I'd be feeling better with Leon there to cover my back.

I took a quick look down the side street. I didn't want to just walk right down to the railroad tracks. Not yet. I turned at the corner, made a loop, and came back onto the main street. Cars kept going by, but I didn't see anybody stopping. Nobody turned down the side street.

Then I saw the car.

A powder blue Pontiac Bonneville with a big dent in the front right quarter panel. This had to be Mrs. King's sister's car. This had to be Darryl King behind the wheel.

I didn't panic. I didn't try to hide. He had no reason to suspect I'd be there, and apparently he wouldn't even recognize me anyway. So I acted like a man who has transacted whatever business has brought him to this lonely corner of the city, and now he's walking back to his truck. The car turned down the side street, toward the tracks. I waited a few beats. Then I made my move.

I walked down the side street to where the railroad bridges would pass over it. I walked quickly, a man with purpose. I had my hand on the flashlight, ready to swing it if I had to, but as I passed by the parking lot behind the wholesale distributor, I saw the car parked there on the far side of a big Dumpster. It was the perfect hiding place. No cop would ever think to come down this dark road to nowhere and look in this one lonely, half-hidden spot.

I kept walking, past the lot, under the first bridge. I went past the trail in the sumac and under the second bridge. Then I took a quick look behind me. There was nobody there. I ducked behind the far side of the bridge's abutment.

I took a few deep breaths. I willed my heart to slow its beating. I listened.

A few minutes passed. Then I heard the sound of a car door closing softly. Footsteps on gravel, then on pavement, then on dirt. I peeked around the embankment and made out a figure disappearing into the brush. I gave him another few beats. Then I was back on the move again.

There was nothing on this earth that would have gotten me to follow him up that trail. He'd hear me coming and then he'd have every advantage. So I went over to his car and found the best spot to surprise him on his way back. The surprise was for one simple reason. If he had a gun, I wanted to take it away from him. Then once I knew I wasn't going to be shot, I would start trying to talk to him.

You've always been good at talking to people, I told myself. Now we're going to find out just how good you are.

I settled down on the other side of the Dumpster. The one streetlight back here was burned out. That worked in my favor. There was a half-moon that kept hiding behind the clouds and re-appearing again. My eyes were fully adjusted to the dark now. I was ready to finally meet Darryl King.

The minutes ticked by. At twelve fifteen, I heard the footsteps again. He had given up for the night. He wasn't going to see his brother. I couldn't help wondering, how long was he going to keep doing this before he gave up hope? A week? A month? That can be one of my first questions, I thought, because it's just about show-time.

I waited for his feet to hit the gravel of the parking lot again.

Step. Step. Crunch.

That's when I came around the Dumpster, turned on my flash-light, and pointed it in his face. He was a bigger man than I had been counting on. In the photo he looked soft, but now that he was here I could see he must have spent the last year or so getting himself into shape.

"Stop right there," I said. "If you have a gun, drop it. Right now."

He stepped back in surprise. Then he held up his hands to shield his eyes from the glare of the flashlight. I knew he wouldn't be able to see me yet. For all he could tell, I had a bazooka slung over my shoulder, pointed right at his head.

"Right now," I said. "You got a gun?"

"No! I don't have no gun."

Some handcuffs, I thought. That would have been a beautiful idea, about two hours ago when I was out shopping for the flashlight. Now I'll just have to rely on my natural charm.

"My name is Alex McKnight," I said. "I talked to you on the phone."

He stood there, still shielding his eyes from the light.

"I'm working for your mother," I said. "All I want to do is talk to you. Are we cool?"

"We're cool. Please get that light out of my face."

I pointed the beam at the ground.

"How did you know I'd be here?" he said.

"Brilliant detective work. Or maybe just a lot of luck and a little help from your mother."

"Where is she?"

"She's at home. Where else would she be?"

"I thought I told you to stay away from her."

"She's worried sick about you. You were only home for like five minutes. Then you disappeared."

"I told you . . ." he said as he came closer to me. He'd figured out that I wasn't armed. Either that or he didn't care.

"Don't do something stupid," I said. "Neither of us needs that right now."

He was already committed. I shined the light back in his face, but he was quicker on his feet than I ever would have thought. He blindly grabbed at me, and as he got a hand on my jacket I brought the flashlight down on his forearm. Not hard enough to break anything, which may have been a mistake because he started swinging with his other hand and caught me on the side of the head. The flashlight went dark as it hit the ground. I ducked under another wild swing, then I tackled him and drove my shoulder into his gut as we both went down.

I rolled off of him, scraping my knees on the gravel as I went for the flashlight. Operating or not, it was still the best weapon I had. He tried to grab me, but I threw an elbow back in his face. I knew I hit something vulnerable, because he let out a cry of pain as I finally found the flashlight and got to my feet.

"You've got two choices right now," I said. "You either talk to me like a man, or so help me God I'll beat you until your ears bleed."

A shaft of moonlight fell over us. I could see that his nose was bleeding. He sat there in the gravel and looked up at me. My right shoulder hurt like hell. When you get shot in the shoulder three times, you're not supposed to be wrestling with ex-cons in parking lots.

"I've got nothing to say to you," he said. "This is none of your goddamned business."

"For your mother's sake," I said, "you're going to talk to me. So tell me what you're planning on doing when you find your brother."

He shook his head. He was still holding his nose.

"Are you going to kill him?"

"Why would I do that?"

"Because you took the fall for him. You spent a lot of years in prison, just so he wouldn't have to."

"Says who?"

"Says the man who helped put you there. I know you didn't kill Elana Paige."

"Now there's a thought that would have come in handy a number of years ago."

"Look," I said, "if you want me to apologize, I'll apologize, but you confessed to the murder. That usually ends the whole conversation right there."

"I was going down for it. No matter what I said."

"No, *somebody* was going down for it. You just made sure it was you."

"So what do you want me to say? Huh? What do you want from me?"

"I want you to come back to your mother's house," I said. "So we can all figure this out. I believed you when you told me you didn't kill Detective Bateman. They have no proof you did, apart from the motive. and I know you've pretty much blown your parole, but if we can get a good lawyer, we'll overturn the original conviction."

"Says the white man from the suburbs. You think that's the way it's gonna work for me?"

"Your mother deserves a few years of her life with a son who isn't in prison."

He let out a bitter laugh at that one.

"Yeah, that was the whole idea," he said. "Tremont was supposed to stick around and take care of her. He wasn't supposed to hop on the next train and disappear."

He had things to do, I thought. More people to kill but this is probably a topic I should approach carefully.

"He wasn't supposed to turn into a serial killer, either."

Or maybe not so carefully. Even in the near-dark, I could tell that one got to him.

"Now you're talking nonsense," he said.

"Am I? Let's start with Elana Paige. Did your brother kill her?"

He looked away.

"I asked you a question," I said. "It shouldn't be that hard to answer. Did your brother stab Elana Paige to death in the train station?"

"I didn't think so. Not at the time."

"What about now?" I said, a little surprised by that answer.

"Tremont was always a stranger to me, okay? Even when we were sleeping in the same room. One thing prison teaches you is that people will do things you never thought they'd be capable of doing. Not in a million years."

"So what are you saying? Is it really possible that you went down for your little brother? That instead of thanking you, he abandoned your mother and went off and kept killing people?"

"What?"

"If that's true," I said, "then not only did you spend all that time in prison for something you didn't do . . . you also helped your brother do a lot more of it."

"What are you talking about?"

"There were more murders," I said. "Just like Elana Paige. All over the country."

"No. That wasn't Tremont. I don't believe it."

"You're willing to believe he might have killed one woman, but not more? Is that what you're trying to tell me?"

He was staring at me now. Burning a hole right through me, but he didn't answer.

"So I'll ask you my first question again," I said. "What are you going to do when you find him?"

"I'm going to ask him if it's true. Any of this. All of it."

"And if it is?"

"Then I don't know. I'll do whatever comes next. Whatever I feel like I have to do."

"Sounds like my kind of planning," I said, "but I have to admit, I'm kind of curious myself now. You really think he's going to show up here?"

"Yes, I do."

"That little hut up there, by the tracks. That's the breadbox."

"There was a bakery that used to put their day-old bread by the back door. They did that instead of selling it half price, because I guess that's the kind of people they were. Which explains why it's not there anymore, but we'd go pick up the bread and eat it in the shed."

"And watch the trains."

"Tremont would. I didn't care one way or another. Until one day, he said, 'Watch this,' and then he ran along the train that was coming by. He reached up and grabbed something and held on. It scared the crap out of me. I was sure I'd have to go back home and explain to Mama why my brother had been cut in half by some train wheels, but he kept riding, all the way down to the station. Then he jumped off. I didn't see him again until that night. He acted like nothing had happened."

He stopped talking. Like he realized that for one moment, he actually sounded like a man who was proud of something his little brother did. It was a sentiment he probably didn't feel like he could afford anymore.

"So what are you going to do?" I said. "Keep hiding out all day, come back here every night?"

"That's the plan, yes. Until I see my brother. Until I can talk to him."

"What if I say I'm taking you to your mother's house right now?"

"You're not going to do that."

"How about this?" I said. "I'll come back here tomorrow, *with your mother*. She can take you by the ear and drag you all the way back herself."

"You're going to promise me you won't do that," he said. "Right now. Or I swear, I'll kill you."

"And here I was thinking you weren't a murderer."

"I already did my time for a murder I didn't commit," he said. "I figure they owe me one now."

I almost laughed at that one. It was that strange a night.

"Look," he said. "Give me a couple more nights. If Tremont doesn't show up, we'll talk about doing it another way."

"I think you're wasting your time, and meanwhile—"

"I'm not. There was a guy I knew in the joint. He rode the trains himself, for years, so he knows about this stuff. He said if you send a message, it'll get there. It might as well be Western Union. When Tremont hears it, I know he'll come here as soon as he can."

I looked up at the moon. If I was expecting to see the answer written across its face, it wasn't there.

"I'm going to leave now," he said.

"I don't think I can let you do that. Not alone."

"You can't stop me."

"I'm pretty sure I can. If I have to."

He was back on his feet now, facing me.

"I have an alternate plan," I said. "I've got a motel room on Michigan Avenue. You come back with me. You have something to eat. You could probably use a drink about now, too. I know I could. We'll sit down and figure this out."

"You'll just take me to the police."

"I'm not a cop. I haven't been for a long time. I won't take you anywhere else, I promise."

I could tell he was thinking it over. He'd probably been living in that car for too long now. Not much money left. Maybe none at all. Running out of gas. No food. If nothing else, I'd be able to keep him alive for a few more days, unless he really wanted to put on a mask and start holding up gas stations.

"My aunt's car is here," he finally said.

"I don't think they'll mind," I said, looking around the empty lot. "Worst they can do is tow it. She'll get it back eventually."

"All right," he said, "but I'm coming back here tomorrow."

"Like I said, we'll figure that out. Let's go."

I took a few steps down the street. He looked at the car he was leaving behind for a moment, then he shook his head and started to follow me. Nobody would have confused us for long-lost best buddies, but it was better than fighting again.

When we got back to the main street, I pointed in the direction of the auto parts store. "My truck's over there."

He nodded, didn't say a word, but he kept following me. It occurred to me then that a suspicious person would have been a little more wary of this whole situation. He could have been playing along, planning out when he'd take my money, and maybe my truck, too. I had about three seconds to think that one over.

Then we both heard the train.

It was coming from the southwest, still picking up steam as it came out of the big turn from the station. It was going on twelve thirty at that point. A little late for the rendezvous, but Darryl King looked at that train, and it was obvious he had the same thought I had. He turned and ran back down the side street. Now it was my turn to follow, and once again to chase him, all these years later. Somehow he had gotten a lot faster than me.

Down the incline, past his car, to the bottom of the street where the two railroad bridges passed over. Then he stopped dead.

He was looking at that one spot, where the trail ran up to the breadbox.

Darkness. No movement.

Then something.

I was still a good thirty yards away when I saw the man step out from the trail. Even from where I was I could see that he was a twig of a man. He was a sliver. The two of them stood there looking at each other. I stopped running.

I waited to see what would happen. After all these years.

That's when the vehicle came barreling down the side street. I looked back and was blinded by the headlights. Everything that came next happened before I could even think about how to react.

I recognized that same green minivan, made the connection with Ryan Grayson. I heard the screech of the tires as the vehicle came to a sliding halt. The driver's side door opening and Ryan Grayson himself practically falling out of the car. The dull thud of the gun hitting the road, then Grayson picking it up and waving it wildly at the two men on the sidewalk. Darryl King grabbing his brother by the shoulders and pushing him to the ground, as Grayson came closer and aimed the gun at both of them, at point-blank range now. Nothing could stop him at this point. Just one more little movement of one finger and it would be done.

But it didn't happen.

Everything frozen in that one instant. Darryl and Tremont King on the concrete, waiting to see which one would get shot first. Ryan Grayson with the gun pointed and then the look on his face of a man about to pull the trigger. Then the bewilderment that it wasn't happening. That a bullet wasn't tearing into flesh.

I saw Tanner Paige through the passenger's-side window. He was looking out at the whole scene with his hands on his head.

That's when the second vehicle came. A sleek dark SUV. Then the third and the fourth and a few more that I stopped counting.

The agents came streaming out of their vehicles, all wearing black bulletproof vests with FBI on the back in white letters. They yelled at Grayson to drop the gun and to lie down on the street. They yelled at Paige to exit the vehicle with his hands on his head. They yelled at Darryl and Tremont King to stay exactly where they were, not moving a single muscle. Everyone complied.

An agent came up to me and told me to put my hands on my head, just as they had done to Paige. It was all still an underwater dream to me, but I knew enough to cooperate, and a moment later I felt the cold sting of the handcuffs being put on my left wrist. Before he could do the other wrist, I heard a voice from behind us telling him to let me go.

The handcuff was removed. The agent pushed by me to assist his teammates in securing the area. There were at least seven, maybe eight vehicles now, with their headlights blazing from both ends of the street. The whole scene lit up in sudden bright clarity like a nighttime movie shoot.

I still hadn't made the connection. How all of this could have happened. How Grayson and Paige could end up here, first of all. Here on this lonely back-alley street that I had only discovered myself a matter of hours ago. Then a whole goddamned team of FBI agents, right behind them.

But of course, I knew that voice behind me. The familiar voice of the agent who ordered me uncuffed. I turned to see her face.

"It was you," I said to FBI Agent Janet Long. "You set me up."

CHAPTER TWENTY-FOUR

It was my first time inside the McNamara Federal Building. The FBI occupied the twenty-sixth floor. Everything was gleaming and immaculate. The room I sat in was worlds away from the old Detroit precinct interview room, where you'd find food wrappers, coffee stains, and a wobbly table and chairs that should have been put out on the street years before.

I sat there with my hands folded together on the table. The door opened. Agent Fleury came in. Janet's partner. I didn't look up.

"How are you doing?" he said. "Can I get you anything?"

I didn't answer.

"Look," he said, sitting down across from me and putting his leather portfolio on the table. "You have to understand something. This is a person who brutally killed seven different women in seven different states. Now possibly eight women in eight states, if the information you've developed is correct."

He sat there and waited for me to say something. I didn't.

"I'm really curious, Alex. What did you think we were going to do? Just sit around and wait for something to fall in our laps? After we've been working on this guy *for years*?"

He opened up his portfolio, took out a piece of paper, and slid it across the table. I didn't bother looking at it. I was reasonably sure I knew what it was anyway.

"For the record," he said, "this was my call. Not Janet's. The law is very clear on this point. We contacted the judge. He verbally approved the warrant. We don't have to have it in our possession. We only have to know it's on the way. So that part was covered."

"Is the GPS tracker still attached to my truck?" I said, finally speaking up. "Or are you going to track me all the way back to Paradise?"

"The device has been removed."

"You said this was your call."

"Yes."

"Was it your call to have Janet take me for our little walk around downtown, so you'd have the chance to attach it?"

"Once again, Mr. McKnight . . . I mean, here's where I should apologize for the deception, but I'm not going to, because sometimes the ends really do justify the means. In this case, it's not even close. It's the easiest decision I've ever made. I'll sleep like a baby tonight."

"I would have brought him in," I said. "What else did you think I was going to do?"

"There were two of them. You were unarmed. If I gave you those odds, knowing the stakes, would you take them? For anyone else?"

"Are we about done here?"

"Just about. You care to tell me how you figured out where they were going to meet?"

"You guys are supposed to be the smartest group of law enforcement officers in the world," I said. "I'm one ex-cop in a truck. If I were you, I'd be embarrassed to ask that question."

He smiled at that one.

"I knew you'd get somewhere," he said. "I knew you wouldn't be able to leave it alone, and I knew you'd find a way to the end of the maze. I *knew* it. That's why I scrambled to get that GPS on you. You've gotta give me credit for that much."

"Good hustle, Agent Fleury. The two of you will richly deserve your big raises."

"She thought you were really going back home this time, Mr. McKnight. She was sure of it. I guess that means I know you a little better than she does."

He folded up his portfolio. Then he stood up.

"For what's it worth," he said, "you helped us catch a serial killer. I will always be thankful to you for that. No matter what you say to me."

Then he left the room.

I sat there a while longer, looking out the blinds at the darkness. I knew it was beyond late now. I didn't even bother looking at my watch.

The door opened again. Agent Janet Long came in and sat down across from me.

"It would save time if you guys talked to me together," I said. "You don't have to send in a parade."

"Stop it," she said. "I'm sorry for the way this worked out."

"Why are you sorry? Everybody wins. All you had to do was play me like a drum. Which I guess must have been pretty easy, seeing as how I never would have suspected it."

"It wasn't my idea."

"Yeah, I know. Your partner copped to that."

"I'm pretty sure I told you to go home, too. More than once."

"You did."

"And I'm pretty sure you promised me you would."

"I'd have to review the tape," I said, "but you're probably right."

"I wasn't straight with you, Alex. I admit that, but you weren't straight with me, either."

"Can we stop?" I said. "I don't want to do this anymore."

"Fine with me. You want to talk about what happened?"

"To be honest," I said, "it's still just a blur to me. How did Ryan Grayson and Tanner Paige show up?"

"I was hoping you could tell me."

"They must have followed me. The old-fashioned way, I mean. I'm sure they didn't have a GPS device they could trick me into carrying around."

"I thought we were going to stop."

I raised a hand in surrender.

"Wait a minute," I said. "Of course they followed me. It was easy. The last time I talked to them, I told them I was staying in a motel on Michigan Avenue. They already knew what my truck looked like."

"You didn't notice them on your tail? *All day?*"

"I guess I was preoccupied."

"You realize, they forced our hand and almost blew everything. If Grayson didn't have his safety on . . ."

"Are you serious? Is that why his gun didn't shoot?"

"For once, thank God for clueless gun owners who have no idea what they're doing."

"They promised me," I said. "No more stupid behavior."

"Yeah, I guess lots of promises got broken this week."

"So what's going to happen to them?"

"Grayson and Tanner have both been charged with obstruction. Grayson's also been charged with unlawful use of a weapon. Which is a lot better than attempted murder. I'm sure he'll get a good lawyer and end up with probation and a fine."

"What about Darryl King?" I said.

"We've got him for aiding and abetting, which I imagine will get dropped, but the state wants him for all of the parole violations, and I'll be honest with you, they still like him for the murder of Detective Bateman."

"Maybe he'll confess again. For old times' sake."

"As far as Tremont King goes . . . Well, that'll be a project and a half right there. We've got a lot of ground to cover."

"I imagine. Has he said anything?"

"Not a word."

I nodded at that. We both sat there.

"My partner did thank you," she said.

"He did."

"It's a good night, Alex. I hope you know that."

"I think you'll have to ask me that tomorrow."

"Fair enough," she said. "I'll call you?"

"Okay."

We both sat there for a while again, looking at each other. Then I got to my feet. She took me to the elevator and showed me to the main entrance. We said good night. We didn't touch each other. I was pretty sure we never would again.

My truck had been brought over from the apprehension site, or whatever you would call that place now. The keys were on the front seat. I started it up and drove out of the lot.

I went right to Mrs. King's house. The place was completely dark. I saw a note taped on the front door. It was for me. An FBI agent had come to tell Mrs. King what had happened. Her sister had come to take her away for a while. She'd call me the next day.

I sat in the truck for a while. Then I drove back down to the main streets and tried to find a bar. They were all closed now. It was after 2:00 a.m.

Eventually, I went back to the motel. I lay on the bed with my clothes on, looking up at the ceiling. After everything that had happened that day, I didn't even want to sleep. Then I closed my eyes and the day beat me again.

My shoulder hurt like hell the next morning. A souvenir of my little tussle with Darryl King, which should have been more than enough excitement for the night right there.

I got up and took a hot shower. Then I checked out of the motel.

I gave Leon a call to tell him everything that happened. He was just as amazed that an amateur had been able to follow me all day long, which certainly made my morning. When I was done with Leon, I called Tanner Paige. He spent the first minute apologizing. Literally saying, "I'm sorry," about twelve times in a row.

"I didn't know he had a gun in the car," he said, when he finally moved on from the apologizing. "I didn't know he was going to run right into the middle of everything like that."

"Sounds like he was pretty lucky," I said, "but I still don't get why you guys were—"

"Following you, I know. *I know!* He was the one following you all over the place, you realize. Then he finally called me last night. I kept telling myself, I was just going along with him to make sure he didn't get himself killed or something, but I gotta admit, Alex, I guess I was just as curious as he was to see what this guy looked like. If he was really the man who killed Elana."

"Well, you'll probably never get a chance to ask him to his face. Not now."

"I know. I guess it really is time to move on now, too. I never want to live through something like these past few days again."

"You were released last night, I take it. What about your brother-in-law?"

"Yeah, they held him a little longer. He has a bunch of hearings to go to in the next few days, but he's home now, at least. I'll go see him, make sure he's okay."

"I was just going to call him."

"Give him a day," he said. "I think he's pretty shaken up. He'll probably be at his lawyer's office all day anyway."

"Okay, fair enough."

Tanner Paige apologized a few more times. Then he thanked me and wished me a good trip back home.

I tried calling Mrs. King. Her cell phone was apparently turned off. I wanted to see her, but I didn't think I could stand one more minute in the city. I'll catch up with her on the phone, I thought. I'll probably come back down, too, as soon as I figure out how I can help.

That made me think of Detective Gruley in Houghton Lake. It was finally time to call him back. I was thinking maybe I could stop in at his post on the way home, too. Explain everything in person.

I looked across the street one more time, at the vacant lot where Tiger Stadium once stood. It seemed like a fitting farewell, at least for the time being, as I pulled onto the road and made my way to the freeway.

Something wasn't right. It was that feeling you get, when you leave the house and you *know* you've forgotten something, but I couldn't put my finger on it.

North to the edge of town. Eight Mile Road. That feeling still there.

Then I saw the exit for Twelve Mile. I pulled off the freeway.

I was in Southfield now. I thought back to that trip I had made this way, all those years before. Detective Bateman and I, coming up to see Elana's parents. I went west. It was right off this road somewhere. I flashed back on the conversation I had with Ryan Grayson and his brother-in-law in the bar a couple of days ago, after I rousted them at the end of the street. He was still living in the same house. In fact, he even offered to let me stay there.

I found the side road that led to Grayson's house. I drove down the long driveway. It was the same big house, just as I remembered. Except not quite. As I got closer, I saw that the lawn needed cutting. I saw that the windows all needed cleaning and the white columns on either side of the door needed a good pressure-wash. Grayson's green minivan was parked out front. Next to that was Paige's cream-colored SUV.

I parked behind them and got out. A few seconds later, Tanner Paige came out the front door. He was carrying a box.

"Alex," he said. "What brings you out here?"

"I was on my way home. I just thought I'd stop by." I looked up at the house. "You're seriously telling me he lives here all by himself now?"

"Ever since his kids moved away. Then his wife left. Yeah, it's kinda sad now, after all the things that used to go on here. All the parties and everything. This place was a real hot spot, back in the day, when Ryan's father was ruling the world. Now it's just . . ."

He looked up at the house, just like I was doing. Then he opened up his trunk and put the box inside.

"I've got to take this stuff over to the lawyer's," he said. "It's a bunch of old news clippings from Elana's murder. The lawyer thought he should have them, just in case."

"Just in case what?"

"He's pretty sure Ryan will get off clean, but just in case he runs into a judge that doesn't understand his state of mind . . ."

Paige looked down at the box and shook his head.

"He's really been hurting, Alex. This past week has been so hard on him."

"So let me just ask you something," I said. "About yesterday . . ."

"It was insane, I know. Apparently, Ryan followed you from your motel to, wait, let me get this right, to Darryl King's house, then to the library? Is that right?"

"Yes."

"Then down to Michigan Avenue somewhere, then up to that corner of Warren and Grand River. Then, what did he say, you went somewhere else after that, before coming back . . ."

He looked up, like he was playing it all back on a tape recorder.

"Yeah, back to the Kings' house, he said. Then back to Michigan Avenue. Then *back* to Warren and Grand River, for God's sake. Or something like that. I might have the order mixed up. I think he was running out of gas at that point and he almost lost you, but then you went and ate somewhere, and that's when he called me."

"So you went to meet him," I said. "So you could keep him company while he stayed on my tail."

"I believe I've already apologized for that, but yes. That's what I did. Like I said, I thought I was looking out for him, because I sure as hell couldn't have stopped him, but anyway, you went to a hardware store. Then you went back to that corner, for like the third time that day, he said. Although that was the first time I saw it, of course. I was thinking, why the hell would you come here? Then you walked down by where the railroad tracks went over the road. Ryan was getting really anxious then. He figured you were up to something important."

"I still don't get it," I said. "Why did he go to all this trouble? He put his whole life on hold so he could follow me around all day?"

"He was convinced you'd lead him to the man who killed his sister, Alex. I mean, after what you told us yourself . . . That's what he thought, and you have to admit, in the end he was right."

I stood there looking at the house, waiting for it to make sense.

"You really didn't know he had a gun," I said.

"I had no idea he even owned one, no. I swear."

I took a few steps toward the front door, then came back.

"Wait a minute," I said. "Why did he choose that exact moment to come down the street?"

"I don't know. I'm trying to remember. The two of you were running, right? You and Darryl? Running back to the tracks?"

"Yes."

"That's what made him go. He figured something was happening. I tried to stop him, Alex. I really did, but he was out of his head at that point."

"He knew that was Darryl I was with? Even though he'd hadn't seen him in years?"

"I think he was just assuming, yes."

"Then when Darryl's brother came out of the woods . . ."

Paige just stood there, looking at me.

"How did he know?" I said. "How did he know that was *the man*?"

"I don't know what to tell you, Alex."

"He was ready to kill him. He was that sure."

I looked back at the house, one more time.

"It doesn't add up," I said. "Unless . . ."

"Unless what?"

"Unless he already knew Tremont King."

He thought it over for a moment.

"Oh my God," he said. "Of course. That would make it all work, wouldn't it . . ."

"It would, yes."

"That son of a bitch." Paige reached into the wheel well of his trunk and brought out a tire iron.

"Put that down," I said. "You stay here. I'm going to go inside and talk to him."

Paige pushed by me and grabbed the handle on the back of the minivan. Then he raised the rear door.

"What are you doing?" I said. Then I saw what was inside the vehicle. The backseats were folded down. There was a plastic drop cloth spread out on the floor. There was something else, wrapped in more plastic.

A body.

"No need to go inside," Paige said. "Ryan's right here."

Before I could even react to what I was seeing, I heard the sound of that thing moving in the air, behind my head.

Then I was out.

CHAPTER TWENTY-FIVE

Sounds. Movement. I'm rolled one way, then back the other way. A wave pushing me toward shore, then pulling me back.

No. I'm in a vehicle. I'm lying down, feeling the momentum of the turns. I'm on plastic. It crinkles every time my weight is shifted.

A voice.

"Hey, Alex. How're you doing back there?"

God, my head hurts so much. I can't move. Why can't I move?

"Settle in, buddy. We've got a little drive here."

My hands. I can't move my hands. I try to open my eyes, but everything is too bright and spinning too quickly. It makes my head hurt twice as much.

I'm trying to sit up. I have to sit up. I have to get out of here. I have to remember what happened and then I have to get out of here.

My hands are behind my back. Why can't I move my hands?

God, my head hurts.

The vehicle swings into a big curve. I'm rolling right. I hit something. More crinkle of plastic.

I open my eyes.

I see three other faces. Then two. Then one.

I focus on Ryan Grayson. His dead eyes staring at me.

Then I'm out again.

I opened my eyes again. I didn't know how much time had passed. The vehicle wasn't rolling me from side to side anymore. There was just the steady hum of an engine maintaining a straight, level speed.

I tried to speak. A groan came out.

"Alex, is that you?"

I couldn't make words anymore. I'd forgotten how.

"We're almost there."

I tried one eye. Just the right eye squinting open. I saw Tanner Paige behind the wheel of the minivan.

"I'm glad you're awake, Alex. Finally. This would have been a whole lot better with someone to talk to."

My hands. I still couldn't move my hands.

"I apologize, by the way. I know that doesn't make it one hundred percent better, but I hope it helps. I'm really, really sorry."

I tried to sit up again. It was impossible.

"I was starting to like you, Alex. I thought we were really on the same wavelength, you know? I really liked Arnie, too. I hope you realize that. I'm not a monster."

My hands are tied behind my back, I thought. I'm tied up in the back of this minivan, and Tanner Paige is driving it somewhere.

I opened one eye again and saw the dead body of Ryan Grayson next to me, haphazardly wrapped in the green plastic, the face exposed through a gap at the top. Bloody and bruised, the nose broken, the front teeth knocked out.

It's only the women he kills with knives, I thought. The men, he just bashes their heads in.

So why am I still alive?

"He kept in touch with me all those years, you know. He was a good guy. Ryan and I even went up there a few times. We'd always take a ride on his boat. Did he tell you that? You were there, too, right? Did you take the exciting ride on his boat?"

I looked up and saw the sunlight coming through the windows. It was still daytime.

"Mostly we just talked a lot, and I think it was good for both of us. Made us both feel less alone, I think, and for him, it was always a good reminder, too. Getting that confession was the highlight of his career. I'd always tell him how much it meant to me. I knew that made him feel good. I was happy to do that for him."

My ears were still ringing. Every sound had an edge to it. I tried to shake my head . . . Big mistake. Don't do that.

"If they hadn't released Trey's brother, none of this would have happened, you realize. That's where all the trouble began. Right there with that cockamamie decision. That's what got everybody all stirred up again. The last time Arnie called me, he said he probably shouldn't say anything yet, but he had to talk to somebody. He said you were trying to cast some doubt on the confession. Which didn't make him happy, but then he said he was getting the old files out and going over them. I guess he drove down and looked at the old confession, too. On tape, I guess? That was the day before Arnie passed."

I hadn't really been listening, but that part broke through. The day before Arnie passed? Did this man really just say that?

I struggled to get my hands free. It didn't feel like rope. It felt more like something rubber, with a little give to it. It was tight. But maybe . . .

"It kinda got a little funny there. Maybe just my overactive imagination, but he was saying how if Darryl King didn't kill Elana, then he wanted to find out who did. Make up for the big mistake he'd made. He said he'd owe me a big apology if that ended up happening, because he knew it would be a shock for me. Kinda funny he would say it that way, looking back on it, but he asked me if I thought Ryan should know, and I said no, not yet. That's why Ryan was so surprised when you brought it up."

I had to close my eyes again. I had to lie still for a while, let the pounding in my head settle into some kind of rhythm.

"Poor Arnie. You really got to him, Alex. When we were done talking, he said he had to make the hardest phone call of all. He had to call you up and tell you he was wrong. Or might have been wrong. Was probably wrong. Whatever. It was really eating him up. Although I could tell he was kind of excited about maybe the two of you guys working together again. Going back over the old case, just like old times. I told him it sounded like he was trying to bring back those days when he was a young hotshot detective. Back when he owned the city, but he said no, he just wanted to make things right."

Those words again. Even now, those words haunting me. To make things right.

"As far as Ryan goes . . . Yeah, poor Ryan. He passed today, too. As you can see. So that got me to thinking, maybe it would be better if people thought he ran away. Couldn't take it anymore. You see where I'm going with this? His safe is open, all the cash is gone. Yeah, if he just goes, and this car goes . . . That'll probably be easier for everyone to deal with."

I could feel the minivan accelerating. I looked up and saw a truck on the right side. For one brief second, the face of the truck driver. Another human being who could theoretically help me. Then he was gone.

"I do feel bad for Ryan, but maybe this was all for the best anyway. He was in such pain, Alex. He was so obsessed about finding the man who killed his sister. Kind of funny, again, looking back on it. That I would be helping him, but he made it easy. All I had to do was point to Trey and say, 'That's him!' He didn't even think about it. He just reacted."

The back windows were tinted. A fact that just came to me then. Even if we passed another truck, I don't think anyone could see inside.

"Of course, after all the dust settled, Ryan asked the same question you did. It finally came to him today. How did you even know who that man was? That's when I realized that, no matter what I said, it would only be a matter of time until Ryan started looking a little deeper. How I was alone that day, the day Elana passed, supposedly playing a practice round at the club. Good excuse to disappear for four hours, by the way, but then also all the traveling I've been doing. I'm a manufacturer's rep for a golf club company. Don't know if I told you that. I've got the whole eastern half of the

U.S. I'll go and do a demo day at a golf club somewhere, pack up and go somewhere else the same day. Go south in the winter, where people are still playing golf. It keeps me pretty busy."

I concentrated on my hands. This is why a cop handcuffs you this way, because it makes you pretty much useless. Even getting to my feet would be a monumental chore right now, but if I can get these hands free . . .

"It gave me a chance to work things out, too. All that time on the road. It really helped me. It was good therapy, reliving that day, seeing if I could be a little less angry each time. A little more in control of myself."

His words breaking through again. Good therapy? Reliving that day? Is that what he's really calling it? Murdering seven women?

"Do you play golf, Alex? You look like you could be a good golfer."

Focus, God damn it. Your hands are tied crossways. There's something looped around them in both directions . . .

"Ryan was terrible at golf. No patience at all. He was about as good at golf as he was at shooting a gun."

If I can flex my wrists. Work them one way, then the other. Back and forth.

"Although, I'll be honest with you, Alex. I'm kinda glad he didn't kill Trey. It's been a long time since I've seen him, but he still looked like that old kid in the train station. I'd meet him there at the station most every Saturday morning. It was a lot better than playing golf with those guys at the club, believe me."

Trey. He keeps calling him Trey. His pet name for Tremont?

"You should have seen him back then. What a sweet thing he was. My God did I love that kid."

Stay calm. Work your hands. Ignore the way your head feels. Ignore the bile rising in your throat. Just stay calm and work your hands.

"He wasn't supposed to be there on a Thursday. That part wasn't planned. I was not happy with him, believe me."

Damn it damn it damn it.

"I told Trey, I said, this was supposed to be between Elana and me, and nobody else. That's why I told her to come down to the station because I was going to surprise her, and not to tell anybody because I knew we weren't supposed to be up there, but there's this place in the old part of the station where the light comes through those big windows and I knew she'd love it and be able to get some great shots there, you know? And she really did love it, I gotta say, I mean I totally nailed it, but then that's not why we were there, not really, which kind of became obvious, I guess."

Don't listen to him, I told myself. Don't get sucked into this. Just keep concentrating.

"So when Trey was there, I was like, you and I have a secret now, my little sweet thing. We're in this together now."

Work the hands. God, my head hurts so much.

"That was a long time ago, Alex. I swear, things were really getting better. I was in such a better place mentally. I'd worked it all out of my system, I think. I was even ready to forgive her for what she did to me."

Shut up, you goddamned psychopath. Just shut the hell up.

"None of it would have happened if she wasn't planning on leaving me. You realize that."

It's working, I told myself. You can move your hands a little bit more now. I was rubbing them raw, but I was making progress.

"Her family never thought I was good enough for her. Not rich enough, not successful enough. I wasn't a County Amateur champion like her father, but that stuff isn't supposed to matter, right? I thought me and Elana had something there. I thought we had something bulletproof."

You're going to get free. Then you're going to crawl up behind him and you're going to grab him by the neck. Even if that means sending this vehicle right off the road.

"Listen to me. I just got done telling you I'm finally ready to forgive her, and now here I go again. I guess I'll never really be over it, huh?"

I felt the vehicle slowing down. Then turning right. I had no idea how long I had been out. Five minutes or five hours.

"You want to hear something funny? You'll like this. We're going to this golf club where I did a demo day in the spring. The pro there, thinks he's a real hotshot, thinks he's got the greatest little gem of a golf course, the best in all of Western Michigan."

Western Michigan. A piece of information, not that it will do me any good.

"He's got this house across the river, raised up a little bit so it's got a little view, right? All you can really see is the water treatment plant, but I wasn't going to say anything to him. I was just like, oh yeah, this is so nice. Anyway, he takes me out to the back of his property, down by the river. There's a bend there and it gets kinda deep, and he actually says to me, he says, 'You could dump a body back here, huh?' Can you believe that? He actually said that to me."

The vehicle was slowing down again. This time we came to a complete stop. I looked up at the hazy sunshine coming through the tinted windows. I wondered how many minutes of sunlight I had left.

No, do not think this way. You still have a shot as long as you're breathing. As long as you're thinking. Keep working those hands.

"He's golfing in Scotland this week. Think he was bragging about that trip a little bit? Even six months beforehand? But now it all kinda works out, so I hope he's having a good time."

The vehicle turned right again, then left. Then it slowed down almost completely.

"Now, where was that turn again?"

I slowly brought my knees up toward my chest. I knew we had to be getting close. I'd be lucky to get one chance to do something. If I got that chance, could I even move?

"Ah, right here."

He turned hard to the right, sending me sliding against the side of the minivan. I hit my head and everything went out of focus again.

I lay there for the next minute, just trying to get my head back on. Then he turned hard to the right again. He was driving slowly now. I knew I was running out of time. I gave up trying to sit up. I closed my eyes and tried to work my hands free. I was sweating, and I could feel the blood on the back of my head, running down my neck.

The vehicle left pavement. We were on gravel. I opened my eyes and looked at Paige. He was leaning forward in the driver's seat, staring out at the road. I heard branches scratching on both sides. Then we hit a series of bumps that had me bouncing up and down. I cried out in pain, despite myself. A line of blood came trailing out from Grayson's head.

"Sorry about that," Paige said. "We're almost done, I promise."

I felt the incline. We were rumbling down one more stretch of rough road. I knew whatever came next would happen in a matter of minutes. My hands still weren't free. I didn't have any options left.

Except one. Maybe.

The minivan came to a stop. The driver's side door opened. Paige got out. He closed the door. I could hear his footsteps coming around to the back. The rear door opened.

I stayed still. I kept my eyes open. I kept my mouth open. I did my absolute best impression of a man who had just breathed his last breath.

"See, it's perfect," he said. "The town's right over the hill there, and yet nobody can see us here."

Eyes staring dead ahead, looking at nothing. Not a muscle moving. Not a breath taken. I am a hunk of meat here, just like the hunk of meat lying next to me. You will look at me and realize this. Then you will let down your guard. You will pull me out of this minivan, thinking I'm nothing more than dead weight now.

Then I'll have my only chance.

"I know they'll find this thing eventually. I'm not an idiot, but it should be a while, I would think. By then I'll have figured out where I need to go next."

What did he just say? What is he going to do?

"Alex, you there?"

I felt a sharp jab on the back of my knee.

"Alex. Hey. Wake up."

Come closer, I thought. Come see if I'm really dead.

The seconds passed. Then there was a loud thud as the tire iron landed on the floor next to me. Before I could even realize what he was doing, the rear door closed.

I heard the footsteps again. The driver's side door opened, but he didn't start the vehicle. Instead, he hit the gearshift, and then in the next second he was out and the door was closed. I felt the vehicle moving. It was rolling downhill. Faster and faster.

It was going into the water.

I felt the jolt as the front end hit. The momentum reclaimed the vehicle, only now the movement was smoother and even more down-hill. I slid up against the back of the driver's seat. My head slammed against it, then my shoulder, then my arms, still pinned behind me. Everything just a riot of pain as I was folded into a ball. The dead body hit me a second later, pinning me against the seat as the weight of the engine pitched everything forward. The vehicle was pointing almost straight down now, and as I looked back and up at the rear window, I saw the last of the daylight disappearing.

It wasn't done moving. Down and down it went, impossibly deep. The pressure built in my ears and made my head pound even louder. It was getting darker. I could barely see a thing now. Then the one last interior light blinked off and it all went black.

I'm not dead yet, I thought. I have a little bit of air left. I need to gather whatever strength I have left. I need to get out of this thing and get back up to the surface. Yes, even with my goddamned arms tied behind my goddamned back.

It was time to move, no matter what it did to my head. I let out a loud yell as I moved my shoulder against the dead body. Nobody to hear you now, I thought. You might as well scream all you want.

I tucked my knees into my chest. I pushed myself up. God, my head was hurting so much. The water was starting to come inside the vehicle now. The dashboard was underwater.

The windows are closed, I thought. I need to break one open. I rolled over onto my back. I was on top of Ryan Grayson now. I kicked at the window. Then again and again, but I couldn't get enough leverage.

The tire iron. I need that tire iron.

I spun over onto my stomach. I moved my body over the rum-pled-up plastic, feeling with my face for the heavy weight of that tire iron.

I have to find it. Or else I will die.

I willed my body to move, to cover every inch I could reach, no matter how much it hurt.

Find it find it find it.

There.

I grabbed the thing with my teeth, feeling the cold sting of the iron. Then I worked myself into a sitting position and dropped it into my lap.

That's useless, Alex. You need it in your hand.

Even then, can you hit the window hard enough?

I rolled my body and caught the tire iron as it hit my hand. The water was coming higher now. Soon the air would be gone.

I gripped the tire iron and turned around so I was facing away from the window. I started swinging the iron at the glass. I felt it hit. The glass didn't break. I swung again. Then again. Then again.

I felt the water on my legs. It was cold. I swung the iron. I fumbled with it, nearly dropping it. Then I recovered and swung again, trying to use my whole body to get more force behind the blow.

The water was rising. Shockingly cold. I was shivering already.

You are going to die, Alex. You are going to die right here with this other man. This fellow victim. They won't find you for weeks, maybe months. Tanner Paige will go on killing while you slowly dissolve in this cold dark river.

Swing again. Like you mean it. Like you want to live. Like you want to get out of here and go find him.

I swung the iron. It hit the glass and broke through before falling from my hand. A rush of water hit me, wrapping its icy arms around my chest. I gasped for my last breath of air as it overtook me completely. Then I was under.

Get out. My only thought. The only two words in the language. Get out.

I kicked against Grayson's body. I kicked against the seats. I felt my head knocking through the rest of the broken glass as I kicked again and again. My face out of the vehicle now, then my shoulder. Another kick. Another. My last breath dying in my lungs as I finally put my knee against the frame of the glass and pushed myself into the open water.

I didn't know up from down at that point. I was moving, but I was in my wet clothes and it felt like I would sink to the very bottom.

This way, I thought. No, this way, this way, and now my breath is gone, and the next thing that goes in will be the river itself, no, I must hold on for the air but I'm going the wrong way.

Then I saw light. I was going to the surface after all. It came closer and closer as I tried to dolphin kick, even with my hands still tied behind my back, with my lungs on fire now, until finally . . .

Air! I gasped for breath, my face just above the surface. I kicked and sputtered and took a breath of that beautiful air and filled my lungs with it. Then I gasped again and gagged on the river water. I spit that out and coughed and wheezed, keeping up my dolphin kick somehow, finding the strength to keep my face above water.

A second breath, a third, a fourth. It was all I could do to keep my body in a position to keep breathing, but as my breath came back to me, I knew I had other problems. I was still in the water, still unable to swim. For all I knew Paige was standing on the shore, watching me and figuring out what he had to do next to deal with this last problem.

From somewhere in the back of my mind, I remembered a technique for breathing in water. You arch your back and turn your face up so that your nose is the high point, and any buoyancy you have will naturally keep that one point above the water. You can do this without having to tread water, so you can regain your strength.

A fine theory, that may or may not work if you're fully dressed. Worth a shot. I arched my back and put my head up.

Nice and easy, Alex. Stop kicking. See if this will work.

Yes. I think we've got something here. As long as I stay perfectly still.

Breathe. Yes. Breathe. Relax.

I did that for a full minute. Then the cold water started to get to me. It was time to move again. It was time to take whatever strength I had recovered and see if I could get to shore, and hope that Paige wasn't waiting there for me.

I dolphin kicked one time, hard enough to drive my head up over the water. I took a quick look. I saw where the road led down to the river. What must have been the boat launch. I didn't see

Paige anywhere. I went back under, then dolphin kicked again, looking in the other direction. I was actually closer to the other shore.

I tried to flatten out my body on the water, but I was too bottom-heavy. I kicked and kicked and got nowhere, feeling the strength draining away again.

Turn over, you idiot. Do this on your back.

I flipped over and looked at the sky. I sucked in the air as I kicked and thrashed and finally started making progress, eventually settling into a cadence. Kick breathe kick breathe.

Until finally, I felt the bottom of the river under my feet. I turned over and went down to my knees, then stood up and stumbled out. I collapsed on the shore, feeling myself sinking into the black mire on the side of the river. I looked back behind me. I didn't see Paige anywhere. He had left. The son of a bitch had turned and walked away, thinking I was already dead. Or if I came to, that I'd be dead in another few seconds anyway. Whatever, I didn't even care. All I knew was that I was here on the shore, feeling like my head was about to explode—but alive.

I lay there for a while, until I started to shiver. When I finally rolled myself back up to my knees, I felt my hands shift. I gave them one great twist and felt them come free. When I pulled the thing around to look at it, I saw that it was a set of jumper cables. I threw them on the ground and looked at the raw skin on my wrists. Then I tried to get up.

Whoa, that's not going to work, I thought. Standing is one thing I'm not ready for. That's when I remembered my cell phone. I reached into my pocket and grabbed it. I turned it on. Nothing. Goddamned cell phone can't survive one lousy dunk in the water. Without another thought, I tossed it into the river.

I started to shiver again, so I put one hand on the ground and tried to stand. One more time, I thought. You can do this.

I got one foot under me, then the other. I took a step and almost went down, caught myself, took another step. I had no idea where I was. I had no idea where I could go for help. I just knew I had to move.

I reached around and felt the back of my head. There was a big lump there. The skin was broken and I felt blood. A cold rational voice in the back of my head made the general announcement that I surely had a concussion and could use some medical attention as soon as possible. I took another few steps and felt everything spinning around me.

When things came back into focus, I saw something just down the shoreline. A large facility of some sort. A building and a pair of great round tanks set into the ground. The water treatment plant. He said something about that. Something about the view from this house, and the man being in Scotland. A useless detail, and yet I remember that part.

"Where are you, Paige?" I asked out loud, my own voice sounding strange and faraway. "Where did you go?"

He drove the minivan all the way out here, after all. He said we were in Western Michigan, right? Didn't he say that? That's a long way back to Southfield. How's he going to get there?

I kept putting one foot in front of the other. The ground was more even here. It didn't feel like I'd fall with every step. I was walking through the facility now. I found the sidewalk that ran between the building and the tanks. I didn't see anybody there. I kept walking.

I need to get out of these wet clothes. I need to get warm. I need to get my head looked at. I need to get the police on Paige's tail. The checklist was right there in my head, yet I kept walking and walking. Out of the facility, down a street lined with houses. I could have stopped at the first house. Banged on the door, collapsed in a heap. Asked them to call 911. Yet I kept walking. Because I saw something ahead of me.

A railroad bridge. Yet one more goddamned railroad bridge, this one crossing over the river. It was pulling me toward it. One more bridge that meant something. I didn't even realize what yet. Until I got closer and I saw the tracks.

I could hear the train. It wasn't moving yet. It was sitting at the station, just a quarter mile from the bridge. Not a freight train. A sleek Amtrak train, sitting there at the station, hissing and humming, ready to go.

This is how he's getting back home, I thought. This is part of the plan right here.

I started walking down the tracks. I could see people getting on. A porter helped an elderly man with his suitcase. What a lovely day for a train trip. What a beautiful lovely perfect day.

I must have been a sight. I was soaking wet and half covered with black slime from the river. There was blood running down the back of my neck. Yet nobody turned to look at this monstrosity, until I was finally right there on the platform.

It was a quaint little station made of bricks. A quiet little out-of-the-way stop on the Amtrak line, from Chicago to Detroit. There was a sign there, but I wasn't sure if I could even read it. Then the letters came together. NILES, MICHIGAN. I was three hours west of Detroit, close to the Indiana border.

"Excuse me, sir!" A voice coming from somewhere. "Excuse me, do you need help?"

No, I thought. I'm just practicing to be the Swamp Thing, for an upcoming movie. I grabbed on to the metal handle, almost missing it. Then I hauled myself into the train.

"Sir! You need to stop right now!"

I was in the rear car. Everyone was settling in for the ride, arranging themselves in the seats. Heads started turning toward me. A woman gave out a little scream.

I could hear the porter outside, yelling at someone to call the police. Yes, please do, I thought. That's right here on my list. Call the police.

I went up the aisle, looking for Paige. He's on this train somewhere. I remembered doing something like this a million years before, looking for someone on a train. Then a new wave of pain washed over my head and my knees buckled. I had to grab onto the seats to keep myself up—but I kept going.

He wasn't in that car. I went to the next. He wasn't in that car. Everyone was looking at me now. Mothers were holding their children. Nobody tried to stop me. Not yet.

When I got to the last car, the conductor was standing in the aisle, blocking my way. I couldn't really hold him in my vision at that point. He was too fuzzy around the edges, and he wouldn't stand straight up and down.

"Sir, you need to get off this train right now," he said. "I really think you need some help, too."

I looked past him. I saw a man sitting at the far end of the car. I pointed in that direction.

The conductor turned to look. I grabbed him by the shoulders and threw him into the seat.

I went up the aisle. One step at a time. In the distance I could hear the police siren.

I came up beside him. Finally. I looked down at him. He was wearing sunglasses. His head was tipped back against his seat. Even without seeing his eyes, I knew he was dozing. Exhausted from his labors.

I stood there for a moment, waiting for him to realize that I had come back from the dead. At that moment, I was every single one of his victims, rolled into one person.

"Mr. Paige," I said, putting a hand on his shoulder. "I'm here to punch your ticket."

CHAPTER TWENTY-SIX

You ask the right questions at the right time. It's basic police work. Detective Arnie Bateman didn't ask the right questions when he had the chance. A man went to prison for a crime he didn't commit. The man who did commit the crime lived to kill again. I can't blame Detective Bateman for this, of course. I didn't ask the right questions, either.

Elana's brother, Ryan, finally did ask the right questions, but at the wrong time. He paid for that mistake with his life. I almost joined him, but in the end I survived and, after an eventful few hours at the Niles, Michigan, train station, I was there to see Tanner Paige taken away in handcuffs, thanks to a few phone calls to the FBI, and especially to an agent named Janet Long.

My concussion was officially listed as Grade 4. I had lost consciousness twice, once for a few minutes, after Paige first hit me, then later for a good couple of hours in the minivan. It takes a while to get over something like that. If you came into the Glasgow Inn anytime in the month of September, you'd see me sitting by the fireplace, wearing sunglasses. Sudden flashes of bright light really got to me. Just destroyed me. Not to mention sudden loud noises. Jackie had to take it easy on me that month. I think it almost killed him.

When I got over the post-concussion symptoms, I still had a nice new scar on the back of my head. At least this one I couldn't see when I looked at my own face in the mirror.

I took Leon to dinner and told him everything that had happened. I thanked him for all of his help. He said he was sorry he wasn't there to help me in person. Even if his wife would have killed both of us when we got back home.

Janet called me a couple of weeks after the arrest, to give me the general rundown on the legwork she and her fellow agents were doing on the other murders. It was an exhausting process, but they were definitely connecting Tanner Paige to each date and location. She also mentioned the possibility of coming up to see me sometime. She said it was her turn to make the long drive.

She hasn't made the trip yet. I honestly don't know if she ever will. Maybe we both lied to each other one time too many, even if it was always for the right reasons.

I kept in touch with Sergeant Grimaldi. I got back to work on the cabins. Vinnie and I replaced another woodstove. On the first day of October, it snowed. Later that month, I received a visit from the King family.

They rode up in Mrs. King's sister's powder blue Pontiac Bonneville. It still had the big dent in the front right quarter panel. I put them up in one of the empty cabins. I took them down to the Glasgow Inn to meet Jackie and Vinnie. On the second day, I took them to Sault Ste. Marie.

We all had a quick beer at the Soo Brewing Company with Leon. Mrs. King looked tired but happy. Darryl looked like he wasn't quite sure what he was doing in the Upper Peninsula. Or what he was doing with me, but we did shake hands and have a beer together. After all we'd been through, that had to mean something.

Tremont was the real enigma those couple of days. He didn't say much at all. After all those years living alone, out on the rails, he was like a feral animal who suddenly finds himself inside a house with a nice bed and regular meals. Add to that the guilt that he had to be feeling. Whether it was truly justified or not, you could look at him and wonder why he didn't do something about Tanner Paige back then. He was a scared fourteen-year-old kid in Detroit and Paige had every advantage over him, including the threat of lethal violence. So maybe you can't really blame him for running away and letting his brother take the fall for him, but there's a big difference between looking at something on paper and waking up in the middle of the night and thinking about what you could have done, if only you'd found a way. I could tell Tremont would be living with that for the rest of his life.

When we all bundled up and went up to the observation deck overlooking the Soo Locks, there was a big freighter coming through. The flag was Australian. Mrs. King and Darryl were both shivering and already looking at the stairs, obviously ready to go back to Paradise and sit by the fireplace, but Tremont looked out at the big boat that had come all these thousands of miles to be here, and I could tell what he was thinking. I knew he probably wasn't done riding on freight trains. I just hoped he'd always come back, now that he had a place to come back to.

On the day they went back to Detroit, Mrs. King gave me one of the biggest hugs of my life. I promised I'd call her. I promised I'd come down to see her again soon.

"Maybe you'll move back to the city someday," she said. "Detroit needs more good people. Otherwise, I don't know if she'll survive."

I promised I'd think about it, but I knew it would never happen. Paradise was my home now.

On the night before Halloween, we got more snow. I lay in my bed that night, listening to it fall. I thought about Detroit. The Motor City. Motown. A great city that could still be great again.

Then I remembered what night it was. Devil's Night. The night they burned down the empty houses, all over the city. It would have been a hard night to be there, watching the sky glow red above every corner of the city.

Watching the city I love burning to the ground.